Role Played

By

J.T. McNair

ISBN: 979-8-9940984-1-7

Cover design by J.T. McNair and J.L. Van Dyke

Current and Future Works

Fiction

Should I Go On? - 2025

The Worm Has Turned - 2026

Hell Is A Farm (with J. LeMay) - 2026

Henry - 2027

Non-Fiction

The Four Rules: How the World Works - 2027

For Lisa.

She would be proud.

Muse: Jamie Lynn Van Dyke

1

Telepy Teletherapy

Somewhere—anywhere—in Louisiana, there is a television on. And on that television, a commercial break occurs to show the viewer something they would rather avoid having to sit through.

As the advertisement fades in we see a young woman looking despondent, though she has perfect hair, perfect makeup, a perfect couch, and a coffee table in a perfect apartment. All colors are muted to an almost light gray. With her head in her hands and shoulders slumped, one might think she had lost her newly wedded husband in a car accident.

We hear a female voiceover, "Are you experiencing signs of depression; fatigue, irritability, the inability to enjoy the simple things in life? Have you thought about therapy but the idea of going to an office and seeing an in-person therapist only seems to make your symptoms worsen? Maybe you've thought about teletherapy but decided it just wasn't for you."

The camera slowly pans to the woman who takes her head out of her hands and looks longingly at the camera, breaking the fourth wall of the screen, as the sun begins to shine through the side window and on to her face.

The voiceover continues, "At Telepy teletherapy, we make it easy for you. Telepy gives you the opportunity to select the therapist that's right for your needs. The right fit at the right time and at the right place; your place. In the comfort and privacy of your own home you can experience a caring and nonjudgemental therapist today."

As the color of a new and mentally healthy worldview is added to the scene, the actress is now shown smiling, smiling at the face of another actress on a laptop screen. She is in a crisp white shirt and is nodding and smiling back as if all her problems were solved in the first few seconds of the session.

The voiceover continues as the camera pans to the back of the laptop and fades to a scene of the earlier sullen-looking actress now walking her dog and smiling at no one in the park. The colors we see now are overly saturated to signify pure nirvana.

The voiceover concludes, "You choose the date, time, and the therapist that fits you best. Most major insurances are accepted. Why not book today? With a fifteen-minute introductory session, what do you have to lose other than your symptoms?"

Your life. You could lose your life.

2

A Deep Breath

Margot Landry, a woman in her mid-thirties with long blond hair, blue eyes, and perfect features dusted with the lightest of makeup sat in front of her laptop at five minutes 'til six. She had finished her day-job and rushed home on the I-10 from Ochsner Hospital. There, she worked as a clinical social worker who helped patients come to grips with the five stages of death and, for the families, the same five stages of grief. She was waiting for her own therapist, Mike Martyn, a Licensed Professional Counselor, to join the connection. It was their usual Thursday. She had been seeing Mike for the last three months.

Mike Martyn had been a therapist for decades. He relished in his skills of picking just the right moment to challenge a person's inappropriate coping mechanism or catastrophizing thought patterns just as much as knowing when not to. Though, nearing his seventies he still had most of his hair and most of that wasn't gray, it was a dusty brown. His blue eyes were piercing though only clients who were in recovery from addiction and talking nonsense would get to see just how piercing. He, like many of his clients, was in recovery from drugs and alcohol and suffered no fools.

His work with Margot had become a little frustrating; a little stagnant. The two often got bogged down with her being sorrowful about her patients or irritated with her new job of only six months. Mike would caution her that she was overly emotionally connected to these families and their grief. She agreed with Mike on that point.

When she wasn't dealing with grief and loss from the patients and their families she was dealing with her own boredom.

Mike popped on the call right on time.

"Hello Margot! How are ya'?"

"Not too shabby, Mike. And you?"

"I can't complain. Wouldn't matter. No one would listen, anyway."

"Not unless you paid them to and sometimes, not even then."

"Ain't that the truth. So, how was your week?"

"It was fairly typical. I mean, I didn't feel like anyone was sucking the marrow from my bones, at least. But I'm still longing to do more clinical type of work. I only have a few clients on Telepy, and some are actually interesting cases; some that have real trauma to work through."

Mike decided to jump at the chance, "Excellent! Then how about we start to work on your own trauma?"

"Well, that escalated quickly."

"It sure did. Of course, unless you count all of our other sessions where you avoided it. Look, you know I won't push you too hard, but I also won't continue to take your money. We both know you came here to work on your own trauma, unless you want to talk more about the plug-pullers?"

"Oh Mike!"

"Hey, you know me. You keep coming back because I'm blunt."

"And you're fair. Harsh, but fair."

"Well? Are you ready to work on you or do I need to fire you as my client?"

Margot took a deep breath and let it out slowly, "Okay, so the toad…"

"I'm sorry?"

"Look, do you want to hear this story or not, Mr. Martyn?"

"Toad?"

"I refuse to use his name."

"Well, that's one way to keep him in power."

"Or it's one way to keep him from having any."

"Fair enough."

"Anyway, the toad, and he is even listed in my phone that way…"

"I would stop you and ask why you haven't taken him out of your contacts but I'm afraid it would only cause you to stop this process."

"It would."

"Then consider it off the table."

Margot spent the next forty-five minutes pouring over the relationship that started with a flash and got abusive just as quickly; not physically, but emotionally.

Mike started to close out the session, "Welp, that's a good start. I've been waiting to hear that history for quite some time. You did well and you have much to be proud of in sharing it. I know that wasn't easy, but I believe it will be a good springboard for our work next week and for a while thereafter. It will bring you toward building up grit. Grit should help you in your work with the plug-pullers."

Through the tearful relief of finally sharing the ugliness of her relationship with the toad, she allowed herself to laugh, just a little, "Okay, that's a little funny. Harsh, but darkly funny."

"You know in our business we need to allow ourselves a bit of dark humor—and some grace. Please allow yourself some, will ya', Margot?"

"Allow myself grace or give into dark humor?"

"Both. Definitely both."

"Will do. Thanks Mike. See you next week."

"Absolutely," Mike said cheerfully, and ended the connection.

3

The Plastic Casket

Margot wasn't in her tiny office at Ochsner hospital long enough to do more than put down her purse, get a sip of her Starbucks and check two messages before the call came through. It was from new parents of their only child in the NICU.

'Baby Leia' was born premature and with multiple defects. She was on a respirator, and the opinion of all her generalists and specialists was that she wasn't going to pull through. Margot's supervisor, Prestin Wilcox had given her the run down with an apologetic tone.

"Okay, I'll be right over," Margot said with a deep exhale and replaced the receiver.

These cases were the hardest. It would be her third since she had started working at the hospital. None of them were easy— no matter how young, nor how old, the person was. But the older they were, the more likely that most of their family and friends were much more accepting of the end—and so was Margot. Though, it depended on *how* ready the family was for their loved one to go. Some family members begged for the end to draw nearer because they had caregiver fatigue.

Certainly, the financial drain—for some—was a component. A spiritual component was usually in the mix somewhere. If it wasn't, it just wasn't discussed. If it was, it was almost *all* that was discussed.

For the young ones who did—or were about to—lose their lives, spirituality usually wasn't mentioned because the parents, or parent, were angry at their higher power. And the older family members who stood around the acrylic bassinette wringing their hands, knew not to bring it up. Margot could read a room quite well and this one was no different.

As she used her badge to gain entrance into the NICU, she saw them almost immediately. The man that was embracing his sobbing wife, both were in their mid-20's, made it evident in what part of the NICU Margot was needed. They were standing over a small enclosure that held their only child. An RN in green scrubs was standing on the opposite side of the crib, hands clasped and looking at the floor.

It was time.

The three looked as if they were already at a funeral and the enclosure held the decedent. However, Baby Leia had not yet left this world. There were tubes, machines, and a rhythmic beeping. The most deafening sound, even more than the quiet sobbing of Leia's mother, was that of the anticipation.

"I'm Margot Landry, the healthcare social worker, and I'm so sorry to meet you at a time like this. I'm here to be supportive in any way that I can be for you and your family."

"Can you make her live?" Leia's mother asked.

Margot was already feeling the lump in her throat. She knew Leia's mother wasn't serious, just desperate and angry. Her husband held her tighter as she asked the question. Neither looked up at Margot, they wouldn't let their eyes leave their only child. And as it would turn out, the only child they would ever have together. They would divorce three years later under the stress as neither would recover from their loss.

Margot struggled to answer the rhetorical question, "I...I wish...I wish I could."

Her husband spoke, "She knows you can't do anything. No one can."

"I'm so very sorry..." Margot was going to finish with the familiar term 'for your loss', but thought better of it as this was not the moment. Truly, no moment ever would be.

The RN, Bethony Thompson, spoke up, "Ms. Margot's here to assist you to..."

"Assist in what!? Getting over the loss of our baby before we have even..."

"Shhh-shh-shh," Mr. Billingsly looked up at the ceiling and started to get teary. "She's only trying to be supportive."

"I know what she's here for, Tom!"

"Okay, okay. It's going to be okay."

"It's NOT going to be okay!"

"I know, honey. I'm sorry."

Lisa Billingsly pushed deeper into her husband's chest and relented, "I know, I know. It's not fair for you, either. We're both losing our baby." Lisa looked over at Margot and spoke through her heaves of sobs, "I'm... I'm... sorry."

Margot spoke quickly, "No, no. No apologies are necessary. This should never happen to a mother, nor a father, and certainly never to a baby," Margot finished as she looked down at Leia.

"I didn't even get a chance to be her mother," Lisa said softly.

"But you did. And you are. And you always will be…her mother." Margot took a step closer. "She will never have another person in her life love her as much as you have in this very short time. There are children that grow into adulthood and pass as elderly that never feel the love that she must feel from you right now. I can feel it. We all can feel it. I know we do."

Bethony, the RN, kept her head down and nodded "yes". She was grateful that Margot was there because this wasn't her strong suit as a nurse.

"This little girl. This baby. Your baby, Leia, will pass knowing and feeling that she was loved deeper than most people are ever loved by anyone and at any time in their lives."

Lisa started heaving with sobs again as she buried herself so deep into her husband's chest that the two became one. Margot had hit home, tears streaming down her own face, now.

No one said a word for two minutes or more as Lisa calmed and looked over at the see-through casket where her baby had lived and would now die.

Bethony looked up to see Leia's mother looking down at her. Lisa's tears were tapping like rain on the dome as she looked at her baby girl one last time. Then she looked up at the nurse and nodded her head. She was ready.

Bethony asked softly, "Would you like to hold her hand?"

"Yes, please," Lisa responded, beginning to softly cry through a smile then looked at her husband.

Slowly and carefully, Bethony lifted the cover that had protected Leia for all but a few minutes of her ten days on earth. Both mother and father reached out and took their baby's hand, his under Lisa's and Lisa's under Leia's, and cradled it. It was no bigger than a penny.

Bethony then slowly put her hand on a switch and looked over at the parents. Lisa waited, smiled at her little one that wasn't to be, looked up, and nodded twice. With a loud *click*, the whir of the machines keeping Leia Billingsly alive came to a halt, and all in the room waited for the beeping of the heart monitor to stop. When it did, Thomas Billingsly broke down in a way most people never see any man do. Margot held still with her hands behind her back where she dug her thumb nail into the flesh of her other—hard.

She pulled a card from her front pocket and laid it on a nearby cart after waiting for a full five minutes as the two parents' cries had grown cold with anger. She turned and left the room.

Margot couldn't get to the ladies' room fast enough, heels clicking the whole way, rushing past her boss who had earlier given her the call to death and had been watching through the window the entire time. Once she got through the door, to a stall, and locked it, she allowed herself to let out the grief that had just impregnated her body.

She never heard from the Billingsly's again.

4

Intervention

Prestin Wilcox sat and waited for Margot to finish her emotional purge and exit the restroom. When she emerged, she didn't notice him. He caught up and joined her as she hurried back to the office.

"I know I don't have to tell you but those are always going to be the hardest, but you did excellent."

"Oh, you saw that?"

"Yes, I could see you through the window, but I couldn't hear anything. All the body language in that room told me all I need to know about how well you did. I could see how the parents appeared to begin to accept their loss."

"What good is it all? They're going to be traumatized, and you know that couple is in grave danger of not staying together more than a few years."

"I know, but you got them through the moment. A moment is often all we have with these cases, if you want to call them that."

When the pair rounded the corner to the bank of elevators, Margot spoke with more than a hint of anger, "I'm not sure I do. And I'm not sure I want to even work with any of these types of situations. I'm calling them that, situations; not cases," Margot finished with a definitive bang on the elevator button as she looked up and around to see how long she would have to remain in hell. The NICU was always that; it was hell for adults and Heaven for the children.

Prestin continued, "That's the issue. They're not cases to you. I know this isn't the first time that you have struggled with one of these. Don't misunderstand me Margot, you're amazing at what you do. Just a few sentences and you get the patient, the family, shit, even the staff, right where you need them to be. But these *situations* stick with you. And maybe that will go away over time, and you'll settle in."

"And maybe it won't!" Margot banged on the up button again, knowing that it wouldn't make a difference in the speed at which the elevator came to her nor in how she felt.

"Okay, true! Maybe it won't. But you are too good a therapist to be doing this if it's going to grow like a cancer and darken you."

"Are you saying you want me to quit?"

"Absolutely not! But I do know that you don't have enough self-awareness to let *me* know *you* should quit. You are so fucking good at this that me and this ramshackle department will use you up, regardless," Prestin finished as the elevator doors opened and an elderly couple, both with walkers smiled and trudged out, taking the rest of their lifetime to exit. They smiled back at the couple as they shuffled away. Neither spoke until they were in and the elevator doors had closed.

"Use me up?"

"Yes! Anytime someone is this good and they have no clue when enough is enough until it's too late for their own mental health…look, I'm just saying that, and I'm only going to say this once; if you do not build up the emotional callouses OR you don't quit on your own…well, you are just too good to lose so just know I won't go firing you for your own mental health!"

"So, basically toughen up or get fucked," Margot said as the elevator doors opened to find another elderly couple. This time the husband was pushing his wife, who looked to be in her late 70's, in a wheelchair. She heard the last part of what Margot said and winked at her then commented, "Amen, honey! That's the way the world works!"

Prestin finished, "Exactly, ma'am!" then looked at Margot, "Exactly."

Margot returned home that afternoon. She lived in a modest house in Algiers on the West Bank of New Orleans. To her, it was good enough. Since she was only renting at this point, it didn't matter to her the location nor the size of the place because it was only her and her cat, Adler. He was named after Alfred Adler, the noted psychiatrist. The white and light orange Scottish Fold cat had been with her since she picked him up from the breeder seven years before while she was still married to the toad and they had money.

As she unlocked the door, Adler was already mewing in rapid succession and trying to kill her by interlacing himself between her legs, "Okay! Okay! I'll feed you in a second. Let me get in the damned door you little creamsicle!"

After putting down her bag, mail, and dumping her keys in the bowl she kept on a credenza in her entryway, she did exactly as Adler commanded. Wet food had spoiled him and she knew it would take two months to break him from acting out like that. Dry food never caused that reaction. So, she stroked his head for a few seconds as he growl-ate and then went to her cupboard and got out her wineglass.

After the first few sips started to ease her out of the day and into some comfies, she turned on the television and ruminated on what she and the Billingsly's had endured.

Margot was so deep in thought about little Leia, she didn't even notice the 6pm news opened with a top story about bones having been found in a wooded area by a hunter in Baton Rouge.

5

Goodness-Of-Fit

Margot was building her private practice. She took Prestin's feedback to heart long before he even gave it. She had been talking to her own therapist, Mike, about building enough clientele so she wouldn't have to do hospital social work. She longed to get back to providing deeper, more meaningful, clinical work; work she found more rewarding than the drive-by-therapy she was perpetrating at the hospital. She felt it was important work and should be done, but Margot wasn't so sure it should be done by her. She was finding out that she could not stay objective enough for the work of setting up hospice one day and watching a baby die the next. It was becoming far too much—far too quickly.

Telepy was going to be Margot's way out. First, she would start by taking on the clients that the site sent to her, the company would take their large cut and then pay her a pittance. As word of her reputation spread, she would leave their "practice" and take those clients with her. Sure, she had her own website, but it hadn't caught on yet, and she wanted to be approved on more insurance panels first before leaving the enormous conglomerate of the ones that Telepy had. She still accepted a few insurances that were left over from her private practice days before she closed it down.

The toad had convinced her years before that she didn't need to work. He said he would take care of her. It was one of his ways of controlling her ability to leave anytime she got good and ready. At least she had kept a few trap doors to escape through; her licensure, the panels, and a few clients. But she needed more. Telepy was her way of clawing back to her real passion; regularly scheduled clinical work.

Though, for business reasons, she never cared much for the fifteen-minute introductory sessions that were meant to gauge if there was, what is called in the therapy business, a goodness-of-fit, between client and therapist. It was part of Telepy's business model, and she had agreed to it by electronic signature; that was the easy part. Stealing clients away from them was going to be a little more morally difficult. Good thing that Margot had a little bit of a rebel streak in her when she put her mind to it; and even when she didn't.

Margot sat in front of her laptop screen in her dimly lit home office space; she loathed using a faux background. They were always off-putting and never worked well. Once she accidentally had put the makeup filter on and ended up with a false eyelash on her cheek while she counseled a poor widower. She told him his Lost Lenore would always be a part of him. He canceled the following week and never rebooked. She wasn't sure if that's what his cancellation was all about, but she made sure to always check for that stupid shit before starting the session. "Telepy shouldn't have that nonsense activated via their session videos, anyway," Margot said out loud to herself after that session was over.

Tonight, Margot had one of those sessions scheduled; the 'goodness-of-fit' fifteen minutes of infamy was with a prospective client named Connie Minae. And unlike most new clients, she was right on time. That first fifteen minutes was the beginning of what would change the trajectory of their lives forever. Well, it was the beginning for Margot. Connie's was already going down that path.

When the session started, Margot saw Connie and immediately thought she was reminiscent of Uma Thurman's character in Pulp Fiction; Betty Bangs and all. Connie was sitting in her kitchen with her laptop perched on the island. To her right there could be seen a countertop that led to a half-foot dropdown space where one might sit to do bills. It was stacked with magazines, papers, and Brick-a-Brack. There was a wall to her left. Margot couldn't make it out due to the fairly low lighting, but it seemed that directly behind her, there was a hallway that probably led to bedrooms or a bathroom or both.

There were times when Margot liked teletherapy. It gave her an idea of where and how a person lived. Although she preferred her old office from a few years back, this was one of the perks of teletherapy; that and she didn't have to pay rent, or slip and fall insurance, or decorate a space.

"Good evening, umm, Connie, isn't it? Do you mind if I call you Connie?"

"Not at all. Oh goodness, I'm so glad you are on here. I have reached out to so many therapists the last few days and most have ghosted me. I just don't understand why."

"Well, let me let you in on a little secret. See, ever since the pandemic, there have been plenty of therapist that have more online work than they know what to do with."

"Oh, I see. They don't need the money or they prefer their freedom."

"Nice reframes! We may get along well in our work, should you choose me."

"We just might, Margot. May I call you Margot?"

"Absolutely!"

"Well, Margot, I suppose this is a type of dual interview. If you don't mind, would you tell me a little about yourself?"

"I don't mind at all. So, I'm a graduate of Tulane where I received my master's in clinical social work. That basically means that although it's traditionally thought of when one hears 'social worker', well, let's just say that it conjures up thoughts of those that take children out of abusive homes and place them in foster care. Or, in some cases, grassroots social work where those who graduate with a degree from a nonclinical program might work to change systems that are thought to oppress people and cultures."

"Umm, hum"

"Uh, yeah, so sorry, anyway someone from a clinical background can get licensed to actually do therapy on many issues that a client might be struggling with."

"Like relationships or, let's say, trauma from past or current relationships?"

Margot gripped her chair slightly, "Yes, that would be one of the many issues."

"You like working in trauma, Margot?"

"I, I do." Margot gripped the chair even tighter. A few minutes in and she was already lying to a perspective client. "I like working with most topics that might come up during our work together as long as the client would find it helpful."

"I have trauma, Margot. I have trauma from a relationship that I'm still in."

"Oh, okay, I see. Well, that's not easy work and takes time. Are you interested in taking the time to do that...I mean, depending on how deep the trauma is and how long it has gone on," Margot thought, *Because I sure ain't willing to do that work on my own shit.*

"Oh yeah, I can't wait to work on it. It's why I have been searching for the right one. But how do I know that you are her? How do I know you are the right one for me?"

"Well, I have worked with many people successfully using traditional methods, such as Cognitive Behavioral Therapy, or CBT, and some other work using uncommon methods such as flooding."

"Flooding?"

"It's basically where we flood you with thoughts and even images, depending on where the trauma originated, that elicit an emotional response and then work through the feelings that come up until they are benign."

"Hum, what about this new stuff I've been hearing about; EMDR?"

"Well, I was trained in it after Katrina when I was just coming out of grad school and I must tell you; I'm not a proponent of that style of therapy. If you are looking for that I would have to refer you out."

"Oh, I didn't know it had been around that long."

"Yep, it caught on after 9/11 first responders started to note how effective it was for them."

Connie questioned in a condescending tone, "If it's effective, then why do you not use it in your practice?"

"That's a longer story than the time we have scheduled for today. Just suffice it to say that the best explanation I have heard regarding EMDR was this, and I'm quoting and stealing here but I can't remember where I read or heard it, 'the things that work regarding EMDR are not new. And the things that are new, don't work'."

"Well, I dunno. I've done my research and I'm interested in that, I think. How 'bout I get back to you after I check around a bit."

"I totally understand. However, I hope that I have not been off-putting by being honest about my work."

"Oh my, no. I appreciate the honesty. I guess that does lead me to want to ask one more question since we have time."

"Please, go right ahead."

"Margot, have you worked on your own trauma?"

Margot paused and her mouth slowly opened as she thought about answering a question that was in the grey area of therapy etiquette and in the dark area of malpractice. But Connie noticed that her possible new therapist was about to struggle and swooped in, "I'm sorry, I mean, if you have ever had trauma to work on. You know, I just shouldn't have asked that. I'm so sorry. I just don't have many boundaries, nor do I have much of a filter."

"No, it's fine. Let's just say I have positive feedback from the clients I have worked with who have experienced trauma. I really believe I can be helpful. Though, it will be a bit more like relationship work with only one part of the couple, or, well, if you are in a polyamorous relationship, more than a couple. Anyway, the point is, when one person that is in a romantic relationship comes into therapy without the other partner or partners, they usually break up or divorce or whatever the arrangement is."

"Thank Christ for that! Because I believe that is how this is going to end, anyway."

"I can help with that, too. We don't want you dragging the last relationship into a new one."

"Honestly, Margot, the only place I want to drag this relationship is to court."

"Oh, do you have a lawyer? Are you working toward divorce?"

"Let's just say a separation would be welcomed. However, we aren't married."

"I can help with that, too. I have worked with people who are leaving their situation to find greener pastures elsewhere."

"Well, I'm still going to investigate EMDR further. I'll let you know. I promise not to ghost you if you promise not to ghost me in the meantime."

"I promise I won't do that. And yes, please let me know if you have found someone that's a better fit. That's the most important part."

"Will do, I'll reach out regardless of my decision. But in the long run, I think you are going to work out just fine."

"Thanks so much. Talk soon. OH, I almost forgot, I imagine you looked at my profile before choosing to have our short chat today, no?"

"Umm, hum…"

"Okay, good. You may have noticed in my standards of practice, that you signed, that I record my sessions using Telepy's encrypted video and audio methods."

"Umm, hum…"

"Not every practitioner does that and I wanted to make sure I put it out there. Full disclosure, it helps me with keeping notes. Sometimes I also like to refer back to sessions prior to our next one to make sure I am keeping up with all the connections that we need to pinpoint in the work you are doing. It also, and I'm embarrassed to say, it helps protect both of us. It is strictly confidential, though, should you feel the need to sue me for malpractice or, should I…oh I hate this part…should *I* feel the need to protect myself from a frivolous lawsuit…well, you know how some people can be these days, not saying you—not at all—but it's a practice that is becoming more standard. Please think of it like residential treatment. They have cameras that record…anyway, you get the picture…just know that I would lose my licensure if I were to share it with anyone without your consent. Or, well, a court order, just like any therapy note."

"I did read that before logging on. It does make me a bit squeamish, I have to say. I mean, when I go to the doctor these days, they do have those A.I. devices that record everything but that's only audio. Though, I guess I really don't care one way or the other. I mean, the video, though…I dunno."

"I can assure you; I can't share any of your information with anyone. Except, there are a few caveats like, you know, like…"

"Right, I read that, too, and that's standard. The 'if I'm going to hurt myself or someone else or..'"

"Yes, that's right…all that. But look, if we choose to work together, we'll get all that squared away and you feeling comfortable—no worries, no pressure, no rush."

"Thank you, Margot. Maybe I'll talk to you, again soon."

"Looking forward to it," Margot finished with a tightlipped smile. She knew Connie Minae wasn't coming back. A silly therapeutic gimmick and video recording would seal this one up tight. Connie was going to find someone else, and Margot was glad because she could tell this one was going to be a pain in the ass. She was going to be the type of client that all therapists called "a help rejecting complainer". Some therapists would gladly take a client's money to have their helpful suggestions ignored, but that wasn't Margot.

"You take care now."

"It's the video that I'm worried about because I don't want him to see it."

"Yes, I understand. If we work together, I assure you, it's encrypted, and I'll share it with no one. Just like your doctor doesn't play the audio they recorded for anyone else. It falls under HIPAA law."

"Yes, I know, but…never mind, I've taken up enough of your time."

Margot would have usually prompted a client to continue their thought but didn't want this one, anyway, "No worries. Talk to you later."

"Thanks. Buh-bye."

"Buh-bye now". Margot couldn't close the lid of her laptop fast enough.

"No thank you very much! I'll have none of that," Margot said, aloud.

Margot knew something was going to go wrong if she took her on as a client. However, she felt it unlikely that Connie would ever schedule another session. That was her hope, anyway. It was Margot's hope that tonight would be the last time she would ever see Connie Minae again...

...and it almost was.

6

Margot And The Mall

It's the simple pleasures in life. A soft pretzel and people-watching at the mall were two of those pleasures. They helped her take her mind off her original emotional trauma that she felt she had from her marriage to the toad and the most recent loss of a baby that she didn't birth. Though, these distractions were only roadblocks to the shedding of her own suffering more permanently. Roadblocks can become brick walls. It has been said by nearly everyone that time heals all wounds. Time does nothing of the sort. It's what one does with that time that heals. But for Margot, and for right now, people watching while snacking would suffice.

After making the purchase of her pretzel and Coke Zero, Margot found herself sauntering through the dying mall. It was alive enough that she still found a good mix of slack jawed gawkers, mall walkers, lurkers, and couples. Couples were her favorite. Mall walkers offered her only an inner smile but nothing in the way of predictive story telling. The gawkers were no different than her, though she figured they were not doing it as a social science. Not on the same educated level, anyway. At least that's what she like to tell herself. Lurkers she liked, not as much as couples but lurkers at least had the potential to show some pathology she could spot and watch. Not only that but watching a lurker who was thinking they were hidden gave her a little jolt of excitement as she was hunting the hunters. Especially when they spotted her tracking them and moved on.

Oakwood Mall was, without question, a dying mall. After Hurricane Katrina, it was looted and set fire to. As it clawed its way back from the brink, there were now far more tennis shoe and hat shops and less major department stores that really brought in the couples. Internet shopping had continued to kill it.

She sometimes allowed herself to take the drive to Lakeside Shopping Center that still had it all, including the couples with money. But today, she didn't want to make that drive across the river. Margot just didn't have it in her this Saturday.

She sat herself center court in the middle of where the mall branched off into different corridors. At the dead center of the mall was a coin fountain that was a favorite place for Margot to people-watch. She was not disappointed. Almost immediately a couple started with the body language she craved. Margot saw them near one of the pagodas that sold cheap gold trinkets. A wispy dark-haired girl, barely out of her teens, bent over with hands placed on the glass display case. He was just as scrawny and so tightly shaven that only the thinnest of lines created a silly looking beard on his square jaw. His cap cocked sideways and standing erect on his head. He was not looking *with* her but around her.

And we're off, Margot thought. *She's looking for something she wants and if she has already found that something, he doesn't want anything to do with it. Next, she will point to it, and he'll feign interest then stand back up and continue looking around like a meerkat.* And on cue, the young woman did just that and his reaction was just as Margot had predicted. *Now she will stand straight up and look at him to make sure he knows she is interested in a little token of his love.* Again, Margot was correct in her assessment.

Now she must up the ante'. She's going to have to ask him something with a little stink face on. She thinks maybe that will do it, but it won't... and it didn't.

Oh boy, here we go. He won't meet her gaze, and she will fold her arms.

Again, her prediction was correct. She was almost halfway through her pretzel already. Usually she had to pace herself, but this had gotten good quickly.

Once the wispy girl's arms were folded the rest got even easier to assess and predict for Margot.

Now his arms will go out to his sides, palms flat out in a 'why are you mad?' pose. She will wave him off without looking into his eyes and turn. He'll try and look her in the eyes by scooting around to position himself in front of her turned face and she will allow none of it. Yep, there she goes, and there he goes, and so it goes.

Margot took a sip of her drink and finished the last bite of her pretzel, stood up, walked over to the trash receptacle, wadded up the pretzel bag and tossed it in.

Yup, still got it, she thought to herself as she walked away from her success.

The rest of Saturday was filled with washing clothes and watching inane shows while flipping through Vogue.

On Sunday morning, Margot started to get ready for her week. She had a distaste for Sundays because they signified that the weekend was over and it was time to get ready for Mondays.

Flipping open her laptop to check her evening schedule load of clients for the following week, she noticed that she was scheduled for Friday at 7pm. *I really need to close down my Friday availability*, Margot thought with a groan while she searched to find out who it was. Connie Minae's name populated the slot when she opened her full Telepy schedule.

"Well, maybe I don't, 'still got it'", Margot said with a slight bit of surprise in her voice and took a sip of her chamomile tea. She sighed, "Well fuck me runnin'."

7

The Woods After Midnight

The week had been fairly benign, as was Mr. Henson's biopsy in room 235. It had been a 'plug-pulling' free week. But the week wasn't over yet. It was Thursday and Mike Martyn was, as usual, on time.

"How are ya, Margot?"

Margot started right in, "I have a client I don't want who booked Friday at frickin' 7pm."

"Ew, that's even worse than someone who books Thursday evenings at *6pm*," Mike quickly shot back.

"Nice…look, at least I'm not a…" Margot trailed off and looked up at her home office ceiling.

"Uh oh, looks like you have already found some similarities between the two of you."

"I hope not. I was going to say 'a help rejecting complainer'"

"Oh no, you don't complain so there is no comparison there. One outta two ain't bad, though."

"You really feel I reject help?"

"Oh, heavens no. You don't even ask for the help to reject. Look, I'm just giving you a hard time. Last week was a great session. But I don't think it will be lost on you to note that we aren't even five minutes in this one yet and we are already talking about work. At least it's work you are passionate about. What is it that she wants to work *on*?"

"She's in a relationship with an emotionally, maybe even physically, abusive man."

"Oh shit. Yeah, there is always that one that is working on something that we, ourselves as therapists, are or should be working on. Though, like Albert Ellis wrote, I shouldn't 'should' on people. Sorry, anyway, it's a double-edged sword, as you know. Always hearing ourselves give them feedback we 'should' be taking."

Margot just stepped right over the meta-feedback Mike had just laid down and continued.

"And she seemed concerned about him getting ahold of session recordings and notes."

"Yeah, I'm old school. Took me nearly losing my practice during Covid before I was willing to offer services via teletherapy. Got to where I couldn't afford rent in the high-rise, so I shut it down."

"So, for the clients who were still willing to do face to face therapy, what did you do with those? You weren't willing to offer services in that swanky uptown house of yours, were you?"

"Ha, fuck that noise, no indeed not. I take it you weren't willing to budge on the video recording."

"Ha, no, fuck *that* noise, especially with the vibe I was getting from her. She's exactly the type to sue. She even noted that she couldn't wait to drag him into court. He probably deserves it, but I'll have none of that. And if she does…or if she complains to the board, as you know, all bets are off, and I can show them that my work was solid."

"Fair. Well, maybe she won't show. You probably spooked her enough. Fuck it, you'll find the right clients for you soon enough. Then you can give up the 'plug pulling' job."

Mike said it to be funny and settle into the session but watched Margot's expression quickly dissolve.

"Was it something I said?" Mike asked as his face changed to match hers and he quickly switched to Rogerian therapy from his usual, "shoot the shit", style.

Margot collected herself, "The day after our last session there was a family I had to visit in the NICU…"

"Oh no, I'm so sorry."

"Yeah, it wasn't good."

"I can't even imagine."

"If it wasn't for the fact that this week was easy…"

"I just bet…"

"And just when I thought I was outta the woods…"

"Margot, let me tell you something. We live in a tent in the woods among zombies. They shuffle around while we follow behind and tell them they are in the woods. They only know they don't want to be there, but they don't believe that's where they are. It's a dichotomy. Or they believe they can live in the woods and still be at the beach. Each week we find them pissing on the same tree at 7pm on a Friday. Sure, we work to get their permission to take them by the shoulders, turn them around, and attempt to bring them out of those woods—the woods they created or got trapped in. But where our problem lies is that we turn right back around to go get the next one only to find that for weeks or months or even years they continue to wander right back in the woods behind us. It's like herding cats."

Margot looked down at Adler and smiled through her drying tears and wiped her face.

Mike continued, "Sometimes they even run past you and beat you back into the forest and to the same tree. Then you have the ones that are in pairs and even quads, whole families of 'em, just fighting to piss on the same bark of that magnolia."

Margot allowed a tiny laugh to escape.

"And off we go runnin' to find the ones who are now setting the whole forest on fire. Just shittin' and pissin' everywhere they live. And all we're trying to do is get them to that fuckin' beach."

"I want to go to the beach, Mike—to continue your metaphor. Although I hate the beach, I do take your meaning."

"Margot, there are three types of therapists. There are therapists that are great at herding cats, or in this case, zombies. I know I have never seen you work but you know as therapists we can just tell the quality of others' work just by talking with them. And you also know how many of them suck. Most of the therapists I have met and even worked with, professionally and privately, they just suck. They shouldn't even have a license to drive an automobile, much less one to lead zombies to the promised land. And then there are the therapists that are great, you being one of them, who take on all the yuck. It sticks with them. You stay in the woods when the clock carved out of the pissing tree strikes 10pm. And it's dark in there. Real dark."

"So, what's the third type?"

"The third type are great therapists, *and* they come out of the woods. They come out of the woods refreshed. They don't live in there."

"So, what type of therapist do you consider yourself?" Margot asked.

"Me? Oh, I'm the pissing-tree. I'm the pay toilet. I'm just someone that clients pay to piss on, and they walk out on their own. I don't just visit that forest or camp in a tent. I'm a permanent resident. But, I *can* live in the woods. I guess I *am* the woods. Well, a lone pissing-tree in the woods. I make up the old guard. We love it in here. We love the dark. We are the dark. And when it's too bright outside, we just provide shade so the mushrooms can grow; mushrooms and the saplings. The saplings are the younger therapists when their feet get stuck and we know they aren't going to leave the forest. They're gonna become part of it…" Mike trailed off and then continued.

"Margot?"

"I know what you are going to say next, Mike."

"And what is that?"

"Don't become a tree in the forest."

"And that's how I know you are one of the good ones. Now, let's uproot you, little sapling, and get you out of that bad relationship you still haven't left yet."

8

The Waiting Is *Not* The Hardest Part

Margot had made it through her week only having to deal with
the more mundane part of her job, and she was grateful for that.
What she wasn't grateful for was that every time she looked at
her Telepy schedule, there she was, Connie Minae. Should
Connie cancel, her name would disappear from Margot's
electronic scheduler. It hadn't and it wouldn't though she held
out hope that Connie *would* ghost her.

Clients do it all the time, Margot thought as she fed Adler.
Please, Jesus, don't show up, she begged. She had been
begging all day, and it was still only 5:45pm.

Long ago Margot had quit locking Adler out of her office
before she started her evening sessions. He would mew and
scratch on the door, anyway. At times, he would jump in her
lap while she was counseling a client and though it would
break the mood, whatever that mood might be, it always led to
a good place. When working with clients that had been with
her for a while, she would simply let him stay in her lap and
she would pet him until he laid down. It was only a real
problem when he would try and walk on the keyboard or even

lay on it. More than once, he had disconnected the client by stepping on a button or two. The house was small enough that even if she closed him in another room, he could be heard.

Margot had already settled in, laptop open, and was gripping the chair in irritated anticipation of the Minae session. Adler was in a crouched position getting ready to jump into her lap.

"Look, you little creamsicle, I don't want to even be in here right now but if you're good, I'll give you an extra…you know what? Wait right here." Margot went into the kitchen and pulled out a can of wet food and slipped it in her pocket. When she came back, Adler had already settled himself on her chair. He looked up at her, put his head back down, and readied himself by digging his claws in the cloth covered seat.

"Oh no you don't, you little shit. I'm not playing this game with you."

Margot tried to pick him up and he dug his claws in deeper, nearly bringing the chair with him when she tried to pick him up. She instantly stopped pulling when he meowed loudly in irritation because he wasn't getting his way. She pulled out the few claws he still had in the fabric and put him on the floor then quickly sat down. He jumped into her lap just before she could scoot the wheeled chair so that her legs were under the desk.

"Damn it, Adler! Stop!" Margot said as she tried to place him back on the floor. Now his claws were dug into her pants and skin. "Ow! Knock it off!" She screeched and pushed him off her lap then grabbed a belled ball cat toy from the top of her desk and tossed it over her shoulder and against the back wall. She pushed herself under the surface of the desk while he chased the toy.

As Adler pushed the ball around—and it jingled as he did—Margot waited. First, five minutes…then ten. The rule, as it was written in Margot's standards of practice on her website; if you are fifteen or more minutes late, the session is cancelled and there is a cancellation fee. Margot looked at the desk clock that read 7:12pm.

"Come on, come on…" she said as if she were calling a horse to the finish line. She was calling to the clock and not to the client. There's not a therapist in the world who hasn't done this when they wanted to avoid a session, regardless of the reason.

With a flicker of the screen, Connie's head nearly filled the entire space. She was sitting in that same kitchen with that same creepy hallway behind her. It was an image that Margot would come to loathe looking at.

"Sorry, sorry, sorry…am I too late?"

Margot fought back showing any disappointment that Connie had made it to the session in the nick of time, "No-no, it's fine. Life happens…it's all good, no worries."

"Oh, okay, good," Connie did a faux wipe of her brow and let out a 'phew'. "I was concerned I wouldn't make the 15-minute deadline."

"You did fine, no worries. Are you okay?"

"Oh yes, my boyfriend, well, partner…I dunno, I mean, my whatever. We haven't gotten married, and we won't. He asked, I said I needed to think about it, and it resulted in him… ya know, let me back track just a little."

"Okay, just take your time, no rush. First, just as a standard of practice, I need to ask you to share your address."

"Oh yes, 2112 Oak St."

"Thanks for that," Margot chirped while writing it down on her desk pad. "Okay, now, why don't you tell me how the two of you met so I can get some history."

"Well, I was working at a coffee shop and Bradly…that's his name…Bradly LeBlanc. Anyway, I was working in the coffee shop, and he came in once in a while; once a week. I noticed his eyes right away; he has striking eyes. Light green eyes until he gets rageful. Then they grow darker," Connie looked down for a moment to gather herself. "Anyway, they are just noticeable. But, like I said, he didn't come in often. He worked, well still does but I say that because I don't work at the coffee shop anymore," Connie sighed, "He started coming in more often after I gave him one on the house and I guess he could tell I was into him. By the end of the month after that free coffee, he was coming in every day and being flirty. Then one time, he only worked half a day, came in, ordered, and then sat and waited. I caught him tracking me."

"Tracking?"

"Yes, you know, kind of creeper-like, but he was always dressed nice and had a Chronoswiss watch…ya know, those are expensive watches…anyway, so I was intrigued. I didn't know where he worked at the time, but I knew he had money. And here I was struggling to make a living wage. So, I admit it, I was flattered. He had taken an interest in me, and he was, well, is, good looking. So, because of all that, it wasn't creepy that he was tracking my movements and eye-fucking me."

"Umm hum"

"Yeah, so, if he had been broke or not attractive…oh, I just sound so shallow but…"

"No, I totally get it."

"Yeah, thanks for that. So, I get off at three and I go to walk past him, and I smile and he offers to buy me a coffee if I'll sit and chat. So, yeah, I'm like, 'okay, why not', and we sit and chat. And, like wow, he's like charming and good looking and he's flashing his watch and talks about working in the building a block up...oh, I forgot to mention that we are in the CBD and so, like, he works up the street with an investment firm, Huntly and Danials. We are forty-five minutes in, and he hasn't taken a breath. He keeps talking about what he has and how he's moving up the corporate ladder and heee's charming and heee's goodlookin'...oh God, there I go again...this sounds so bad."

"Look, let me jump in here real quick. Please don't feel any guilt whatsoever that you were feeling doted on by a wealthy and goodlooking man. As women we grow up wanting prince charming, right?"

"Yeah!"

"And we think about 'him' and wait for 'him' and some of us even try and hook 'him' in, right?"

"Yeah! I mean, I wasn't trying to hook him in, but yeah."

"No no, right, I know you were just minding your own business, right? I mean, it's okay if you showed some interest and, obviously, he noticed that interest."

"Yeah! I mean, I did show some interest. I didn't expect it to go anywhere. And I certainly didn't expect it to end up how it is right now."

"Say more about that."

"So, now...well, I dunno. I dunno if I'm ready for that just yet."

"Totally understand, trust me I do."

"You do? I mean, well, of course you do because you work with people all the time that have these issues, I would imagine."

"More than you know. And it takes time to unpack this stuff. We may choose to unpack it at another…"

At that moment, something caught Margot's eye in the background. It was unnerving. So unnerving she forgot what she was saying and looked over Connie's shoulder and down the hallway.

"Connie…um, that door, the one behind you…in the hallway, it's slowly opening."

Connie didn't even turn around at first as she explained, "Oh, yeah, this is an old house. It's over a hundred years old. If there is a draft or a window cracked open or when the air kicks on…oh, and the house leans a little and needs to be shored up and that door almost latches but not quite…well, not all the time, anyway. So, it just does that. I close it every time I see it because it's a mess in that room. I store stuff in there. Anyway, it's nothing but it did scare me to death the first time I noticed it. Bradly just laughed and laughed. Asshole. He explained what was going on. Suction or some sort then made some shitty joke how I could take a lesson from…well, you get my point."

"Ouch!"

"Yeah, I know. But it's not because of, well, this is a bit embarrassing, but it's not because of any skill level. It's because…"

"No, sorry, I didn't say 'ouch' because of his shitty statement; it's not that. It's my cat, he just figured out I have a can of wet food in my pocket to keep him quiet and still, should he start

44

acting up. He can smell it right through the tin. I'm so sorry, give me one second."

"Awwww, what kind of cat?"

"He's a Scottish Fold, ya know, the kind," both women said in unison, "With the folded ears."

Connie continued on after Margot said, "Yep."

"Awwww, let me see him, please."

Margot, picked him up, "Okay, buddy, it's your big debut."

Margot, put his face in the camera.

"Well, ain't he just the cutest thing? What's his name."

"Adler."

"Oh, after Alfred Adler, right?"

"Oh, you know your psych history."

"Well, only a little. I took psych 101 at UNO years ago, but, well, I never got a degree."

"Okay boy, down you go." Connie heard the can pop-top wrench and click. Margot tossed the top of the can in her trash next to the desk, "Anyway, where were we?"

"Fellatio." Connie said so deadpan it was almost creepy.

"Oh, um, yeah, okay so…yeah, door that opens from time to time on its own."

"Yes, but mostly that I wasn't giving him enough."

"Understood."

"Yeah, so, like, I wasn't giving it to him because he had become cruel and I was no longer, ya know, feeling it."

"I totally understand."

Connie paused and just staired at the camera. Like she was offended she had been interrupted.

"Do you, Margot?"

"Well, um, I understand that with couples, sexual desire can wane for many reasons."

"Many? Reasons?"

"Uh, well, yes. It happens when women are no longer emotionally connected to their partner." After hearing Margot's explanation, Connie suddenly was fine again.

"Yes, yes, that's it! He was being mean, and I didn't want to bring him any pleasure at all. More than that, he was being…ya know, never mind, that's for another session."

"Absolutely. No problem. Just know that you never have to be more detailed than you are comfortable with."

"Good. That's good. I'll just leave it there for now…" Connie sighed, "Ya know, I just don't want to talk anymore. Let's end this session early. Thanks, though, you have been helpful and maybe this is a good start."

"Okay, that's fine. No worries."

"You keep saying that."

"I'm sorry?"

"You keep saying, 'no worries'."

"Oh, it's a bad habit. Just a colloquialism that I use too much."

"Okay, well, see you next week. I'd like to book this time again. Fridays at seven."

"That's, well, that's fine."

"Oh, that time not good for you?" Connie said with a haughty tone.

"No, it's fine. Just let me know if it can be any earlier, though," Margot was starting to have a tone of her own.

"It must be this time. It's when he is gone every week. It's ritualistic for him. He leaves at 6:30 every Friday to make his weekly card game. I was late tonight because he took too long to leave. I wanted to be sure he was gone before I got on here with you."

Margot softened a little as she felt Connie was likely worried about getting caught and she had surmised he was physically abusive to her, "Sure thing. This time works for me."

"Good! See you next week!" Connie said and shut the laptop before Margot could say 'goodbye'.

"Bitch." Margot hissed, though, it was under her breath just in case the connection hadn't yet been broken.

9

The Friend

Joan Pierse was semi-retired and worked in the giftshop at Ochsner Hospital. Margot Landry had wandered in after interviewing seven months ago. The interview, of course, was for the job she now held and detested. But it was a full-time job, and she needed the income after the break-up with the toad. She had kept only a handful of private clients during the marriage. Moving forward, Margot knew that she would need several weeks or even months to build up her clientele list again. To make matters worse, the job she had was slowing her progress down in a way she didn't expect.

It may have slowed the process down further, but Joni and wine always made it better. Her name was Joan but if she liked you, and you knew when she didn't, it was Joni. And she knew instantly when she didn't like you. And she liked Margot right away. They struck up a conversation the morning of Margot's interview and even had coffee. Margot wanted to know more about the hospital and the people within it. Joni couldn't wait to give her all that juicy gossip—and did. She even left the shop closed with an *On Break* sign hung on the door for a full hour so she could spill all the hospital tea.

Joni was in her mid-sixties and everyone who knew her, and even some that didn't, considered her a spitfire. Short gray hair with lowlights and always in a dress that hung just at the knees. Costume clip on earrings, real pearls, and flats rounded out her look. She could scoot around faster than most women half her age. Her quick wit got quicker with a nice chardonnay. She was every bit of what people would call a "dame" had she been the age she is now but living in the 1940's.

It was Saturday evening, and the ladies had decided that Joni would be having Margot over for a little dinner with wine.

Margot came to the door of the converted shotgun-double nestled in old Algiers at 4pm sharp, rang the original doorbell buzzer, and Joni greeted her with a smile and a wise crack, "Ayyy, who kicked ya cat, toots?"

"It's been a fucked-up two weeks, Jonesy."

"Well come on in and let's crack a bottle up against that week. Like the Titanic, let that shit set sail off into the sunset and sink."

"I brought some," Margot held up a twenty-five-dollar bottle of grape she brought from home.

"And I drank all mine so it's a good thing you came packin'," Joni joked. She actually still had seven bottles in the rack.

"I'm going to need this whole bottle to myself."

"Well, if you don't share it then you'll be drinking it from the neck of that bottle because I have the glasses."

"Fine, I'll give you a swig."

"Give me your bag and let me put it up for you after I root through it. I know yesterday was payday."

"You can have anything you find in there."

"Then I know it's just bills, and I got enough of those."

"You and I both," Margot huffed as she flung herself on the chaise lounge, kicked her shoes off, put her feet up, and held out the bottle which Joni took dutifully with a snatch.

"You ain't messin' 'round. See, this is what happens when you don't come see ol' Aunt Joni during the week. Last week was bad enough. What happened this week?"

"I got this new fuckin' client that is going to be a pain in my ass. I just know it."

"You have great intuition. I'm surprised you didn't listen to it and just dump her with one of your patented excuses."

"I need the money, I need to practice, and, well...," she looked over at Joni who had retrieved the bottle opener and was going to work on the cork, "...I'm intrigued."

"Sounds like how I got into my third marriage. And we both know how that ended. So, if that's any indication..."

"Yeah, curiosity killed the cat."

"And someone already kicked yours. What's your client's name...oh wait, I can't ask you that."

"Let's just say that her name rhymes with Cunt-y Bidet"

Joni bent over laughing, "Oh yeah, sounds like you got a winner there, honey! Spill it! What's wrong with her?" Joni finished with a pull of the cork and started filling the glasses she had already laid out.

50

"I dunno, she's just, odd."

"Ain't that what you do for a livin'? Fix 'odd'?"

"I dunno about *this* brand of odd."

"That sounds like my fourth husband."

"Fourth!?! How many times have you been married, Joni?"

"I quit counting after four."

"Well one is going to be enough for me."

"Yeah, I'm sorry baby girl," Joni said as she handed Margot a glass of wine, "That toad of yours didn't turn into a prince."

Margot finished her first full swig of the grape and asked, "Why did you ever marry again…especially all those times?"

"Oh, none of it was their fault that we didn't stay together. It was mine. Well, or they died."

Margot was mid second sip, "That's a first."

Joni sat on a chair that was directly across from the chaise, "What's that?"

"Do women usually take responsibility for the marriage being over?"

"No, but I do. I'm witty and charming and fun but no one can live with me. Once women are old enough, or men for that matter, we know what's what. I can't be lived with, and I know that. And I simply enjoy the pleasure of my own company, so I don't give a shit," Joni said with a wave of her glass then put it up to her lips, her eyes toward the ceiling.

"Well, I'm not charming nor fun and I think that I can be lived with."

"And there you've gone and proven my point…you're not old enough, yet."

Joni was an amazing cook. Chicken Marsala with mashed potatoes was the dish of the evening and Margot, who didn't cook much of anything, found it divine.

"Joni, this is sooo fuckin' good."

"Thank you, my dear. So, how's the book coming?"

"And there goes my appetite."

"What? I'm just giving you some gentle nudging like any good aunt should—related or not."

"It's not going well at all."

"If I thought it were, I wouldn't have asked…anyway, you have some great stuff to share that will be helpful to others."

"Pfft, I can't even work on my own shit. How am I supposed to write anything about trauma if I can't deal with my own?"

Joni put down her knife and fork, put her hands on the table, then leaned forward, "May I level with you, pumpkin?"

"Uh oh, here it comes, I don't know if I like the sound of that."

"You can feel free to tell me to mind my own my own business…but I won't."

"In that case I won't say shit, I'll just listen."

"As far as I can tell, you haven't gone through any trauma."

"JONI!"

"Wellll, honey, you haven't. Unless there's some shit you haven't shared with me in the time I have known you. To be fair, it hasn't been long but…"

"I've shared nearly everything regarding the toad, and he is the bulk of my trauma."

"Then I repeat myself," Joni said as she wiped the corners of her mouth and placed the cloth napkin back in her lap.

"I'm almost offended."

"Yeah, 'offended' is a word that I'm not even sure should exist. It only means that your feelings got hurt. Although, you probably have been offended in that marriage and divorce, but I'm not sure about traumatized."

"Joni, where is this coming from?"

"Look, all I'm saying is you need to write about what you know."

"I…I know a lot about how to work with trauma."

"Oh, dear, I'm not talking about your formal education nor professional experience. No question, you are very smart and have much to teach, just like I said. No, I mean about *feeling* it. Look, I'm no professional, you know that. I mean, who am I, I can't stay married and I'm working in a giftshop after years of working in finance. But I know what trauma looks like. I lived next door to a family that was the epitome of trauma. And I know how that family, with their shitty father, turned out because of them not working through that trauma after he went to jail," Joni took a sip from her glass as Margot waited, "Trauma is near death, seeing death…"

"I've seen death! It wasn't the first time, either. You know last week I watched a baby die!"

"*A baby,* not *your baby*…not even a family member's baby. Car accidents or, dare I say the word, 'rape', or even constant verbal abuse of a child. No, hon, you went through a bad marriage. That's what happened to you. And please forgive me, because I adore you and don't want you hurt by what I'm saying, but you went through a drab marriage with him talking shit for a few years. My main point is you've given it more weight than it deserves. Work on that shit; get it out. But the more you call it trauma, the more power you are giving what amounts to nothing more than a bad memory of a shit marriage."

"You sound like my therapist, Mike."

"Mike sounds smart."

"Fuck," Margot exclaimed with a slump of her shoulders while looking in her plate.

"That's the spirit! Now eat your chicken. It's getting cold."

10

Book Trauma

On Sunday, Margot sat at her desk in her home office, laptop open, and stared out of the window that faced her. She was looking without for inspiration when she needed to look within. However, looking at her own life after speaking with Mike, and now Joni the night before, left her feeling flat. She contemplated how both could be so right and both be at slightly different angles. Mike wanted her to work on something that Joni said wasn't there. Margot felt it was both. She knew Joni was right and she half-heartedly resented her for it. *Resentments are simply unmet expectations,* she thought, *and I expected Joni to be on my side no matter what.*

Joni saw Margot's marriage for what it was. Not several trauma-inducing events but just drab, as she called it. Though the toad was an ass and said shitty things, he didn't traumatize her; he controlled her. Even worse was that she was the one who allowed it. He didn't have any power over her that she had not given to him. And for that, she resented herself.

Mike was right, too, though. Margot called it trauma, and Mike went with it. But it was really about being stuck; stuck in her own shit. As a therapist, it always resonated with Margot about how right her professors were. She thought back on the times they would talk about how easy it was to spot other people's issues and giving them feedback about those issues, but it being much more difficult working on one's own struggles. It wasn't even a therapist thing—it was a human thing. That same road always led to the same place: realizing that seeing faults in others was so much easier than seeing one's own.

Still lost in her window of thought, she was also now realizing she had used the term 'trauma' as a crutch or badge of honor. It gave her an identity that replaced the one she lost during that marriage. An identity she clung to like a life preserver. Then she visualized herself clinging to a large yellow blow-up ring around her body with a big duck face on it. In her vision she read the words printed on the floaty, 'NOT TO BE USED AS A LIFE SAVING DEVICE'. She laughed at herself and looked down at the blinking cursor on her laptop and immediately frowned.

Margot was dealing with imposter syndrome and non-writer's block in a jelly roll. She wasn't an author at all. The only thing she had ever really written was her thesis. And it was only a regurgitation of other more talented peoples' work topped off with, she believed, a heaping helping of pagination. She loathed writing her thesis. Margot had considered it a waste of paper and ink. Not because she thought she had done a bad job. It's because it was the equivalent of busy work used as an exclamation point of proof that she deserved her master's. The imposter syndrome was coming from now knowing why she couldn't write this book in the first place. It's because Mike and Joni were right. She was stuck in the woods even though she hadn't lived there long enough to become rooted. And what she had lived wasn't traumatizing. What was worse was that she wasn't happy about it.

Now what? Margot asked herself.

She had no idea she was going to get that trauma she so desperately wanted to cling to.

11

Open Door Policy

It had been another uneventful workweek for Margot. She primarily stayed in her tiny office each day. And those days were filled with more of the mundane tasks of the job rather than the grim specter of death and wailing mothers of lost sons and daughters. It was generally traditional social work.

Margot had not gone to see Joni since Saturday night. Not in her home nor in the giftshop. She was still smarting, somewhat, over Joni being as blunt as Joni always had been. But she missed her friend and wasn't mad at her for being direct. And she wasn't mad at her for being right. For that matter, she wasn't even mad. She was just being protective of her ego and didn't want another dose of that kind of medicine. She longed for her friend's company, though. So, just before lunch, she made her way down to the giftshop.

"Well, well, well and here I thought you were avoiding me after our dinner. Didn't even answer my call three days ago."

"Your message said you were fine and just checking on me. That was sweet. And thank you. But my fragile ego was hurt."

"So, you *were* avoiding me."

"Yes, but not because of you. It was because of me," Margot finished by picking up a candle and sampled the scent named 'candy apple'.

"Hon, please forgive me. I meant no harm."

"No, I needed to hear it, you were right."

"It's okay, you'll get used to it."

Margot smiled, "Or I'll get right."

"In your mind or in your head?"

"Both! Wanna go to lunch?"

"I knew you'd ask."

"No you didn't"

"Okay, I'll admit it, you're right."

"You'll get used to it," Margot said with a wry smile.

The two ladies walked arm and arm, whispering and giggling as they went into the cafeteria. After walking up to the grill, they began to give their orders to a girl that looked to be twenty-something, one they hadn't seen before.

Margot spoke up quickly, "I'll have a patty melt."

"And I'll have a tuna melt."

"Ew."

"What?" Joni said with her hands splayed out.

"Hey, it's your mouth but hot tuna?"

"When you are over sixty you stop eating like a teenager. You eat things that'll put hair on your chest."

"I would never!"

"Don't mind her honey..." Joni said to the pudgy twenty-something, "...when you get to be my age you'll eat it, too."

"Don't listen to her, they won't even make nastiness like that when you are her age," Margot made a 'yuck' face as she punctuated her point.

The young girl turned and went to give the cook the order without even acknowledging the whole exchange.

Joni semi-whispered, "Well, I'm sorry."

Margot bit her lip as the ladies leaned into each other and giggled.

That evening, at 6pm, it was time for Margot to come clean with Mike regarding the wisdom Joni had shared.

"Well, hello there, youngster. How are you?"

"Good, and you?"

"Doing well, thanks for asking. What you got for me this week?"

"Well, let me get right to it. I don't have trauma and I'm not describing what I *do* have as 'trauma' ever again."

"Oh, thank Christ," Mike exclaimed with a slap of his hands together. "Look, I mean no disrespect, but I just couldn't even...please, excuse me, I mean, well..."

"No, it's fine. I get it. The term is overused these days in our field, anyway. But really, I've come to the conclusion that it should be reserved for the real stuff. Not shitty marriages that…well, you get it."

"Oh yeah, I totally get it. So, how did you come to that conclusion?"

"Joni."

"Wait, your friend from the hospital?"

"Yes. Well you, too, of course. Your woods analogy stuck with me and then Joni followed up with a great volley and it all just all came together."

"Good, okay, so if you don't have the 'T-word', then what do you have to work on?"

"My shit."

"Yup, that's more my speed, me being a junkie and all."

"Reformed junkie."

"Oh, no ma'am. Once a junkie, always a junkie. I want to get high right now…it's the consequences I don't want, and I know they will always show up if I pick up."

"Ah, so that's how that works."

"Yes, and also how it doesn't."

"Understood. Well, I have some shit to work on."

"Let's get to it, then."

"Now I'm getting bored with work."

"Aw, for fuck's sake."

At almost the same time, Adler mewed and jumped in Margot's lap.

"No, it's not like that. I don't miss two weeks without the 'plug pullers', as you like to say. No, but it's either the patient deaths or the boring paperwork or setting up hospice or…well you get the picture."

"The kind of job where you are damned if it is and damned if it isn't."

"Right!"

"How's the book coming?"

"That has been suspended for the moment. Maybe I'll try fiction," she looked down at Adler in her lap, smiled, and petted him on one of his folded ears.

"What about?"

"I dunno. No clue, really. I do have that new client…"

"Oh, really? You mean the shitty one you didn't want to show up in the first place? She present some interesting stuff to work on? Is that the one; the one that has you considering writing fiction?"

"I'm not going to say the 'T-word', but she is going to trump anything I went through. At least it seems that way because she's scared of her boyfriend."

"Sounds like they're still together. Yeah, that'll make it interesting."

"Yes, but that's not quite it. She's…well, like I said last time, something's off with her. I mean, I'm not blaming the victim, so-to-speak. It's just that I just get this vibe from her that something's not right."

"You've seen her once, correct?

"Only once after the freebie."

"Normally I would say that you needed to take your time and not jump to conclusions with both feet, but we have talked enough about cases together for me to know that your instincts are good—damned good."

"Thanks for that. But I dunno," Margot said with a huff of insecurity, "I'm going to just keep my eyes open on this one."

"Well, I know you are a bit more risk adverse than most so I'm sure you have your recording going and her permission to do so, right?"

"Yeah, she signed all my online forms and it's in my standards of practice."

"You'll be fine, then."

"I suppose. She's…she's prickly! That's it. She like…I'm getting the vibes of a borderline with childhood tra…'T' word, ya know."

"Not to diagnose someone I have never worked with and someone you have worked with only once, but how about a psychopath?"

Margot got a chill.

"How about a borderline with sociopathic features?"

"Yikes."

"Yikes, indeed. But that's what people want to read about and so that's why I'm thinking maybe turn her into fiction."

"Yeah, they may want to read about 'em, but almost no one wants to work with 'em," Mike said with his eyes wide open.

"Well, since she intrigues me, I may not be as risk adverse as you think I am," Margot said with a lilt in her voice.

"You might want to be," Mike said in all seriousness.

Even though Margot knew what Mike was saying and what he meant by saying it, she asked anyway, tongue in cheek, "Be what? Intrigued or adverse to the risk?"

"You can be both."

"Fair," she said, as she didn't expect the "both-and" answer.

"You may have made a good junkie. Though, I'm glad you weren't and aren't. Don't do drugs, kids," Mike said with a smile and a wink. Had he had a beard he would have looked like the Coca-Cola Santa Claus in that moment.

"I'm not sure I get your meaning."

"Dope fiends are often skittish with a side of rebellion."

"Ah, understood. Yeah, that's me."

It was Friday night and nearing 7pm. Margot meant it when she told Mike she was "intrigued" by Connie. She was totally risk adverse and had been most times in her life and in most areas—she lived nervously. But, then again, there was that streak of rebellion.

Margot sat with the laptop open, the Telepy app ready, and the 'record session' button already pressed. The checkbox and explanation of when the client electronically signs all initial Telepy paperwork is there for a potential client to either click, leave blank, or run for the hills should they want none of it. Margot was sure she had lost some clients due to it. However, that was a hard boundary for her, and she was going to stick to and record all sessions.

Margot was sued in her mid-twenties. At that time, she had rented a room at a group practice after receiving her newly minted license to practice. She accepted only evening sessions occurring after her work at one of the local adult psychiatric hospitals. She had clients three evenings a week in the little Mid-City New Orleans collection of offices with an attached waiting room.

The suit centered around her treatment of a teen who was on the spectrum. At the time it was generally diagnosed as Autism or Asperger's syndrome for those that were on the outer edges of its symptomology. That's what became Autism Spectrum Disorder. However, Margot had not worked with a teen, nor anyone for that matter, with those symptoms. She struggled with his case and his parents. They had not had him diagnosed before nor did they know what was causing his odd behavior since he was four or five. From that age on, it continued to become more pronounced, and they were frustrated with his lack of progress with any professional they had brought him to. They expected him to be "fixed", like parents often do, when they bring their child in to be assessed and addressed.

The group practice allowed her to use their space and, because they took money from her for the use of that space, everyone in the building was named in the suit. It was two months and eight sessions in before she had diagnosed him and the parents sued the group for malpractice. Margot was insured and her insurance company gave her a lawyer from the one of the top five law firms in the city. He was perfect. He knew nothing about therapists or how it all worked, but he allowed Margot to explain the profession and the process. He chipped away at the case before it was ever set to go to trial.

Because the lawyer representing the family was so poor at understanding how the therapeutic process works, and after five years of back and forth, that included a long deposition process, the entire mess was tossed out with prejudice. However, although the practice was let out of the case, the family's attorney simply began to focus on Margot and rewrote her argument as a malpractice suit specifically against her.

Margot would go it alone because, not long after that process began, the practice asked her to take her leave from the space. She wasn't a partner and was only being allowed use of the office because she knew the psychiatrist who also rented space there. They both worked at the same psych hospital, and he had suggested it to the partners as a way to help them pay the mortgage until a more seasoned staff therapist joined the practice.

Yes, Margot was as risk adverse as Mike and her had talked about, but she believed she was right from the very beginning of being served with that lawsuit and it gave her a sense of righteous rebellion when she finally won outright. Since she didn't want to go through that hell again, if she could record a session and the client agreed, she would. If the client didn't agree, then she would refer them out. Telepy to the rescue, she once thought, but always at a price.

Connie popped up at 7pm on the nose, "Hello, Margot."

"Hello, Connie, how are you?"

"Yeah, just livin' the dream, I guess."

"Okay, so, just a reminder, our session is being recorded, and would you please tell me your address?"

"2112 Oak," Connie said as she rolled her eyes.

"Okay, well, thank you for that. So, how can I be helpful?" Margot asked. She noticed that the door behind Connie was already open. The skittish clinical social worker was happy about that. Though, now it bothered her that she couldn't see past the door frame of the room because it was so dark. She imagined all sorts of things behind Connie. Gnarly faced monsters, wispy ghosts, lawyers.

"You can't," Connie said smugly and then smiled. "I'm sorry, it's just been a tough week and honestly, I couldn't wait to get to session."

"Oh good…I mean, not good that you had a rough week but…"

Connie cut her off, "I get it."

"Okay, so tell me about your week."

Connie stared right into the laptop, quietly, and just when it was awkward enough for Margot to want to break the silence that all therapists are taught not to encroach upon, Connie spoke.

"The truth is, Margot, that he asked me to marry him several weeks back. I mean, he didn't get down on one knee or anything like that, he just blurted out a proposal. So, I told him I needed to think about it. I told him I needed to think about it knowing full well that I had no intentions of entering into anything close to marriage with this man. We haven't fucked in months. Well, except the times he forced himself on me. Rape clearly. Fuckin' asshole!"

"Wait, he has raped you?"

"Oh, Margot, please, no one is going to believe that. It's domestic and you know that the rules are different."

"I know, but I want to make sure that I've got it clear, so I get the full picture of..."

"How much fuller of a picture do you need after I say 'rape'?"

"Yes, I understand that..."

"Well, I would hope so, Margot!"

"Let me stop you here..."

"Excuse me?"

Adler, who had been sleeping in the corner of Margot's office, quickly left the room, he didn't care for the tone.

Margot knew the value of boundaries and though she was shaking when she said it, she was going to erect one and held up her hand to the screen, "Connie, if we are going to work together, I need you to understand me as much as I need to understand you. We are going to speak to one another respectfully and we are going to retain a decorum in space and a modicum of mutual respect, or I will end the session and refer you out to someone who is a better fit for you. Are we clear?"

Connie put her face in her hands and started to cry. Through her sobs she blurted out, "He backhanded me! That was a few months ago. It wasn't the first time he has hit me and it's getting worse."

"Are you looking to get out?"

"No question, yeah, totally. I'm just worried to even try...I'm afraid it may get worse. I'm afraid he might send me to the hospital!"

"That's a valid concern," Margot said flatly. She was still rightly in command of the session, or so she thought.

Connie wiped her red face with angry swipes of her hand from her nose to the back of her neck. It was obvious she was going to test boundaries again but as her face returned to a calm state, Margot knew she had thought better of it.

"I just don't know what to do."

"Okay, so, do you have family that you can go to?"

"No, my family disowned me years ago due to my addiction, but I don't want to talk about that!"

"Fine, okay, I understand. Do you have any friends you can…"

"He cut me off from all of them. I'm so fucking alone! I just don't know what to do…"

"There are women's shelters."

"A shelter? I can't do that. I won't do that."

"What about a hotel?"

"With what money? He controls all the money, and I don't work, I told you…you know, he told me he would take care of me!"

"But he isn't and he won't and you know this will get worse. You said it yourself."

Connie tilted her head downward, pointed her eyes toward her sharp bangs, and got low in tone as she spoke slowly, "I know what I said, Margot. There, I believe that was with a modicum of decorum, no?"

"Do you feel you are currently in danger?"

"He's not here, of course, so no."

"I mean do you believe that in the next 24-hours he is likely to harm you—since you are making the choice to stay there?"

"I'm not making the choice! I can't go anywhere!"

"Women's. Shelter. Connie."

"He would just fucking find me!"

"Okay, okay, let's take a moment. The situation you are in is clearly not ideal. I know you know that," Margot said with her palm up to the screen in a preemptive strike knowing Connie was likely to retort. "But for those who are in this type of situation, what you are feeling is normal."

Connie appeared to be listening and even calming.

Margot continued, "And that's why what I'm about to say next is going to be hard to hear," Margot paused and she was sure why she had. It was because she expected Connie to stop her. She wanted Connie to stop her because she was about to take an Adlerian risk, not the cat but his namesake. When one went well it went great, but when that risk failed, it failed miserably. The streak of rebel made her speak up, anyway. She was going to try a paradoxical intervention; an Adlerian staple.

"Is your health insurance paid up?"

"I paid you, didn't I? What difference does that make? I paid you on the cash app through Telepy. Why are you even asking me that?"

"In case he injures you. We have gone through all the options other than calling the police, and clearly you aren't going to do that. As you said, the rules are different. Different than if you were assaulted by someone you were not in a relationship with, correct?"

"Yeah...so? I mean, what the fuck, Margot? You are worried about me being able to pay a doctor bill?"

"I want to make sure that if you are going to stay that you are prepared for the fallout of what comes next."

"Are you out of your fucking mind? You are really suggesting I just stay and get beat on to the point where I have to go to the hospital?"

"No, I'm not. But you are."

Connie sat and allowed her mouth to slowly open and hang there.

"And, Connie, if it sounds crazy for me to say that, then I can't even imagine how nutty you feel living it."

Connie dissolved again, "I...I just...I just don't know what I'm going to do."

"We need to get you safe."

"I...I know...I know...I...I need to go now...I need to think."

"Okay. Just know I will be here if and when you need to reach out."

Connie just nodded her head without looking up, then did after a few seconds, "Margot?"

"Yes."

"Thank you."

"My pleasure," Margot said with a smile and a sense of pride she had broken through.

After Connie closed the laptop, she looked at the ceiling. A male voice came from behind her.

"A bit much, don't ya think?"

Connie responded softly, "Fuck you."

12

Book It

Margot was sitting on her leather couch, Adler in her lap, and both were staring at the blinking cursor on the screen again.

She was still feeling a bit of victory. She created and held a boundary with a difficult client, was coming closer to a diagnostic conclusion, and felt she had broken through Connie's attempt to reject help and simply complain. Margot was even beginning to feel a bit of compassion for Connie. Compassion for her victimhood as well as knowing that it was likely she came up hard, used drugs, and was now in a relationship that was equally as likely to have mirrored what Connie lived through with her family of origin. Likely a broken home that was financially broken, as well. It was possibly the reason why she was trying so hard to cling to the financial fallacy of being taken care of. And it was equally likely why he was able to control her in that way.

Though, Margot thought further, she did seem to have full control and secrecy in paying for her therapy through Telepy by using a cash app. *Yeah*, Margot thought with irony, *help rejecting complainer. Living in the trauma and not yet a survivor of it.*

Even if Connie got out of this relationship, it was clear she would have to work hard to conclude that she had a personality disorder that needed work. If she didn't, she would probably end up in a string of relationships like this one.

Knowing one is going to be abused if one says the wrong thing, then doing it anyway knowing what's coming; that's about rebellion. Connie was getting something out of it even if it was the only way she could feel powerful. Perhaps it was the only way to feel loved. Perhaps it was the only way to feel; the only thing she knew growing up. Maybe it had become normalized by the time she got into romantic relationships of her own, Margot theorized.

Margot typed on the blank screen, 'Everyone does what they do because they are getting something out of it. Even if it's a sick system, the system is still producing what it's designed to produce'.

Margot sat back after typing and crossed her arms then smiled with satisfaction, "There, I wrote something."

A loud *DING* came from her computer. Her phone and her laptop were linked. Phone calls and texts would pop up to her phone and computer in unison. She leaned in to get a closer look at who the text was from before it disappeared. The message was from the *toad,* and it was labeled as such. Before it disappeared, she was able to make out some of the words that read, *So, how's...* and then it was gone.

Margot opened her messages by clicking the bubble at the bottom of her screen. *So, how's Adler?*

Margot leaned back, her happiness over having written something, anything, that she considered progress on a book that her ex never believed in was instantly sucked right into the black hole that was the toad vortex. She didn't answer and stared off into space wondering why she had not blocked his number. They had no kids, the divorce was final months ago, and she wanted nor needed anything from him.

Shawoop, the sound of a message coming from an open conversational textbox came through.

It wasn't all bad, was it?

"The fuck it wasn't," Margot exclaimed and slammed the laptop shut. Adler popped up with a start. To calm him, Margot petted his head and cooed, "Right boy?"

DING!

"OH MY GOD, ARE YOU KIDDING ME? LEAVE ME ALONE!"

Adler was spooked now and hopped down and pranced away.

Margot opened the laptop just as huffy as she had shut it. She hadn't realized it was a different sounding 'ding'. It was from her Telepy messages. It was Connie.

I need to see you again sooner rather than later! I was thinking about what you said. I'm ready to tell you the story and get it all out. I think it will help me move on. Please see me. Tuesday night is the earliest I can do it. Do you have the time?

Margot thought, *I have the time, but I don't know if I have the gumption. However,* Margot thought with the tilt of her head, *I need to strike while the iron's hot.*

The irony was, both women, and one other person, thought the same thing.

13

Buh-Bye

Adler had begun to crunch on his dried food in his ornate wooden bowl while Margot reread the message.

Woosh!

It was Connie again. This time it was just three question marks.

"Well, I suppose money is money and if I'm going to turn her into a character in a fictional book then I need to know more about her, right Adler?"

Adler looked up from his food then turned his head to his water 'fountain' of a bowl and lapped at the liquid, unmoved.

"Okay, fine, you little creamsicle. I'll do it."

Margot typed back, 'what time works for you that is between 6 and 9pm?'

'Oh thank you so much, yes, 6pm works great!'

'Please book through the app.'

'I'm doing it right now!'

'Great, see you then.'

'THANKS!'

After a few moments the session populated the schedule that was next to the elongated messaging box.

And instantly Margot regretted it.

"Well, if I'm going to succumb to a needy client than I might as well get rid of the other needy person. Right Dreamy?" Margot said aloud and Adler came over to join her by jumping in her lap.

"It's time, sweetie."

Margot picked up her phone, opened the contacts, scrolled to the one marked "toad" and blocked the number.

"Out of the frying pan and into the fire, I suppose."

Margot didn't know at the time, but it was worse than fire. It was hell she was jumping into.

14

Socially Secure

Margot was sitting in the cafeteria, Joni-less, because her friend didn't work on Tuesdays nor Mondays. She had done well enough in her financial job, made smart investments, and was collecting her retirement and social security. Margot had recently learned that Joni didn't have to work. She was low-key wealthy.

Those are the folks that always do well, the ones that can't sit still for long and are always into something that made money. Joni didn't make much working in the gift shop. She had said to Margot once that when her mother was elderly and sick in that very hospital, she had simply wandered into the shop to get something to brighten her mother's day and never really wandered out. The manager of the shop loved having Joni there because she could always sell more than anyone else that had worked there before. Financial dealing was just in her blood and that's all there was to it.

Margot sat with her laptop open and was reading about the world. She took a second to allow her mind to drift contemplating in amazement that a small, thin, but powerful object could give her any bit of information that she wanted. It also gave her a blank void upon which to write nothing, communications that she didn't want, and clients she couldn't stand. She snapped back to looking at the weather report when she heard someone toss something metallic on a table that was on the other side of the cafeteria as she scrolled to see when it was going to rain next.

After lunch and checking on weather that mattered nothing to her, Margot went back to her office and returned her calls. Her cell phone rang, and it was Joni.

"Hello, Jonesy!"

"How ya, toots? How's your day without your favorite unrelated aunt at her post?"

"I missed you at lunch. Luckily there isn't much going on here."

"Well then, I was thinking of inviting you to dinner so we can catch up. No people watching will be included unless we invite over some male strippers."

"Do they even still have those?"

"Maybe not. We can invite over my first husband; he did that for a little while to get through school. Then, it turns out he was gay. On second thought, we'll leave him out of it."

"Ah shit."

"Oh, you want him to come over, anyway? I mean he's got to be in his 70's by now so things might not be in the same place. He was hung like a ho…"

"Ha, no, I'm good. My reaction was because I just remembered that Cunt-y reached out for an extra session."

"Well, that didn't take long. You have the gift."

"Yeah, unfortunately for me. I saw her Friday and now I have to see her again tonight. Maybe that will be enough for her. We shall see. Anyway, how 'bout you come over to my place, and I treat you for a change?"

"Ahhh," Joni said with delight.

"Don't get too excited, you know I don't cook."

"No, but the pizza you get from that place near you is some of the best and it's been a little minute since I had any...pizza that is."

"You're such a Joni! Anyway, what about Wednesday afternoon you just follow me over from work?"

"That'll do, toots!"

"Good deal, that makes my day. I know I've not been available lately and I miss you."

"I miss you too, love...oh, I got another call. I'll see ya tomorrow, sweetie!"

And before Margot could say 'bye', Joni was gone.

15

Rapid and Partially Tangential

Unfortunately, Connie was right on time.

"Margot! Thank you so much for seeing me. I, I just felt like we have got off on the wrong angle and I want to get right into it because I'm not sure when he'll be back...Oh, wait, okay, yes I know the session is being recorded for note taking purposes and my address is 2112 Oak. Okay, so, look, like I said, it was his eyes that caught me at first. He was..."

Margot again became fixated on the long hallway and door behind Connie. She was trying to decide which way she liked it better, closed or open, when she snapped back to paying attention. She had been nodding at words she didn't even hear as Connie faded back into focus and luckily had not come up for air nor asked a question.

"...so we go out and he was charming and money, well, I told you all that already. It was a whirlwind of promises and sex and future talk. Talk I was into at the time, mind you. But then he started to control where and when I went. So much so, I had to stop even going to the bookstore. But I thought it was cute at first. I thought he was just that into me. And I guess he was. I guess that's why guys like that do those sorts of things," Connie didn't wait for a response.

She continued, "He would just say, 'I just like hanging out with you, I just want to be close to you all the time, I just don't want anyone to get you to like them more than me' an' stuff like that. Anyway, he bought me lavish gifts and quickly told me I should move in and quit working. I couldn't help it. I came from nothing, and I had never seen so much spending in my life. Not to mention he lived in this mansion alone. It's on the sliver on the river, as you know. It's survived every storm and flood. He bragged one time that after Katrina, some movie star, you know they had a lot of those move here after that storm, anyway some star tried to buy it from him. I can't remember who. I think it was that guy that was, was...oh what character did he play...umm, well, never mind, anyway, some star, doesn't matter. Now it's worth twice that. But, Margot, it has become more like a prison. But I'm jumping ahead..."

The door at the end of the hallway behind Connie slowly started to open inward toward the room and its black nothingness.

"...and my friends come over and, well, of course they are or were, depending on who and where they are now, in recovery from drugs and or alcohol—I met some of them when I stopped using, anyway, after they all leave he starts saying shit about this one and that one and looking around swearing that this one stole a watch and the other one stole a ring and another took money out of a locked safe. Fucker couldn't count, that was all the same money that had been in there...well, I guess it was, because I don't have the combination. So he keeps me from going out and he keeps them from coming here and after, like, three months they are all off to the races or whatever and I'm sitting here watching stupid shit like...well I don't even know the name of some of those old shows, some 'Gunsmoke' and 'This Gun's for Hire' or some shit, like, Jesus, dude, I ain't 70…no offense…"

Margot shook her head and held her hand up to signify "no offense taken" but, well, she did take at least take a spoon full of offense but not the whole bowl.

"…I'd get up to go to the bathroom and he would ask, 'where you goin' and whatever, and I'd be like, 'I'm going to piss!' I mean shitfire man, can't a woman relieve herself without the questions? I wouldn't say that out loud, but my God! And when it was time to eat it would be an argument. Time to get up, it would be an argument. Time for him to go somewhere and it would be an argument. So, I start, like, ya know, taking up for myself. Puttin' my foot down. And I guess I put it down enough times where he smacked the shit outta me and then leaves. I thought about it right then. Time to go, time to get the fuck. But I, I dunno, I jus' didn't. So, he comes back with flowers and a card and whatever about three hours later. He's all like, 'I'm sorry and I'll never do it again and please forgive me' and this and that. So, I tell him, 'That can't happen again'. And it doesn't…for a few weeks…then it does. And each time he leaves after hitting me it takes longer and longer for him to come back and what he comes back with is more and more expensive. Bags and bracelets and sunglasses. Sunglasses I don't even like. The only thing they are good for is that they are huge and cover up my busted eyes when I'm allowed to leave the house. Now he has me jacked up in this prison and he has this routine—it's every Friday at 7pm. He has this card game he goes to, but he's always home before midnight. I mean, what guy does that? If you're a guy hanging with, well, GUYS, you stay out all night, three or four in the morning, right? That's what would make sense…"

Connie had not stopped talking for five straight minutes. Margot's clinical experience was informing her opinion that Connie was bipolar and in a manic phase. This was going to be tough. This was a classic presentation of a manic episode. But if she was also suffering from borderline personality disorder, and it would be one of the few times that Margot had seen the two combined in her whole career, it was going to be a web of emotions to work through. Though, Margot had decided a few years ago that the pair together was way over diagnosed. Insurance doesn't pay to treat personality disorders so over those years, if a client had seen enough psychiatrists, they would have a laundry list of diagnoses with only one or two of them accurate.

Margot broke in, "I noticed that you are speaking rapidly."

"I'm trying to get all this shit out before he gets home, Margot!"

"I totally get it. That makes sense."

"So now he's been more snappy and pushes and shoves but I haven't been fighting back so he hasn't been outright slapping or punching me. But he keeps threatening..." Connie put her head in her hands. Margot decided to wait until Connie collected herself and just let her keep running with her endless stream of consciousness.

Connie looked back at the screen and through a veil of tears. "...HE KEEPS THREATING TO KILL ME IF I LEAVE!"

"Okay, look, we need to get you out of this."

"I CAN'T, DON'T YOU UNDERSTAND?! I CAN'T FUCKING LEAVE! THERE ARE CAMERAS EVERYWHERE! HE WOULD JUST FIND ME, ANYWAY! He's a fucking animal...and I've had it...I can only think of two ways out that are acceptable. But I can't tell you either one of them because then you will have to report it…FUCK…HE'S HOME!"

Margot had opened her mouth to speak but only saw the lid snap shut.

Connie stayed seated at the kitchen island. She had pushed the laptop away from herself. A voice from that same 'somewhere' questioned, "Do you think that will do it?"

Connie stared straight ahead with a blunted expression that gradually grew into a sinister grin.

"Of course it will. We chose the right one."

16

Sphere of Influence

Margot got very little sleep Tuesday night, but Adler did. He was standing on her back when the alarm went off. Like a horse out of the gate, Adler bolted toward the kitchen. Margot hit the snooze button and fell instantly back to sleep. Adler, not hearing nor seeing Margot getting up started mewing loudly and sauntered back into the bedroom. Margot heard nothing. She was dead to the world.

Her alarm went off again eight minutes later and she smacked it. Then back up alarm she had set on her phone went off. When it did, Margot flipped the covers back in a huff, "DAMN IT!"

Adler bolted back into the kitchen and waited for his wet food while Margot trudged over to the coffee maker that had been prepped and set to 'automatic' the night before. It had already filtered the water through the grounds producing the only inviting thing to her that morning.

Margot never drank coffee black, but she did this morning after she couldn't pour it fast enough. Adler still made his presence known until she retrieved the can from the cupboard, popped the top, and shook it up and down over his dry food.

She had never done that before, but she didn't have the patience to get out another bowl while he caterwauled. Adler looked up at her and then backdown at the food. He walked away after shaking his paw and not eating a bite.

"Good morning to you, too, Creamsicle," she said and finished another sip of her black.

Margot got to her office late but went through her morning routine just the same. By noon, Margot went down to the giftshop to visit Joni.

"Well, hello, my friend. Would you be a lamb and hand me that box over there? It shouldn't be too heavy," Joni pointed to a small opened cardboard container with an order of Bric-a-Brac. Margot brought it over and Joni could read her expression.

"What's got a bug up your tuchus this afternoon?"

"It's that client, again."

Joni whispered, "What did Cunt-y do this time?"

"Extra. A whole lotta extra. But I don't want to bother you with it…at least not right now," Margot looked around and saw a couple with a little girl in a stroller just as they came in. The man had a three-day shadow on his face and mom looked equally disheveled.

"Understood, honey."

Margot went into it anyway, "She is just so, geeze, I think I'm getting a handle on this case but honestly, Jonesy, this woman doesn't need a therapist, she needs the police and a safe haven."

Joni took an open bag of balloons from the box, "God, they don't even bother to give you a new bag of these anymore. Sheesh. Anyway, what kind of case is this turning out to be?"

Margot lowered her voice even more, "She's in an abusive relationship and I believe she is either contemplating harming herself, or him, or both—and, based on the diagnoses I'm contemplating, all possibilities are on the table."

Joni placed a balloon on the helium canister nozzle.

PFSSSSSSST.

"That sounds like husband number...all of them."

"No, really Jonesy, this ain't good. I have all these recordings, and I can't get rid of them now because they are all part of the record."

Joni tied the balloon like a pro with a *SNAP*. She was cutting the ribbon to tie to it when she asked, "What? She say something that could get you in another one of those legal jams?"

"Depends on what happens and who is still around to do anything about it. I mean, she hurts him, and his family sues, he hurts her, same thing...they hurt each other...it's got shit all over this."

Joni tied the ribbon she had cut to the balloon knot and then added a weight on the other end.

"She say something on the video?"

"What didn't she say. Look, I shouldn't do this. I could lose my..."

"Show me that shit. You know who you're talkin' to."

"Shhhhh!"

"Okay, okay," Joni took another flaccid balloon from the bag and loaded it on the nozzle.

PFSSSSSST, the balloon filled and Joni removed it. As she started tying it quickly, Margot continued, "I'll show you the video from last night. But you have to swear…"

"Who would I tell anyway?" Joni said with a shrug and cut another ribbon then repeated the task she had done before.

"I know but, you know, I'm a rule follower…until I'm not."

Joni pulled another balloon from the bag and loaded it on the helium tank spike and stopped with her hand on the nozzle handle.

"You know, I really think you ought'ta consider another line of work. Come work with me down here at the shop."

"Joni, we can't all be millionaires in disguise."

"How did you know, honey?"

"Please…"

"Okay, you got me," Joni turned the handle. She only had the final mylar 'Get Well Soon' balloon left for the order after this one.

PFSSSSSSSSSS

As the balloon started to inflate, Joni went back to look at Margot and continue talking about that "new line of work". But Margot's gaze never left that balloon. The bigger the balloon got, the wider her eyes became. Joni looked at the tank and then allowed her eyes to follow up to the message in latex.

The letters 'H.H.' were written in black marker. Underneath the letters, was a crudely drawn skull with the number 33 on its forehead. The words 'THINKING OF YOU' were written beneath the jawline. Both ladies just watched with mouths agape while that number, that skull, and that message got larger and larger.

POW!

The balloon burst, the mother in the store gasped, and the baby started crying. Joni and Margot hopped up a half foot from the floor.

An employee from the hospital was walking in and dropped his keys on the tile just when the balloon burst and scattered its tattered message at Joni's white flats.

"You ladies alright?", asked the middle-aged hospital employee as he was picking up his keys.

"All good, thanks." Margot said, still stunned.

Joni started to pick up the red pieces of rubber and lifted her head from below the counter, "Yup. Just a busted balloon. Nothing to be alarmed about."

"Okay then," the man said then he turned and continued walking while whistling a tune down the wide-open space. The little stroller girl could still be heard crying off in the distance.

Margot looked over the counter at Joni picking up the pieces and tossing them into the trash, "What are you doing?"

"I'm cleaning up our excitement. Won't be the first time."

"This has happened before?"

"Oh, yeah, maybe you didn't get my joke."

"Ah, yeah, I get it…look, what the hell was that? Who does that?"

"Listen, you know my heart dear so I can say this to you but those balloons and every single item in this shop comes from China. All those little buggers are children in sweatshops makin' these things and one of 'em got a sense of humor."

"Oh, you think that a kid from China drew that shit on the balloon?"

"Of course, toots, who else?"

"Joni, I know I've been a little out of sorts lately and I'm no detective, but that box was open, the bag was open, and I'll be damned if some child in China—one with good English and spelling skills—knew this balloon would end up in America, in a hospital gift shop, and so decided to write a condolence message with a skull on it."

Joni thought for a moment, "I see your point," Joni pulled the scraps out of the trash and slid them into her pocket then gave it a pat, "Safe keeping. I don't have an ex-husband that would pull this nonsense but, well, let's just say there are more exes of mine running around out there than were ever my husband."

17

Girls Night In

The doorbell rang and Margot answered it while Adler ran for the back bedroom. It was Joni holding up a bottle of wine in each hand, "I figured we were going to need both. You have a story to tell, and I have a mystery balloon in my pocket."

"I'm half a bottle in of the two bottles I bought on the way home from work."

"Lady, you need to pace yourself."

"Did you bring your overnight bag?"

Joni started to cross the threshold, "You bet I did. I just left it in the car for now. But we'll be lucky to make it to work tomorrow anyway with all the bottled grape we have."

"I already ordered the pizza so it should be here soon," Margot noted as she shut the door behind Joni and locked the deadbolt then slid the chain latch across the metal slot.

Joni took notice, "You expecting someone that shouldn't be showing up here?"

"Jonesy, I'm spooked," the slightest bit of slur in her speech coming across as she said it.

"What you got to be worried about?" Joni asked while placing the dual bottles of wine on the dining table and taking her handbag strap from her shoulder.

"That client and that balloon."

"Oh, dear," Joni said while placing her hand on her friend's shoulder, "I don't believe the two even know about one another. I've given it more thought, and I still think it was some kid's prank. Kids come in that store all the time. All they would need to do is draw that and then put it back in the bag."

"Well, I've been thinking more about it, too…" both women sat at the dining table. Margot started to pull the cork from her half drunken bottle that was almost as half-drunk as she was. She wanted a top off and she wanted Joni to catch up, "…and I figured it this way because there are three things that bother me about that whole balloon thing."

"Okay, shoot your shot, dear heart."

"The first thing is that I don't know if Connie's boyfriend is controlling enough to try and keep me from seeing her and at what lengths he would go to do it—silly shit like a balloon trick."

"Okay…"

"And second, it's that number 33. That's more like a message than a prank."

"Humm…I can hear that…but what's your third?" Joni asked as she took her first of many sips of the evening.

"Pull the scraps of that balloon out and let's spread 'em on the table."

Joni stood up and pulled them from her pocket. She palmed the half dozen or so pieces and spread them on the wooden surface.

"Okay, so look. What do you see?"

"I see a party that we were invited to but didn't want to be at."

"Seriously, Joni, what do you see?"

"I see a busted balloon, honey. I'm sorry, I just don't know what you are driving at."

"Joni, look at the lines of what is written. You can't hardly make them out at all, can you?"

"Well, not in pieces like this."

"Okay…" Margot stood up and leaned over the project, "…lets spread them out a bit, stretch them so I can make my point." Joni took a sip and leaned herself closer to the makeshift workstation. Margot started to lay out the picture and the message but left relatively large fissures between all the pieces. Some were curled and hard to lay flat. And the half bottle of wine she already had in her made it even more difficult. She pushed them into the wood of the table and that caused some of the pieces to stick and lay flat. After forty-five seconds, she had her mosaic laid out the best she could.

"Do you see it now? Because I'm even more sure than ever of my assumption that I've been ruminating on all day."

Joni looked at the pieces with tilted head, looked up at Margot, then back at the pieces.

"You see it don't you?" Margot asked.

Joni began to think aloud, "When I was a kid, sometimes I would draw faces on balloons. I guess all kids do…"

"You steppin' in what I'm laying down girlfriend?"

"…and I noticed that the color of the pen or marker was always darker after the balloon was deflated…"

"Uh huh," Margot said with a bit of excitement in her throat, "annnnd soooo?"

Joni looked up at Margot, "Since this was written with, what appears to be, a large-tipped marker…"

Both ladies said in unison, "Then the balloon had to have air in it first."

"CORRECT," Margot finished with the slightest bit of an alternating up and down shoulder dance.

Joni finished her thought, "And no one could have done that in the store without me noticing."

"CORRECT!"

"Okay, fair, but sweetie that still doesn't explain a thing about where it came from, when they wrote it, or who wrote it."

"True," Margot said with a slump of her shoulders that a few seconds ago were dancing, "But there's something else."

"Ooo, I'm intrigued again."

"Well, I wouldn't get too excited."

"You mean you led with the best part? Honey, that's not very feminine."

"Be serious, Jonesy. I need you to look at something else. But only if we can see it and I'm not so sure we can."

Margot picked up the two halves of the balloon pieces that looked as if they were part of the skull and handed one to Joni who put her wine glass down and looked up at Margot.

"What do you want me to do with this?"

"Come over here to the lamp and I'll show you."

Joni followed behind Margot who had already started to make her way to a floor lamp in the corner of the dining room. She unscrewed the shade and sat the bolt on the China hutch next to the lamp.

"Oh good, I could never understand why you had this hideous shade on an otherwise stunning lamp," Joni said like she was in a black and white movie from the 40's. The lilt in her voice was as if she were trying to sound "continental". Margot didn't say a word because she knew her friend was trying to keep the mood light. Joni was getting spooked, too, and didn't have the amount of grape in her that was required. Once the shade came off, the room and their eyes filled with unfiltered and blinding light.

"Yeesh, now I know why," Joni said while tilting her neck and shielding her eyes. Margot's pupils were slightly restricted, so it didn't affect her as much.

"Okay, now take your piece and stretch it out. I'll do the same with mine and then we put them close together."

"Honey, I like you but I'm into men. Well, there was this one time in college…"

Margot slowly looked, with blunted affect, at Joni.

"Okay, okay, I'll be serious. Sheesh."

Margot and Joni, in unison, stretched the pieces as far as they would go until their hands touched. Before them it looked like a jumbled mess. Had the ladies not been there to see it blow up to scale it would have been hard to make out. The crude skull looked even more hideous than before.

"Yep, I knew I remembered it correctly."

"Remembered what, honey?"

"Look, let's do it this way," Margot said bright eyed and put her piece down to her side and Joni followed suit. Margot took the lamp and moved it in front of them both.

"Turn your piece around and stand back here with me in the corner."

"I think I see what you are getting at."

Joni started to do as instructed and noticed Margot taking a deep breath. She blew it out in a huff like she was about to serve before match point. She lifted her hands with the red balloon piece and stretched it out then looked at Joni. Joni complied with the silent request.

Both did the same as before, but this time they were no longer looking at the balloon pieces directly. They were looking at the shadow cast on the far wall. They were looking at the shadow of the skull.

Both said nothing after aligning the grotesque picture on the dining room wall as best they could with the makeshift projector. After a few seconds Margot spoke, "See how everything is drawn and remember how the message was written?"

"Yes, and it's all giving me the heebies."

"The words were written in perfect script."

"So, this is a lesson in penmanship?"

"Damn it, Joni!"

"Okay, I'm sorry, I don't get it!"

"Look at the '3's."

Joni looked for a moment with her head tilted, "They are scratched at angles like they are not one stroke like the rest of the message."

"Correct!"

"So, what does it mean?"

"I don't know," Margot answered while shaking her head.

A shadow cast across the skull and numbers. It was coming from the half-window of the front door because Margot had left the porch light on.

The shadow pounded on the door and Margot didn't move. Joni nearly lifted out of her flats.

Margot looked over at the spooked Joni and calmly said, "You hungry?"

"Je-SUS! I need to catch up with where you are in alcohol level."

After eating, discussing what little clues they had to the balloon mystery, and drinking more wine, Margot and Joni got in their P-Jams. The ladies then retired to the back stoop and watched the frogs eat bugs in the moonlight. Joni pulled a deck of cigarettes from her pocket. She was wearing Tiffany blue pajamas made of silk; printed on the fabric were several strings of pearls in different shapes. Margot had on shorts and a Taylor Swift concert tee.

Joni poked a cigarette in her face and let it bounce around while she talked before lighting it. While waving around an old gold lighter she had received from the firm when she retired, she spoke, "I don't know, Margs. I will concede the fact that the number thirty-three is clearly drawn as stick lines to create those numbers..." Joni waved her hand even more and the unlit cigarette continued to bounce, "...but I don't know if it's a message for us or if it's a message at all."

"Give me one of those."

Joni looked mildly surprised, "I didn't know you ever smoked."

"A little in the bars while I was in college."

"Yeah, that happens. I would have an ashtray full of butts when writing papers," Joni finished by pulling another stick from the pack and handed it over then lit her own before giving up her lighter to Margot who admired it before she lit hers.

Joni continued while taking back her lighter, "Yeah, I just don't get it. Are you sure we're not reading too much into this? I'm getting jittery from all this...or it's the strong-ass coffee you gave me kicking in," she said picking up the mug with a cat printed on it.

"No, I don't know at all if it has anything to do with anything. I don't even know if either of us is who the message was for or if it's a message at all. For me, the H.H. is almost as intriguing as the scratchy looking thirty-three," she said, then took a short draw and coughed out the smoke.

"Smoooth," Joni joked.

Margot's eyes were watery as she waved the smoke from her face.

"I'll grant ya that, Margs. I've been wracking my brain to figure out if there is someone I know or have known in the past, for that matter, with those initials and I can't come up with it. I hate to say it but wasn't there a serial killer by the name H. H. Holmes?"

"Jesus Joni."

"Well?" Joni said with her hands splayed out and her lighter tucked between her thumb and palm in her right hand.

"I mean, yeah, over a 100 years ago," Margot said while swirling her head toward the stars.

"Pfft, well that's all I got."

"I have even less than that."

"Well, ain't we a pair?"

18

Just Another Thursday

Margot texted Mike and cancelled on him after the balloon incident the day before. She just knew she wouldn't be worth two balls of goat shit after what she and Joni had been through.

She wasn't hung over, but she wasn't feeling her best since the ladies had stayed up late and chewed the fat. They had nearly smoked the whole pack of Winstons, and it had Margot's throat feeling funky—but she was at work anyway, and so was Joni.

She got a call from her supervisor, Prestin Wilcox, and he said there was a call for her to go to room three-thirty-three at the Women's Pavilion. Margot shuddered.

"Three-thirty-three? Are you sure?"

"Yeah, I know. You don't need another one of these."

"Can't Nancy or Carla go?"

"I just got two other calls back-to-back before this one, so I sent them to those. I'm so sorry. I'd go myself but a meeting was added to my schedule. Some thirty minute training on a new electronic health record. It's supposed to start in a few minutes. Come by and see me after you get done. Maybe it's nothing more than some consultation regarding being a new family…first baby or something. And, anyway, they asked for you by name."

"Me—Margot Landry—by name?"

"Yup. You must be getting a good reputation. Maybe some pre-birthers a few months back met you and you made a good impression."

"Yeah, ha, maybe so," Margot allowed herself to ease a little. However, her laugh was a nervous one, "Okay, I'll go right up."

"Thanks Margot. I appreciate it."

"No worries."

Margot went over to the bank of elevators at the Ochsner's Women's Pavilion, took a deep breath, and pressed the *up* button. *It's got to just be a coincidence*, she thought, *it just has to be.*

When the doors opened, the elevator emptied while Margot patiently waited then stepped in, alone. She pressed the button for the third floor and took another deep breath. It felt like an eternity—plus one—for those doors to close.

The elevator stopped on the second floor. It opened to find one of the hospital employees looking at his phone. He continued scanning his device as he got in. The employee then pressed the first-floor button three times in rapid succession.

As the doors started to close, he said almost as if he were speaking to himself, "Oh, you're not going down…well, not without a fight, anyway," and huffed a laugh.

Margot pressed herself as far back and to the left of the elevator as she could and only then did her curiosity and rebellion kick in, "I'm sorry, what did you say?"

The elevator went quickly, ascending to the third floor. The man continued looking at his phone. He didn't turn around, nor did he answer her question, saying only, "It's okay, I'll take the ride with you."

When the doors opened, he stayed inside the elevator but didn't move from his position that was only slightly right of the center of the opening. He never looked up.

Margot went to push past him and brushed his shoulder with hers. When she did, she said, "Oh, um, sorry." And hurried out.

When the elevator doors started to close, she heard him say, "No worries."

She turned around, but by then the doors had almost fully closed. She could see none of his features because he still hadn't looked up from his device.

Irritated, Margot turned then marched down the hall toward the unit and found her way to the closed door of room three-thirty-three. She knocked and heard a male voice on the other side say, "Come in," so she pushed the latch and the heavy solid wood door opened slowly.

Standing there was a man in his 30's or so and a young boy not yet in his teens. No one was laying in the bed, though it wasn't made. Before she could speak, Margot heard the toilet flush. She looked over at the door to the restroom and noticed light reflecting on the floor. Just as quickly, she heard someone turn on the sink, so she looked back over at the man and smiled.

A woman exited the restroom and looked at the social worker. Margot realized she didn't recognize anyone in that room. The woman spoke when she started to climb back into bed. She was struggling with her dripline and monitor that was connected to a saline bag on the pole hook she was clinging to—and all of it was attached to her.

"Would you mind helping me back into bed? My husband is a little rough, bless his little heart."

"Not at all," Margot said as she walked over in haste to help ease the woman down to the bed.

"Ahhh, that's better. Thanks. You one of the doctors? You ain't dressed like a nurse."

"Umm, no ma'am," Margot scanned the room again to get a clue as to why she was there, "I'm one of the medical social workers. I was, well, I was called to this room by my supervisor."

"Oh, I wonder why?"

"None of you called me?"

"I didn't. Honey, did you?"

"No. And actually I'm not even sure what a medical social worker does."

"Well, most days, thankfully, it's fairly boring. This is room 333, correct?" Margot questioned as she backed up and stuck her head around the corner of the door to read the number plate on the righthand side.

"I'm fairly sure", the woman said, "I usually get them twisted when I have to come to the hospital, but that's an easy one."

"Yup, it's 333. Hum, well, he must have gotten the wrong number. I'm so sorry to have bothered you folks."

"No bother at all and thanks for helping me back into bed. Honey, will you grab me that pillow over there?" the woman asked her husband as Margot was leaving the room and pulled the door to its latch.

Margot sprinted to her supervisor's office expecting to find him on his training call. She lightly tapped on the door and he answered, "Come in", sounding slightly annoyed.

"Hey, you got a sec?"

"Turns out, I do. I joined that training call, but it was only me and one other fella. Neither of us knew why we were there, so we jumped off the call and then the invite disappeared. It was from some email address outside of..."

"Prestin, who called you and asked for me to come down?"

"Oh, it seemed like a nurse, though, and I'm not being pejorative here, a male one."

"What extension?"

"Hum, lemme look," Prestin said quizzically as he scanned his desk phone, pressed the arrow keys, and then went to a list he had in his desk drawer. Oh, here, it's in orthopedics— extension 2231. Huh, that's odd."

"It is, isn't it? Because why would someone from ortho be requesting that I go to the Women's Pavilion and a specific room to a family who didn't even know why I was there?"

"I…I just don't have a clue."

"Well I'm going to find out," Margot asserted and she bolted from the chair. It was in that moment that Margot noticed she was no longer frightened, she was pissed.

Once in the ortho section of the hospital, Margot realized she didn't quite know where to start. She went over to the nurse's station and asked, "Excuse me, can you help me find where a call I received originated from?"

"You need to use the phone? You can use this one," The charge nurse said kindly because she couldn't quite see Margot's badge and wasn't sure if she was corporate or not.

"No thanks. I need to see where the phone that made the call is actually located. It's extension 2231."

"Humm," the nurse said as she ran her finger down a paper list taped on the station counter, "Oh here it is, but you can't go in there right now. It's a surgical theater and they're performing a bone graft."

"How long is the procedure scheduled to last?"

"Oh, let me see," the charge nurse said as she used her mouse to scroll through the schedule, "It's on the schedule for the next four hours and they started…it looks like about… hum, yeah, ten minutes ago. I'm sorry but, either way, that's where the extension is located."

"Thanks so much. I'll just give it a look-see later."

"You bet. Anything else I can help you with, Ms…" The charge nurse looked closer at the badge and was relieved she wasn't from C-Suite, "…Ms. Landry?"

"Not at this time. Thank you for your kindness."

Margot couldn't get down to Joni fast enough.

When she rounded the corner to the giftshop, Margot noticed the *Back In Five Minutes* sign on the door. However, in true Joni fashion, the 'five' had a line through it and 'ten' was written above it.

Margot waited all ten minutes and still no Joni. While she waited, stragglers peering in the shop window then moving on was all she saw. Margot decided she might check the ladies room but if Joni had been gone for that long…well, she didn't want to interrupt her.

Margot gave up on waiting and went back to her office. She settled into the rest of her workday and decided she would check on Joni near lunchtime—but she never did. She spent the rest of the day returning calls, visiting patients, and setting up aftercare. By that afternoon, Margot thought the whole extension mystery may have been nothing more than a creeper that she fully intended on speaking to H.R. about once she caught the little bastard.

Then it hit her.

She would just go to the security office, request to see the video, and see if she could identify the person who used the operating room phone around that time. *Then I'll have that fucker*, she thought.

At around 5pm she went back to the giftshop. No Joni and the lights were turned off. The sign was gone, too. The whole day had made her a bit nervous, again. Her anger had slipped back into a state of fear. Though she didn't like to admit it, Joni seemed to make things better, less nerve wracking. It was her quips that felt calming. It was her timing that sucked.

She called Joni's cell but there was no answer. Joni was notorious for just allowing her phone to die in her purse and she wouldn't answer if she were driving, anyway.

Once she got home, she tried again.

"Hello, my dear. Where were you all day?"

"Oh, thank Christ! You okay?"

"Of course I am, why wouldn't I be?"

"Let me tell you about my day…"

19

Incongruent

Joni and Margot had agreed the night before that Margot would call security the first thing in the morning, and she did. Charlie Rutherford was at the desk, monitoring all the screens.

"Rutherford, what can I do for ya?"

"Yes, uh, this is Margot Landry. I'm a social worker here at the hospital."

"Yes, ma'am. What cha' got?"

"Well, I need to see if there is any video footage of O.T.-12 from yesterday between 8am and 9am."

Charlie said without hesitation, "No ma'am there isn't."

"Are you sure?'

"Yep."

"Please forgive me for asking so bluntly but, well, how are you so sure?"

"Because what happened is rare."

"Oh, what's that?"

"I was called and told the patient revoked video consent and to turn off any recording of the operating room."

"Oh...yeah, I see."

"Yeah, HIPAA and all that, you know the drill."

"I do. How 'bout just outside the...you know, never mind," Margot finished with a tone resignation. "There would be people in and out of there all morning I bet."

"Oh yeah, all the morning surgeries start around that time so it's like the Superdome before a game starts, ya know?"

"Yeah..."

"Well, when the Saints had Drew Brees, anyway."

"Yeah, I get it...okay, thanks."

"You bet," Rutherford said and abruptly ended the call.

That afternoon, Joni and Margot sat in the cafeteria, sipped coffee, and watched their surroundings like detectives on a stakeout. Nothing noteworthy was noticed by either, just the usual constant buzz of activity.

"Well, this was thankfully a bust," Joni said tossing her empty paper cup into a receptacle.

"Yeah, now all I have to look forward to is my second dose of Cunt-y."

"More like an overdose, sounds like to me."

"You got that right. Call ya later?"

"Sure toots."

As the two women parted ways Margot heard that metallic sound hitting a faraway table again—like she did the other day. When she turned around, she noticed nothing and Joni had kept walking.

By 6:45pm it was that time again. Friday night fun with Connie Minae. *Maybe—just maybe this will be the time she doesn't show up*, Margot relished the thought. She imagined what it would be like to never see Connie again.

She was close to right and yet not right at all.

At 6:58 Connie's name popped up in the Telepy site waiting room.

"DAMN IT," Margot barked as she pounded her desk. Her fist landed with a loud thud, causing Adler to bolt out of the room.

"Well, that was effective. I'll have to remember that from now on…poor little creamsicle."

Margot decided to make Connie wait until 7pm sharp. She wasn't going to give her one more second of her time than she had to. *Maybe she'll bag out of the waiting room*, she thought.

For two whole minutes, Margot glared at Connie's name. At 7pm it was still there. Margot clicked the record icon and off she went to what was to be their last session.

"Hello, Connie," Margot said drolly.

"Hi, Margot. Yes, I know I'm being recorded, and my address is 2112 Oak Street. And how are you?"

"Not too bad. And you?"

"Oh. jus' livin' the dream in this fuckin' prison."

"Give me the rundown of the last two days."

"Same shit, different days. He came home and nearly caught me on the laptop. Luckily, I heard the garage door start to open and it gave me enough time to stow it."

"Connie, I was thinking. I'd like to do a little role-playing with you. That is, if you are willing."

"Role-play? What's that going to do?"

"I want to play him, your boyfriend or whatever you want to call him, and you play yourself. It's to help you be able to speak to him about how things are."

"Like shit will get any better. Are you kidding me?"

"Right now, it's not about getting better. It's about getting out."

"Oh, you *are* kidding me; there's no way…"

"Let's just try it. Now, I'll be…," Margot asked in a questioning tone.

"Brad. His name is Bradly LeBlanc."

"Brad, okay, I'll play him. I want you to talk to me—talk to me like you would him…just freewheel it…just let it go. You can say whatever you want to say and as I'm playing like him you can just correct me when I say anything that he wouldn't."

"He wouldn't say that."

"Say what? We haven't started yet."

"He wouldn't allow any conversation like this to even occur. He would never say, 'You can say whatever you want to say' or 'correct me when…'"

"Okay, you just use me as a body to say to him whatever it is you *want* to say."

"Fuck you!"

"Is that for me or have we started?'

"Can it be both?"

"Whatever you like."

"Okay, we'll start now. Fuck you."

"Keep going," Margot said while trying not to roll her eyes.

"Is that him saying that or you?"

"Both."

"He wouldn't say that."

"You just keep talking," Margot felt her ears get hot as she gripped the chair again.

"Now that, he would say. He would say that just before he had enough."

"Go ahead…just keep going with it."

The door started to slowly open behind Connie. Margot was focused only on her client. By this session she had learned to just ignore it.

"Fuck you, Bradly. Fuck you and the Porsche you rode in on."

"What, are you upset?"

"He wouldn't say that."

"Well, what would he say…"

Suddenly, the door swung open quickly.

Margot's eyes widened.

And there it was. A dark shape sprinting down the hall toward Connie.

The shape was dressed in all black and a ski-mask covering its head. With its right hand, it shoved Connie to the floor. She landed with a thud.

The voice behind the mask growled in a low, dark, and angry tone, "You really want to know what I would say, Margot? I'd say, 'I'm going to kill you'," then slammed the laptop shut.

20

What Just Happened?

Margot stared at the black video screen on her laptop that once framed the face of Connie Minae and the featureless figure that assaulted her. She stayed totally still and slack jawed for a full five seconds; immovable. In an instant, Margot snapped into action by grabbing her phone and dialing 911.

"911- what's your emergency?"

"Yes! I'm a therapist and, um…oh Christ, I think I just witnessed a murder. Or at least a…"

"Okay, ma'am, just calm down and tell me if the person is still breathing."

"They aren't here! They are at…oh, wait, wait…umm."

"They aren't there? Did they leave?"

"They were never here, it's..it's a woman! And then this thing, this man, came up behind her…"

"Where ma'am, where are they?"

"I'M LOOKING FOR THE ADDRESS!"

"Ma'am, just take a breath. What's the address?"

"I'M LOOKING, GODDAMNIT!"

Margot heard nothing but static on the line as the operator sensed nothing she said was going to help.

"HERE, HERE IT IS, 2112 OAK! HURRY! HE'S PROBABLY STILL THERE."

"2112 Oak-where, ma'am?"

"UMMM, UHHH, UPTOWN!"

"There is a lot of 'uptown' …wait, I found it. A large residential house?"

"YES! That's it! They were in the kitchen…I saw it when I was doing therapy!"

"You were doing therapy with them in the kitchen?"

"ONLINE!"

"Okay, I understand. I'm sending over emergency services now."

"Thank you!"

"Just stay on the line with me, ma'am, to make sure we have everything correct and emergency services get to the right place."

"Okay, I will."

Margot listened to the 911 operator speak to dispatch, "…yes, 2112 Oak…Okay, they are in route, and they are close."

"Thank God!"

A few minutes of static and hearing other 911 operators in the background pop in and out from time to time when they were loud enough to break through the squelch.

"...okay, yes, that's probably the one...", a few more moments went by and Margot heard the operator again, "OHhhhh..."

"What? WHAT? WHAT'S THE MATTER! I THINK IT WAS HER BOYFRIEND, WHAT DID HE DO? IT'S HIS HOUSE!"

But the line had gone dead.

Again, Margot couldn't get to Joni fast enough. She dialed.

"Hiya, toots."

"JONI, JONI, I NEED TO COME OVER!"

"WHAT'S WRONG!"

"I THINK CONNIE HAS BEEN MURDERED!"

Joni said with total disbelief, "Oh, come now. You have a nightmare or somethin'?"

Margot steadied herself, "Joni, I need to come over and I'm packing a bag."

"Okay, okay, come over. I have plenty of..." Joni was going to say "wine", but Margot had already hung up.

21

What's Happening?

Bradly Lablanc was on his way back home in his black Porsche 911 Turbo. He pulled up to see the front of his house surrounded by crime tape.

There was nearly a half dozen squad cars and a little white crime-lab van. He parked where he could, because his driveway was full of both cops and their squad cars. A few detectives were going in the house as he got out of his car and tried to run up the lawn.

"Excuse me, sir!" a small black cop exclaimed while she stood in his path, held her right hand up, and rested her left hand on the butt of her service pistol.

"I'm the owner of the house! My girlfriend, Connie, and I live here. What…what happened?" he asked then he put his hands on his hips and started to breathe heavily, half-bent over.

"Sir, where have you been tonight?"

"I've been…I've been driving. I was supposed to be at a card game, but it was canceled so I just, uh, I just drove around the city."

The New Orleans police officer looked over her shoulder toward the front door where a detective was standing and listening, "Wait here. Do not go into the house."

"Oh God, what has she done now?"

"Sir, remain calm. I'm going to have a detective come speak with you," she finished and then started to walk up to the front door of the house to get Lead Detective, Ronnie Bolt.

In the kitchen there was blood everywhere. It was enough blood to cause every detective, and even the least seasoned of cops, to easily conclude that whoever had lost it was dead.

The white kitchen tile was now red. A stool had been knocked over and both Connie and the laptop were gone. The detectives, by this point, knew there was a missing laptop because they knew about the online session from the 911 caller. There were drag marks in the blood that led to the side door and trailing out to the back of the house. It continued in the grass then ended at the blacktop driveway.

"Hello sir, I'm Lieutenant Bolt. I hear you were supposed to be at a card game, correct?" Bolt questioned. He was flanked by the cop who had stopped Brad. She took out her pad and pen and started writing.

"Yes sir…what…what's going on? Where's Connie?"

"We were hoping you might be able to shed some light on that matter. I want to say this delicately but, well," Bolt looked up from the ground to Brad's green eyes and said, "no one is here. However, there is a large pool of blood."

"OH JESUS," Brad exclaimed and fell to the ground with his hands to his face. The cop and Bolt just looked at one another, side eyed.

"Now hold on, maybe everything is fine or it's just a prank or something. You said you live here with your girlfriend," Bolt kept looking at the cop and she nodded her head.

"Yes but...oh God, she...um," Brad looked up at the sky. He had some tearing but not enough to be convincing to Bolt, "She umm, she has cut herself intentionally at times. She has threatened suicide, too, when she gets mad enough. She's on medications for depression and anxiety. She's had an issue with Xanax and...and...OH, she has abused her ADHD meds before."

Bolt responded with a slow drawl "Umm, humm, I see."

"Does it look like something happened to her or that she did something to herself or what?"

"Well, now, that's an interesting question to ask, Mr..."

"LeBlanc."

"Yes, very interesting. Ya see, we don't know where she is to even make that determination."

Brad got to his feet, "Y'all said that but it's only really hitting me now...you mean no one is in the house?"

"Not unless they're hiding. She have the combination to the safe?"

"I never gave it to her...I mean, she's smart, and she may have figured it out or been watching over my shoulder...wait, is the safe open?"

The cop and Bolt looked at one another, again, "It is. Officer, would you kindly get this man some of dem special booties and we'll let him come tell us what's missing from that safe or anywhere else in the house."

"Yes, sir," she said then she went off to retrieve a pair.

"Yeah, we haven't finished processing the murder scene."

"MURDER SCENE?"

"Well, yes. I mean, not to alarm you but it, well, it's enough blood that one would assume…"

"You told me not to worry!"

"You're right. Let's see what we can find out. Maybe they have taken her and will call for ransom or something."

"TAKEN HER? RANSOM? HOW DO YOU EVEN KNOW SHE WAS TAKEN?"

"Look, calm down, let's take this one thing at a time, Brad."

22

What Happens Now?

The uniformed police officer returned with her blue latex gloves on and a pair of white shoe coverings for Bradly, "Here, put these on."

"It's my house, why would I need these, my footprints are all over the place."

"Trust me, if you want to keep those shoes, you need to put these on."

Brad put on the coverings. When he was done with the second one, he looked up and said, "You really think I care about these shoes when you are telling me my girlfriend is missing, and blood is everywhere?"

"You don't seem too concerned about ya girl," Officer Robinson allowed a little of her New Orleans dialect to come out.

"Look, she was getting to be too much for me, anyway. I was trying to figure out how to get her to leave without too much fuss."

"Well, there is a whole lotta fuss in that house."

"Is it really that bad?"

"Yup."

Detective Bolt had already walked back up the lawn and was waiting by the entrance.

Once inside the front door, Brad looked at all the blood in the kitchen. The flash of the camera highlighted the pool of gore and all three detectives standing around as the crime photographer moved to get another angle.

"Bleedin' Christ" Brad blurted out, "ARE YOU KIDDING ME?"

"Look, calm down Mr. LeBlanc. Like I said, we don't have a body or anything. She may be fine. Hell, maybe it's not even her blood."

"Who else's blood could it be?"

"Well, now that I don't know. For all we know she may have dragged someone out that side door and into her own vehicle."

"What makes you say that?"

"You sure are asking a lot of questions. I should be asking you some of those…but before I do, what kind of vehicle does she have?"

"It's a black Escalade."

Robinson wrote that down on her little pad.

"Yeah, we figured it was an SUV."

"It's gone?"

"More questions?"

"Look, I'm just trying to figure out what happened here almost as much as you are."

"Let's go see what got taken from the safe."

The master bedroom was to the right of the living room, and the kitchen was off to the left. They went through the living room that was classically lit and a huge flat screen hung above the fireplace. There was an entrance to a large dining area that was set behind pocket doors that were open. One cop was in there poking around and gave Detective Bolt a shake of the head to signify that he hadn't found anything.

Once in the bedroom, the trio entered the large walk-in closet that was once an attached nursery 70 years ago. Brad bent down and looked inside the safe, "Well, they got the money. There was nearly a quarter-million in there."

Bolt whistled a long and drawn-out catcall. "Wow, you keep that kind of cash laying around?"

Brad turned and looked up at him, "Kept."

"What else is missing?"

"The two pistols that were in there."

"Oh, yeah, we took those out. They are on their way to ballistics to see if they have been fired recently."

"They haven't been. Not in years. And if they have been, they weren't fired by me."

"Brad, don't you think it's a little odd they didn't take the guns or even the rings? I mean, unless you had some nicer ones in there."

"I suppose it is and no I didn't have any other rings in there. Just these and they are more heirlooms than anything else. Fifteen or so grand each. I don't wear gold anymore."

"You really aren't worried about her being gone, are you?"

"I would have paid someone a quarter million to take her but not leave this mess."

"Well, you nearly got your wish."

Brad looked back up after further surveying his safe and frowned.

"Maybe she just left?" Bolt questioned.

"Then who left the blood?" Brad asked.

"Yeah, that's a real puzzler, ain't it?"

"Not really. Connie's loonier than a toon and could have put anyone's blood there."

"Not that amount."

Brad stood up and asked, "May we go to the kitchen now? I gotta see what I'm gonna have to do to get this shit cleaned up."

"My, but you're cold blooded."

"Not really, just practical and a little relieved."

"Even though someone just relieved you of a quarter million?"

"The bank has the rest. If she stays gone, it'll be worth it."

"Hum, welp, you may get your wish and stay relieved. Hey, ya know, I wanted to ask you something. I noticed you have two missing pairs of shoes on your rack. This place is…well, was, meticulous. I figure you are wearing one pair. Over there," Bolt pointed to a rack of different tennis shoes, "there seems to be another pair missing."

"They should be there. I have no idea where those are. I didn't move 'em."

"Well, maybe the burglar or burglars or maybe even Connie herself took them."

Robinson spoke up, "I don't know Detective Bolt, quarter mil can buy plenty of shoes."

"Good point, Robinson. Make sure the photographer gets everything in here, too."

"You got it, Detective."

"Okay, let's go see this kitchen," Bolt waved them both out of the closet.

Once in the kitchen, Brad rubbed his bald head and sighed.

"Yeah, it's bad but it gets worse," Bolt said, exhaling, "Come around here, past this empty laptop bag."

Brad started in as if he were just as confused as the detective, "They don't take guns nor rings, but they take the laptop...and I don't see the power cord... Jesus, what is that?"

"Yeah, they're drag marks and judging by the look of it the person being dragged was small. By the way, how tall is Connie?"

"Pfft, like 5' 4" and a buck-five."

"Petite, huh?"

"Very."

"Then I don't suppose she was the one doing the draggin'," Bolt said. But the way he said it was like he was slightly confused. He wasn't, and Officer Robinson played along.

"They did have that one girl drag that big dude, Detective."

"Oh yeah, the Arias case."

"Yup."

"Well, maybe. Anyway, that doesn't seem to fit the footprints."

"Footprints?" Brad was intrigued.

"Yeah, we found some sized, oh, I dunno," Bolt looked down at Brad's bootie covered shoes, "About that size…what are those?"

"Size eleven and half…and now we are off to the races. Here we fuckin' go."

"Well, there are four of your shoes missing and you only have feet enough for two."

"Yeah, well, if the prints match missing shoes, where are the fuckin' shoes, Detective? And who says that rotten…" Brad stopped himself, "that Connie wasn't wearing them."

"Only one pair of hers is missing and we believe they were on her feet when she was dragged outta here, Brad. And I intend to find out who was doing the draggin'."

"Do your damnedest."

"Brad, wadda ya say we go out the front door and come back around? Wouldn't want you steppin' in none of those drag marks. I want you to take a look at where her Escalade was parked. I'm not saying you did a thing, and you might be able to shed some light on this mess. Oh, you got your phone?"

"Yeah, why? You can have it…look at anything you want on it."

"Oh my, no, Brad, we need to make sure you aren't getting any ransom calls, remember?"

"Sure," Brad said plainly and handed over his phone.

The three went through the front door and around the house. Once they were near where the grass met the black top, Bolt turned on his light.

"You see from the door over there, I'm sorry, I know it's a mess," Bolt mocked, figuring he would get Brad to crack soon. *This will be an easy slam dunk by the end of the night*, he thought.

"Yeah."

Bolt traced the streaks with his light to near where they were standing. "You see this? It's a pretty clean print right here and it looks like they may have loaded her up in the back of her own SUV and left with her body and your money."

"Don't forget the laptop," Brad said.

"Oh right. You seem rather intrigued by that laptop."

"You bet I am."

"Why?"

"Because, like you said, why would someone take a laptop, the power cord, and not the other stuff?"

128

"I didn't say that, you did, Brad. Anyway, you have cameras, don't you?"

"Holy shit, I wasn't even thinking about that!"

Bolt and Robinson side eyed one another, again.

"It's on my phone. It records the outside of the house—front and back. Oh, and the living room!"

"Well, shitfire! That should settle it!"

"Lemme see my phone, yeah, I'll show you!"

Brad opened the app, used the slider. Nothing had been recorded for weeks.

"FUCK!"

"Awww, no good, huh?" Bolt said as he put his hands on his hips.

Brad shook his head, "Damnit!"

"Well, I'm sure we'll get this squared away. Say, you mind if we look through your car?"

"Sure don't!"

"Good, let's go down to the street and once we do that and finish up here, I believe that should give us a good start."

"Yeah, a start toward me as a suspect."

"Mr. LaBlanc?"

"What, Detective?"

"That train left the station when you started talkin'."

Brad slapped his key fob in Bolt's open hand and led them to the car while the detective pulled a cellophane bag of gloves from his back pocket and put on a pair.

"You look all you want. There ain't shit in there but the stench of cigar smoke."

"You smoke cigars in this fine automobile?"

"It's one of the few pleasures I have left in life."

Bolt clicked the front trunk button and slid his hand under the latch release and pushed it up.

Brad had his arms folded and was looking at the detective's back. Both Bolt and Robinson stepped back. Brad stepped forward and looked in his own trunk.

Detective Bolt spoke, "Uh oh, I think you may have just bought yourself one less pleasure."

Grabbing Brad's arms that had just been folded contemptuously in front of him then putting them behind his back, Officer Robinson said, "Bradly LeBlanc, you are under arrest for suspicion of murder. You have the right to remain silent…" D.D. Robinson finished reading Brad his rights while she quickly cuffed him. Detective Bolt just shook his head slowly and looked at the gory mess under the hood of that car. He wondered how someone could have even fit a body in that small of a space.

Brad's eyes were wide open but seeing nothing. Instead, he was envisioning himself in a prison cell just before he spoke lifelessly, "I have an alibi, but it's not a good one."

23

Everyone Needs A Joni

It took every ounce of courage for Margot to stop by the
store—especially at that time of night and after what she
seen—to get wine before making her way to Joni's house to
spend the weekend. It was twenty minutes 'til eight, Friday
night. She was thankful that New Orleans didn't have package
stores. One could go into any grocery store, at any time, and
purchase alcohol.

"Need anything else, ma'am?"

"No. Oh, wait, uh yeah, where do ya keep the smokes?"

Joni may have been happy to see her friend, but she wasn't
happy about the circumstances. Earlier, Margot had told Joni
about what had happened when she asked if she could stay
with her for the weekend. After Margot had gotten to Joan's
place, she set up Adler's litter box in one of the upstairs
bathrooms and changed into a pair of shorts and a Fleetwood
Mac tee-shirt. Joni had been following her around the house
the whole time.

At Joni's request, Margot went over the whole ordeal again while sitting in the living room. Joni said nothing until Margot was finished, "I just can't believe it, Margs. I just can't. I mean I do, but I can't. You know what I mean?" Joni's unlit cigarette bounced up and down in the corner of her mouth, gold lighter in hand.

"Yes *and* no and I went through the shit to begin with."

"Through it? How about in it, honey?" Joni said after pointing to the television. It was on but muted and Detective Bolt and D.D. Robinson were walking Brad LeBlanc, arm and arm, down a hallway in the First District Police Station. A tagline below read, *Uptown New Orleans man arrested under the suspicion of murdering his girlfriend.* Both ladies stood up, moved closer to the TV, and stared as they read the caption under the video showing the outside of the mansion then the Porsche being put on a flatbed tow truck.

"What do they mean 'suspicion'? I saw that shit!"

Joni unmuted the set. Both ladies listened to the familiar cadence of a local reporter.

"…Thanks Rob. Details are sketchy at best right now but we received an anonymous tip that a prominent investment manager, Bradly Ray LeBlanc, has been arrested and brought in for questioning regarding the apparent murder of his girlfriend…" the reporter looked down at a white note pad that was blowing in the wind while he was being drizzled on by a light rain, "…Connie Minae. We have no middle name at this time," the reported fumbled around during that line while looking for the next.

"Police are saying that they have enough evidence to make this a quote, 'slam dunk'. An anonymous source with the New

Orleans Police Department went on to say that the suspect, who you just saw in the clip there, is in custody and the suspect's black Porsche had, and I quote, 'all the evidence needed for a conviction'. Police went on to say, and again, this is also a quote, 'plus, all that was found at his house'. However, Rob, we don't yet know what that evidence is."

"Thanks, Travis, I know you will keep an eye on this story as it unfolds in the days and weeks ahead."

Joni muted the set again, "Why didn't they say anything about the body?" Joni turned to her side and looked at Margot who was clearly distraught.

"Jesus, Joni, I didn't get the police there in time. I called as quick as I could…I think…I dunno, it happened so fast and yet in slow motion."

"Margot?"

"What?" she responded softly.

"Give yourself some grace. You did everything you needed to. If you hadn't been on that session with her, they may not have caught *Brad…*" Joni said in a mocking tone before continuing, "…at all."

"But maybe if I had called just a second sooner, she would have been okay."

"And if we had a time machine, we would be Marty and Doc Brown," Joni quipped, trying to keep it light for her friend and put her arm around Margot's shoulder with her cigarette still dangling from her face. But Margot didn't want to be comforted by friendship yet and pulled the still unlit Winston 100 from her friend's mouth with a huff. She wanted a drink and a smoke first.

"I need something stronger than wine before we talk about anything else."

"Scotch or bourbon?"

"Definitely bourbon. Scotch tastes like smoked meat drippings," Margot said with a twisted stink face.

"Well, I'm sorry," Joni said while she bent down and pulled out two shot glasses from the liquor hutch and a bottle of Four Roses small batch.

Joni plopped the two glasses that were pinched between her thumb and index finger down on the table. They landed with a clank against each other. Margot stared off in the distance as she was watching the movie over and over again in her head of what she had saw.

Joni poured the cherry and green apple hinted whiskey into one shot glass then the other, while looking over at Margot, "Margs, I can smell the hot-buttered popcorn over there. Stop watching that movie in your noggin." Joni slid the glass over to Margot and said, "Bottoms up, toots. I keep this stuff around only for special occasions. It's aged ten more years since I bought it."

Margot took the glass and shot it quickly at the same time Joni did. Margs took a look at the glass the way one would read a label when they are in flavor heaven.

Joni looked over with a smile, "That's some good shit, ain't it? It's like drinking class."

"It's the best thing to happen to me all day… other than you allowing me and Adler to stay with you."

"Honey, I'm staying with *you*. We may be at my place, but you are doing me a favor. After you explained what had happened to you and what you saw…" Joni said as she poured two more shots, "…I didn't want to be here alone, anyway."

Joni took another swig and Margot was still standing and smelling the sweet, aged liquid before taking it in as Joni sat down, took a smoke from the pack, and lit it. Margot looked over at Joni as she finished her shot. Margot gave a surprised look and Joni said, "What?"

"I thought you didn't smoke in the house."

"Honey, I thought you didn't smoke at all, but I know better now," and slid the lighter across the table to Margot.

"I usually don't," Margot said and she lit hers, "But it's not every day you see a murder."

"No truer words have ever been *smokin'*. Let's see if we can keep it that way."

"Well, at least he's in custody and we ain't his girlfriend, so, we have that going for us."

"Speak for yourself, honey. He looks like a guy I dated in the early 2000's. Okay, on more shot and we go to wine, young lady. You will be laid out if you go much faster on this. I don't mind that it's 30 bucks a shot, but I don't want you three sheets to the wind before you give me a better rundown of what happened."

"Fine, hit me again," Margot said after taking another drag. No coughing this time. It seemed that old habits weren't dead.

After pouring two glasses of the wine that Margot brought, both sat, and Joni slowly slid the glass over by the base.

"Okay, spill it. Not the wine but the story."

"I told you everything, Jonesy."

"You told me what you saw in flashes, and I already forgot half of what you said. I want the finer details, if you can call them that."

"Oh, Joni, I dunno…"

"I said spill it, toots."

"It's just all a blur now. I was sitting there trying to role-play with her and…"

"Role-play? They still do that?"

"Yep. What do you know about it, anyway?"

"Third and fourth husband."

Margot gave her a look.

Joni waived her cigarette around in the air and said, "Hey, we tried."

"Yeah…well, anyway we were role-playing and he just came through that door I mentioned to you that gave me the spooks a few times, ran down the hall and shoved her to the ground."

"Did he say anything?"

"Yeah, he said, 'I'm going to kill you.'"

The cigarette that Joni was dragging on got left in her mouth as she spoke, "He. Said. What?"

"Oh, he wasn't saying it to me, it was in response to the role-play."

"I can't even follow."

"Those shots are taking effect for both of us, and it may make it more difficult anyway…and now the wine is following the story more than either of us are."

"Didn't you tell me once that you record those things?"

"Oh, Jonesy, Don't make me…"

"I don't think I'm drunk enough to watch it anyway. But I will be after I finish this glass and pour another."

"I don't know that I'll ever be drunk enough to see that again," Margot said after taking a swig and then a draw and an exhale.

Margot's purse began to buzz. Both ladies looked at the purse, and then one another.

Margot just held Joni's gaze.

Joni spoke, "Well pumpkin, you gonna get that?"

"Who the hell could that be?" Margot started to have a slight bit of slur to her words.

"You keep that purse waiting and we may never know."

Margot got up from the table and steadied herself. She bent over her bag and had a slight wabble, "I've not eaten, and this stuff has gone right to my head."

"You answer that, I've got just what the doctor ordered," Joni shot up and scooted right into the kitchen."

Margot answered the call, "This is Margot Landry."

"Hello Ms. Landry, this is the lead detective in the case that I have been informed you were involved in. I'm Lieutenant Detective Bolt."

"Uh, yes Detective, how can I be helpful?"

"My understanding is you were the one that called 911 and got emergency service rolling. Thank you for that."

"You're welcome but I don't know what it really did."

"Well, it got us a suspect quickly and he's on ice down here in an interview room. We were wondering if we might come by and get a statement from you...I mean I know it's late, but you may have something that would give us leverage in this case."

"You have him in custody, so I take it you found all you needed."

"Not really. I mean, yes, we have evidence, but we don't know if..."

"What do you mean? He's there on suspicion of murder, right?"

"Yes, ma'am but we have a problem."

"What is it and what can I do to help?"

"We don't have a body."

"Wait, what?

"We don't know if Connie is alive or not. It's possible, but highly unlikely. Based on what we found in the house and in his car it's not looking good. Neither for him nor her. We have a...and I'm sorry...a lot of blood on the kitchen floor."

"If there is any possibility that I can help I will. But even if she's not alive, I'll do whatever you need me to do to bring this to a conclusion for the family."

"We don't know if Connie has any family to speak of, but either way, thank you for that. Right now, we just need to know what you saw."

"It's all a bit hazy. It's more like a blur."

"Ms. Landry, and please don't take this the wrong way, but have you been drinking tonight?"

"Wouldn't you after seeing something like that?"

"Every night, ma'am, right after I take the gun and badge off."

"And there you have it."

"Yup."

"Anyway, I don't think my statement would be as helpful as the recordings would be," Margot's thinking was slightly slowed but she caught herself and realized what she had just done.

"Wait, let me understand this; you have a recording?"

"Umm, well, yes but they are protected. I can only acknowledge I know who you are talking about because she is, or was, in danger."

"And she still may be. She may be alive somewhere and anything on that audio may be helpful in giving us clues as to her whereabouts."

"Honestly, I could hand them over either way."

"I get it, patient/therapist privilege. It would probably help to get a court order to protect you, but I'd have to wake up or sober up the magistrate judge as it's well past 10pm."

"That would help but I'd have to download the video so that…"

"Wait, you have VIDEO?"

"Yes…sorry, I thought I mentioned that."

"We are definitely going to want that."

"My licensure board is closed until Monday. It would take forever to report to them and…"

"Ma'am, that's days away…and we may only have hours. I'm sending a tech over right now. What's your address?"

Joni poked her head out from slicing cheese to go with the Triscuits and olives, "He wants the address doesn't he…well, give it to him."

Margot did and Bolt read it back.

"Ms. Landry…"

"Yes?"

"Thank you, I'm coming over with one of my computer guys now."

"Okay, bye," Margot ended the call.

Joni emerged from the kitchen with a large cutting board and sat it on the table. She went back and got a bowl of lemon olive oil with fig balsamic. Margot wasted no time in helping herself.

"I smell popcorn again. You're watching another movie. What is it this time?"

"They don't have a body. She may still be alive."

"Well slap my ass and call me Sally."

"I'll stick with just calling you Joni. But I may slap your ass for this spread."

"How 'bout you tell me what all this is about regarding 'the board not being open'. What's that got to do with anything?"

"I'm supposed to protect my client's info with my life. Well, not quite that."

"You've come as close to doing that as any therapist would want."

"Somewhat," Margot took a Triscuit and a slice of aged sharp cheddar then placed it on top. Swiping it in the oil and balsamic she took a bite and shut her eyes while she took in the symphony of flavors then spoke, "It's better to refuse to hand anything over until there is a court order. But since she may be alive, in danger, and clues may be on that video, I'm protected at this point. So, like I told him, either way, I could hand it over."

"So, they're sending some computer geek and a rugged detective over, right?"

"Right."

"Then tell me, Margot, you a good wingman?"

"Joni, from what I've learned about you over the past few months I don't think the two together could handle you."

"A drunk woman says what a sober woman thinks and it hasn't clouded your judgment one bit."

24

Drag and Drop

The ladies drank, ate, and talked while they waited for Detective Bolt and the computer geek.

Joni blurted out, "I wanna see it!"

"See what?"

"The video."

"Oh, Joni, trust me, no you don't."

"Look, don't you need to download it or transfer it or something, anyway?"

"The computer dude will do that when they get here."

"It's getting late, and I don't trust myself with all this alcohol and men in the house."

"What? You afraid you will fall into another marriage?"

"Ouch!"

"Aww, Jonesy, I mean no harm girly-girl."

"No offense taken," Joni was slurring now, "Anyway, no, I won't ever get married again...'course I said that after number three."

"Me neither, no thanks. I rode that train and jumped off of it while it was still moving."

"Speaking of that, how's the toad?"

"I blocked him."

"PROGRESS! LET'S DRINK TO PROGRESS," Joni exclaimed and held up her glass for a toast.

"TO PROGRESS!" Margot said and clinked her glass to Joni's.

Margot got up from the table and Joni took her sip and said, "Steady as she gooooooes!"

The ladies were just short of smashed.

Margot went over to her bag and pulled out her laptop. "Gotta make sure it's all plugged in annnnn' ready to goooooo!"

"Atta girl, let's see the crime!"

"You're going to regret allowing morbid curiosity to get the better of you. If you watch it, wake me when it's over 'cause I ain't watchin' shit."

"You're gonna have to," Joni said in a sobering low tone.

"Why would I ever have to do that?"

"There's gonna be a trial and you're gonna have to testify."

Margot's face went white. "I didn't give any thought to that at all. How did I not think of that? Oh fuck, no."

"Awww, it'll just be a short little thing. It's not like you were there or had anything to do with it."

"Easy for you to say. It's not like you're involved."

Joni's mouth slowly started to hang open as she looked at Margot while she sat the laptop on the dining table and began to unwrap the cord. Margot noticed her looking ashen.

"What's wrong with you, Joni? You okay?"

"You don't think that balloon has anything to do with this, do you? If it does, then…"

"Oh no, we ain't bringin' that shit up to the cops. That was a one-off. That was a prank of some sort."

"You didn't think that before. You tryin' to convince me or yourself? And the call to room 333? That a 'one-off', too?"

"Look, I dropped that. I have tried to forget about it. My tracking led to a dead end and that's where Imma leave it."

"Fine with me…I don't want to have to testify to shit."

"Yeah, we don't know nothin' 'bout nothin' when it comes to that balloon or messages or clowns or circuses or…"

"Deal!"

Margot plugged the power cord in the wall and then to the computer, sat down, and lifted the top. The Telepy app was still open. Shown on the screen was the usual lavender color of the site and in the center of the screen it read, 'Connie has disconnected from the session'.

Margot hadn't noticed but Joni had gotten up and worked her way around so that she was behind her. Margot hopped up in her seat with a start when Joni leaned in her ear and said, "Elvis has left the building."

"Je-SUS!"

"I'm sorry, toots. I just can't help it. I want to see it, no matter what you say. I'd do it myself if I knew how the site worked."

Margot sighed, "I don't know how to use it, either. I mean, I know how to use it, but I don't know how to download a recording to the desktop."

"Oh, let me see that, honey," Joni said with comical impatience while she attempted to squeeze into Margot's chair. Margot didn't budge and huddled over the screen.

"Joni, I'm not supposed to…aw fuck it. I'm too buzzed to care anymore."

"Buzzed? Pfft. You're fuckin' hammered!"

Quickly, Joni sat in the chair next to Margot, put down her wine glass, and slid the laptop over so that it was directly in front of her. Joni was still comfortable with computers regardless of how long she had been away from the financial world. She had her own desktop in the house and played the market with her "mad money" occasionally. Even though she was jacked on shots of Four Roses and two and a half glasses of wine, this task was going to be relatively easy for her.

"Alright, just give me a minute to see what's what. Where are the session recordings kept on the site?"

"Here," Margot said pointing to the screen. Both ladies were lit up in lavender when their faces got closer to the screen. "Awe, hell, let me get my reading glasses," Joni reached around her chair where her purse hung, dug around, and found another pack of cigarettes and her reading glasses. She smacked the deck of smokes on her hand three times to pack them and quickly unwrapped the box. Poking one in her mouth she pulled her lighter from her pocket, lit it, and then went to work. "Okay, let's see what we got here…"

"Remember, you didn't see or do any of this."

"I ain't seen shit. The firefly cherry bobbed up and down in her face when she spoke. Joni looked over with her reading glasses far down her nose and peered over them at Margot. "Honey, when you work in finance as long as I have, you ain't seen a whole lot of nothin'."

Margot got what she meant.

Joni went back to work, "Here we are. Oh look, that's convenient, it's in a file labeled 'Connie Minae'. That's lovely! I bet we can just….drag….and….drop. Yup, there we go." A progress bar popped up and within twenty seconds, the sessions were on the desktop.

"Now what?" Margot asked.

"Now we watch!"

The door buzzer rang and this time, both ladies did a seat hop.

Joni went to answer the door and Margot stayed seated at the table for fear she may not make it to the door and back. "Hi, I'm Joan Pierse, Margot's friend."

"I'm Detective Bolt and this is our computer specialist, Richie Allan," Richie nodded and said, "Hello, ma'am." He was in his 20's, thin, and had a head full of moppy hair.

"Nice to meet you both. Please come in."

"Thanks. We know it's late and this shouldn't take long."

"Oh, it's no bother. Margot and her computer are over there," Joni said as she was shutting the door.

Bolt strode behind Richie who couldn't get to the table fast enough. The detective flashed a smile, "So, you're our hero, Margot Landry. It's nice to meet you, though, I'm sorry it's under these circumstances."

"You and I both," Margot replied while she was watching Joni checking out Bolt's ass and she was clearly pleased. Margot shot her a look and Joni just shrugged with a smile.

Once Richie got to the table he asked, "I take it this is the computer that you were on when the incident happened?"

"Yes, and Joni already cut the videos and put them on the desktop."

"Okay, good. I didn't know what kind of computer you owned so I brought a dongle to make sure it would fit any port you had."

Margot looked at Joni who had sat next to her and gave her the look of, 'don't do it…don't you dare.' Joni made the same shrug and smiled.

Richie was clueless and the ladies inside "dongle joke" and had already introduced the device to the laptop and went to dumping the videos to the thumb-drive connected to the dongle. "Ms. Landry," Bolt jumped right in sensing the same joke, "I'd like to ask you some questions."

"Okay, look, it's obvious that I have been drinkin' and it's prolly not a good idea for me to give a statement right now."

"Okay, fine enough. May we watch the video with you and see if we have anything to ask you about?"

"Oh no, I don't wanna watch that shit…sorry, stuff. I just don't."

"Okay, how about we watch it, you don't have to, and I'll ask questions?"

"I dunno. I just don't know that I even want to hear it."

"We can keep the audio down," Richie chimed in.

Detective Bolt clasped his hands together and went for broke, "Look, he is in custody, and we need to find Connie quickly. If she's alive, she's likely extremely injured based on all the evidence we found and collected. If she's not alive, this man needs to never see the light of day again. Ma'am, look, we need you right now."

Margot put her head in her hands and started to cry. Through her sobs, she spoke, "She warned me…I thought she was crazy, and I didn't take her as seriously as I should have. She warned me that he would hurt her. I was trying to get her out...I mean, I was trying to push her to make the decision on her own to leave him. And I just…I just couldn't get to her. She left sessions after only a few minutes, she was panicky; all outta sorts. I…I did a shitty job and now she's dead…"

Joni put her arm around Margot, "Stop that! You don't do that. You're great and I know it. This woman didn't want to leave. What did you call her…a self-rejecting complainer?"

Margot laughed snorted through her tears, "Help-rejecting complainer," she corrected.

"Yeah, that…look, that's not the point. The point is…well…what's my point? Oh, yeah, you can be helpful now!

You can help her. She may still be alive—who knows? Detective Volt, thinks maybe…"

"Detective Bolt."

"Yeah, Bolt here," Joni motioned toward him with her thumb. "Yeah. He thinks she might be."

Richie, who was on the spectrum, couldn't deal with all this emotion.

"Detective, let's watch the video and see where we go next. It may not be useful, anyway."

"Margot, are you going to watch this with us?" Detective Bolt asked.

"Yes…no…I don't know…I'll just listen."

"Okay, that'll be fine. Go ahead Richie."

Richie clicked the video, and it popped up immediately. As they began to watch, Margot was listening and looking at their faces. Both men had their eyes darting at specific spots on the screen attempting to "detect" anything that they might find interesting or useful. Yes, they had plenty of evidence. But without a body, it was going to be slightly difficult to get an indictment. It was going to be an uphill battle to get a conviction. Every little bit would help. They were looking for anything.

Margot was so focused on the men listening to the session and waiting to see their reaction to the dark figure coming down the hall, she had not noticed that Joni had slowly drifted around and was watching too.

When she did notice, Joni sipped her wine and gave her another shoulder shrug then a 'what' look. It must have been right at that moment that Bradly Leblanc came running toward Connie because Joni reacted and spit her wine on Richie's back. He didn't move an inch when he felt it.

When the video was over, Bolt looked up at Margot who had her head in her hands again with her elbows on the table.

"He threatened you."

"That's not what he said, Detective. It was a role-play answer. He said, 'I would say "I'm going to kill you"' to Connie, not me."

"Margot, I'll just say that we need to keep him locked up and we are likely going to need you to testify. Not only that, but you are also likely going to be listed as an expert witness. And I won't lie to you…he has money. He's going to have the best attorneys that New Orleans has to offer, but you can help Connie now more than ever. This is your chance."

Margot looked up with anger in her eyes. She knew she was being manipulated by Bolt. But she believed he was right.

"I'll fucking do it."

"I'll drink to that," Joni swished her glass and hips, "Oh, sorry about your shirt, sonny," she said to Richie who had already pulled the dongle out of the laptop and was getting up.

Saturday afternoon, Margot went to the station and gave her statement. Joni and she got soused again and watched the news reports about the bloody evidence and the probability that Connie was buried somewhere or maybe even locked up in a room bleeding and unfed. Mr. LeBlanc was not talking and had lawyered up hard.

Sunday, the ladies slept most of the day. Adler had taken to sleeping with Joni so often she was considering getting a cat.

25

Hall Pass

It was Monday morning, and the ladies were drained. The whole weekend since Friday night had been a complete shit show.

Margot entered her office at 9am sharp. Joni had walked with her even though she wasn't working until Wednesday. She was being very protective of her friend, and they had grown closer in the last few days than they had been over the last several months of lunches and coffees. On her desk was exactly what she needed right now. A potted orchid tied to a long stick to keep it stable. A plastic card holder held a small envelope.

"Joni, you shouldn't have."

Joni held her hand over her mouth, "Honey, I didn't."

Margot looked over her shoulder and saw Joni's worry and concern.

"Joni, I'm not going to read that card."

"Well, I don't wanna open it!"

Margot stared at Joni with the look of "please" written all over her face.

"Okay, okay!" Joni said as she marched over to the desk and pulled the Tiffany blue envelope out with a huff, opened it ,and pulled out the card.

Margot watched Joni's face dissolve slowly into horror.

"What what what?" Margot asked while shaking her hands like they had gone numb.

Joni just turned the card around so that it faced Margot and held it out in front of her. Joni then put her head in her other hand.

Margot's eyes got large. The shit show was now a full-fledged shitcom.

She read the card.

A skull with the number 33 scratched into the forehead, reminiscent of the balloon, was on the card. The overlapped sticks that created the number was filled in with a thin, red-tipped marker. The skull had a cartoonish but creepy frown and three tears "dripping" from its left orbital bones. Under the skull it read,

So sorry for your loss.

With love,

H.H.

After Joni had slipped the card in her pocket, Margot went directly to her supervisor, Prestin Wilcox's, door and knocked in rapid succession.

"Come on!" Prestin said, to call her into his office.

"Sorry to bother you Prestin but I need to take some time."

"I have thirty minutes before my first meeting."

"No Prestin, I mean I need to take some time off work."

"Oh, are you okay?" he asked as he looked over from his computer where he had been typing.

"Have you seen the news about the guy who they think killed his girlfriend? Well, they haven't found the body. They think there is a chance that...never mind. I was providing therapy for the victim, and it happened during session."

Prestin revealed his shock, "Margot...umm...yes, yes of course. Take all the time you need...wait, are you still seeing Mike? I mean, if you don't mind me asking." Prestin had known Mike for years; he was well respected in the therapeutic community and had been suggested by Prestin as a therapist and mentor for Margot once she shared struggling with the aftermath of her failed marriage.

"Yes, I'm still seeing him but that's not..."

"No, I just mean to have him write you a letter for FMLA, so I don't get asked any questions from H.R. and corporate. It's none of their business anyway."

"Yes, of course. Thank you, Prestin."

Margot called Mike and explained some of the details on her way home and he quickly agreed on sending over the letter to Prestin.

"Margot, if you need to see me, please reach out."

"Thanks Mike. I really appreciate this. I'll let you know."

The card that was nestled in Joan's pocket made the decision easy for her to call the giftshop manager and quit with no notice.

26

Writer's Block

Margot and Adler were sitting on their couch. Margot had her laptop open while she stared off in the distance petting her feline. The balloon, room 333, the assault or attempted murder or murder, and now the card with the flowers expressing condolences for a loss. What loss? When were those flowers ordered? How long before that session? Was it from a creeper? Was it from Brad? Was any of this connected at all? Skulls, 33, and H.H. It was a roller-coaster of bullshit that had Margot both scared and pissed. She called Joni.

Joni answered on the first ring, "Before I say *hello,* don't ask me to drive anywhere because I'm into my second glass of wine. Okay, now that we got that outta the way, the second part is I quit the shop. I won't go back to that hospital to have even a lifesaving procedure at this point. That's my story and I'm sticking to it."

"Hello to you, too, Joni."

"What the hell's going on now?"

"I'm thinking too much or not enough."

"That makes two of us. You coming up with any answers as to what the piss is going on?"

"Not at all. I don't know if any of this fits together or not."

"Well, I've come to more questions than to conclusions, toots."

"That's why I'm calling. You kept that card that came with the flowers, right?"

"I'm not being sassy about this but I'm way ahead of ya. I looked at the balloon pieces and the card. Looks to be in the same hand. And really, why wouldn't they match?"

"Not bad but I was gonna ask you about a different idea I had."

"Like I said, honey, I'm way ahead of ya. I called the flower shop. They have cameras and I wanted to see who drew that silly shit and delivered those flowers. Turns out that the delivery fella was just a regular guy that has worked there for years. Some guy named George, but he's a nobody. They say he's never done a creepy thing as long as they have known him. Anyway, I asked about the cameras, and they said it was a phone order…"

"Then what did they do, get someone to draw that fucked-up card based on the order alone?"

"That's the most interesting part. They took the order by phone, and by the way it was a full two weeks ago. How in the world would someone, unless they knew when that session of yours was going to go down, at that time, and on that night? OR, this is some weird coincidence, and you have a slimy admirer—or *we* do—because they didn't know you would be standing there when and if I even blew that balloon up, though, it too, was a phone order. I don't even think I looked at the room number that the order was going to be delivered to that day. I just started to make the damned thing. Anyway, I'm getting off track, point is, the owner said he remembered taking that order because it was an odd one."

"Odd in what other way than creepy as shit?"

"The day the order was taken, the card showed up in a separate envelope with no return address, of course, and a note instructing them to add the card to the flower order. Margot, this bastard knows how to play the game, and we are just figuring out that there is a game being played at all."

"Joni?"

"I'm ahead of you again, toots. Pack a bag—a big one. You are going to be with me a while. I don't want to stay here alone anymore. And bring that big furball with you. I've grown fond of that little shit."

Margot had no intentions of not staying with Joni until the messages stopped and that asshole was in prison for good. She figured both may happen at the same time. This guy was as bad as they come, and she settled on the fact that he was trying to scare her and may be enjoying the act of doing so. Not much of it made sense but he must have wanted her to stop seeing Connie, too. That's the best she could come up with based on what she had.

She saved the two paragraphs she managed to bang out and closed down the book document that was becoming more and more useless at every attempt. Her eyes floated over to the sessions that she had downloaded from Telepy and the computer geek, Richie, downloaded on his "dongle". She hovered the mouse over the file and took her finger away from the track pad, put it to her lip, then bit her nail—hard.

"Okay, Adler, here goes nothing."

Margot knew she need to get through this at least once. For her own mental health and her writer's block that was yet another "trauma" getting in her way of being able to write a book about getting over, well, trauma.

She clicked the file and sat as far back from the screen as she could and looked through her fingers as if she were watching a horror movie—and she was. It was *her* horror movie about Connie.

Once the file played through and the chills wore off. Margot knew two things: something wasn't right, and the other was what she had known for years; to trust her gut. She watched it again. She watched it a third time and kept her eyes closer. She wasn't as nervous about it as the first of the two times. *Systematic desensitization*, she thought. She noticed something and decided to watch the end in slow-motion.

That night, Brad closed the laptop, and the screen went black, leaving only Margot's shocked expression in a postage-stamp sized box at the bottom right of the recording. Margot had noticed nothing in that moment. While watching now, though, Margot could see it clearly even though there were only two frames before darkness and it was mostly covered by Brad's thumb.

27

Trauma Bonding

Margot and Joni huddled together after getting emotionally settled with a little wine and another cheese board that Joni cheerfully had put together before Margot got packed and got to Joni's house. If nothing else, it was so she had a reason other than fear to have a knife in her hand. Adler was settled now, in what had become his familiar settings. He jumped in Joni's lap and purred.

"Okay, I want to show you something and I want your honest opinion," Margot said as she lifted the lid of her laptop.

"When have you not gotten my honest opinion?" Joni picked up her readers from the table and put them on while she spoke, "What we lookin' at?"

"I finally took a look at the video and I…"

"Oh, we've got brave, haven't we?"

"No, just pissed. I want to know who the hell is trying to scare us and if this Brad guy has anything to do with it."

"Tryin'? Whomever is doing this has me sleeping with cutlery under my pillow, so please tell me you've found something."

"It's only two or so frames but I'm going to ask you to look at it…"

"You won't have to ask me twice."

"…and after you watch it, I'm going to show it to you a few more times then ask you what you make of it."

Margot pulled up the video and used the slider to get close to the end, adjusted the speed to as slow as possible, then pressed play.

"Slow-motion?"

"It's going to be hard to make out any other way."

Joni took a cracker and placed a piece of Manchego neatly on the top with a satisfied smile then bit it in half. Margot looked over at her with a "are you serious" look.

Joni chirped away with a mouthful, "What? They're movie snacks. Want some? Whew, this Manchego is nice and funky."

Margot's attention was caught by seeing the laptop starting to close on the video, "Okay, here it comes. Now, I won't say a word, and I want you to pay attention. Tell me what you see."

"I see that bastard in a ski mask."

"We're not there yet…keep…watching…"

Joni was peering, with head tilted, through her cheaters. She got closer to the screen but by then the scene was over.

"I think I missed it."

"Okay, watch again," Margot said with a little annoyance in her voice. She used the slider to bring the video back to where she had started a few moments earlier—right at the point before Bradly had closed the laptop.

"Okay, stay close to the screen this time."

"Honey, if I had an idea of where I was to look and what I was to be looking at and for..."

"I don't want to tell you because if I do, it may taint the experiment."

"I don't like science. I'm fine with numbers but it gets complicated..."

"Damn it, Joni, get serious!"

"Alright! Alright! Don't get your bloomers all in a pinch."

"Now look close, it's coming up."

"Well, that helps a little, I suppose."

Joni watched more intently this time. Once it was over, she asked, "Was that it?"

"What did you see?"

"He closed the laptop."

"Joni, I'll do it one more time..."

"Oh good, a re-run."

"Look, if you aren't gonna take this serious..."

Joni looked at Margot with eyes that were sharper and more pointed than she had ever seen her look before. Joni spoke softly but sternly, "Margot, I want you to listen to me before I watch that video of that masked-covered fuck again."

Margot held Joni's gaze and didn't move an inch as she slowly nodded her head before Joni continued, "I have seen many things in my day. Many things I could not explain, didn't want to figure out, and even, maybe, a ghost once in the 80's," she finished with a shrug. "And then there are some things that I can explain because they were my fault. I've certainly lived through too many marriages. I watched husbands two and four die prematurely of heart attacks. I've seen a few roadside crashes that looked like no one could have possibly walked away from. And as you well know, I wanted nothing more than to watch this video when the cops were here the other night because I've been desensitized. That, and to be fair, it didn't happen to me…at least that's what I believed at the time. I have seen and lived through other things that I will never share with another person. I'll be taking those to the grave," Joni finished as she allowed a tear to escape and looked up at the ceiling to gather herself. But one thing I won't be taking to the grave, and I've never told you this, but I even watched as my sister tried to save her only child, my nephew, as he choked to death when he was only three. I was visiting—she couldn't save him and I was frozen. I never forgave myself for that and likely never will," Joni finished with a shake of her head and eyes closed as tight as her mouth. Margot half reached out her hand to Joni's arm, but her friend pulled back and renewed her stern resolve, "But I want to tell you something right now; I'm shook. I'm shook hard. That balloon was one thing, then the disappearance or murder or whatever the fuck, well, that was another. But that card and those flowers on your desk this morning. That did it. That was enough for me. All those things I have only seen and some I lived through—they were life. But not this. Something is wrong. Someone is fucking with you or me or, most likely, us. And it's either Brad, someone else involved with this disappearance, or not involved with it at all. And that someone has made us a target. And today, when I made a choice to not ignore all that shit anymore, and I quit my job and I called that flower shop this morning and realized this bastard is smart and is still a goddamned mystery to us. Well, that did it for me, honey. Yeah, that fucking did it. You aren't sleeping here for you. Oh, no ma'am. I, for the first time in my life, am scared to death to be alone in this house or anywhere else for that matter. I can't laugh nor joke my way outta this one. This is it. Someone wants our attention and by God that fucker has mine, full stop."

Joni quit talking and just looked at Margot as tears began to form on both their faces. In that moment they were, and would be, bonded forever in a sisterhood. A sisterhood no one would wish on their worst enemy.

She finished without so much as wiping her eyes, "So, I'm going to need you to give me a little grace on this one and I promise, I'll do you the same kindness."

Margot had never seen Joni this way before. And she would never see her this way again, "Joni…I'm scared, too. And I'm sorry, and I love you," Both ladies finished with an embrace that Margot initiated. She leaned back from their hug and said, "Take all the time you need. I'm hoping you see what I see or nothing at all. Either one will make me feel safer; saner."

"Okay, Margs. Let's start again."

By the third pass of the video after Joni's speech of seriousness, she was back to her old self.

"I think I see it, Margs."

"What? What do you see."

"I see a choice of bad kitchen tile."

"Okay, now let me show you another video where Connie shut her laptop in nearly the same way and then tell me what you see."

After only the first slow-motion viewings of that one, Joni looked up at Margot, "Let me guess, they didn't get a tile job within a one-week period?"

"No, Joni. I don't think so."

"Show me the other video one more time."

Margot did as instructed. After a moment, Joni looked up at Margot again, then said, "Well, I'll be goddamned."

She could see what looked to her to be Connie's hair. It looked like a dirty mop, and it lay in a large pool of blood. A pool of blood that Margot and Joni agreed without even expressing it to one another was *too* large. It was that both were sure that blood had to already be on the floor before her body hit that kitchen tile. What was white was now red. Both would later agree that no one bleeds that fast from hitting their head on the floor. And they would also agree that Brad had done nothing more than push her off the stool.

28

Go Fly A Kite

After snacking, a little alcohol drinking, and the computer was put away, both ladies sat chatting with every light on in the house—even the ones in the large closets.

Joni broke the silence first. For several minutes the two had been lost in deep contemplation about what this all meant and if it may be connected to what the ladies now referred to as '33', "So, you gonna call that Detective Bolt and let him know what we think we see?"

"Only if you promise not to ogle his ass again."

"Honey, I'll promise nothin' of the sort."

"I guess you refusing to promise doesn't matter much. That is, unless you come see him with me. I've decided that I'm going to the station to request to meet with him directly."

"The balloons and flower card, too? You taking all that stuff with you?"

"I dunno. I guess. I mean the card is clear cut if the balloon sells. I feel silly showing him only a busted balloon."

"Maybe they will know something. Maybe it will be connected to another case. I mean, it could be, I guess," Joni took a sip of wine and a drag of her cigarette. Smoking in the house had become habit again. She had quit doing that in the 90's.

Joni finished her thought, "yeah, the balloon pieces *would* seem silly unless they have something else regarding '33' on file and connected to other cases."

"I think that's the issue."

"What's that, honey?"

"I don't know that I wanna know. I don't want to know that it's exclusive to just us…that someone is specifically targeting us…that it may be someone who isn't Brad…someone who *isn't* in jail…someone who may still be out there," Margot finished by pointing to the door.

"You said something there. But I also don't know that I want to live like this in my own house waiting for the next message to show up. Earlier today I had hoped that by quitting that pissant job I would stop seeing that kind of shit. But now? Now I'm just worried that this person is so smart, that he, or she, has already found me…or us, for that matter. And if they have— and if they want to continue the torment—they will just send the messages here. Or worse, they might just show up at my fucking door."

"But what if all that stuff was connected to Brad? What if he was just trying to scare me so I just shut down and quit seeing her? Maybe he thought she was gaining her voice while working with me and he got worried she would leave him…feared he would lose control of her? Maybe Bradly was behind all this shit," Margot asked with a sense of hopefulness that Joni was wrong.

"Margs, at this point, I believe that bastard could construct a kite with notebook paper and shoestrings. Then with more of that paper, write a message and tie it on the tail of that fuckin' kite only to fly it right through my kitchen window. And I believe he could do it all while sitting on his bunk in that parish lock up."

29

Run Along, Now

It was Tuesday at 10:45am and Margot had made her way to the First District police station in New Orleans where Bradly Ray Leblanc had been held until earlier that morning. Margot didn't know that and she wasn't there to see him, anyway. Both ladies had decided that it would be best if Joni would cat-sit rather than coming to the station to get another eyeful of Detective Bolt's ass.

Margot walked up to the receiving desk and announced her intentions, "Hello, My name is Margot Landry, and I need to speak with Detective Bolt."

The desk Sergeant was extremely overweight, surly, and Margot detected a hint of lazy contempt.

"And who might you be?"

"Umm, like I said, I'm Margot Landry."

"Yes, but what business do you have with Lieutenant Bolt?" he said with a disingenuous smile.

"As I'm sure you know, he is the Lead Detective in the Bradly LeBlanc case, and I have information and evidence to provide to him regarding such."

The desk Sergeant instantly softened, "I'm sorry, Ms. Landry. We get a lot of kooks around here and, well…I apologize. Let me see if he's at his desk. I know he was in court this morning but should be back by now."

"Thank you so very much," Margot said, giving back just a hint of what the Sergeant had given her.

Margot noticed the Sergeant didn't react to her tone and attitude as if he didn't detect it. If he did, he chose to ignore it figuring that she had earned her ounce of flesh from him after his less than friendly greeting. He picked up the receiver and pressed in Bolt's extension.

"Yes Lieutenant, I have a woman here by the name of Margot Landry…yes, she says she has some evidence regarding the LeBlanc case…okay, will do," he finished and closed the line, "He asked that you wait here just a moment, and to tell you he'll be right out."

Margot simply nodded, turned, and walked to the far end of the open space, then rested her back against the wall. She took her computer bag strap from her shoulder and held it with both hands in front of her. It only took a minute or so before the Lieutenant Detective came from the back to greet her.

"Hello Ms. Landry. I hear that you have some evidence in Bradly's case that you want to share," he finished with a quizzical look.

"Yes," she whispered and looked around, "but I was wondering if we might go to your office."

"We could if I had an office. I only have a desk and it's not even a nice one."

"Is there a room where we might speak privately?"

"Um, yes, of course. Follow me," he finished by turning around and walking back the way he had come. And well, as it turned out, Joni was right.

The Lieutenant led Margot up the creaky stairs to a dingy, medium sized, room, "Please excuse the surroundings. We redid the bottom floor after Katrina—but the top, well, as you can see...," he finished with the wave of his hand as if he were making a presentation on a gameshow.

There was a conference table that had stacks of papers, files, and cardboard banker's boxes strewn about, but there was enough space for her to put her laptop bag down.

"Lieutenant, I want to start off first by saying that what I'm about to share may not be of any value."

"We'll take all the help we can get. However, just so you know, as soon as we found the load of evidence in his car and cuffed him, he lawyered up right away. It's enough evidence that we may not need anything else. And if you are concerned for your safety, the good news is, he was arraigned this morning and is being held without bond near the courthouse at Tulane and Broad."

"What does that mean? How long can he be held?"

"Well, there was a time when we risked him being let out after a few months on a 401. That would be if charges weren't picked up by the parish. However, there was so much evidence pointing to his guilt that the D.A. picked up the charges right away, so he'll be there until the end of his trial. We believe with what we have against him right now he'll be going to Angola for life."

"Okay, well that's great news. However, I wanted to make sure you had everything you needed as soon as I found it."

"Please, yes, share anything you have."

Margot pulled out a Ziploc bag she had gotten from Joni's kitchen, and it held the balloon pieces and the card from the orchid delivered to her office on Monday. She relayed the story and concerns while explaining the timeline of events. She had to explain that her and Joni's fingerprints were all over those items. She went on to share the information regarding the phone call Joni made to the florist and the information she gained from that exchange.

"Well, it's likely, as you have surmised, Ms. Landry, that whoever did this, and it is interesting, would likely not have left any prints, anyway, so no worries there. And I can assure you that Bradly doesn't have any cell phone access where he is. So, they, the messages, should stop if they are from him. But it sounds like, from what you were telling me, you don't know where the balloon and note even came from. A creeper or a prankster is more likely, don't you think?"

"I have to admit that it seems a little silly explaining it to a detective."

"Is this all the evidence you have for me? If so, I'm afraid this wouldn't be useful. And, frankly, we have enough to hang this man twice, body or not."

"I take it you didn't find one yet, have you?"

"No, and if he stored her somewhere for safe keeping, so to speak, she would have likely bled out or died of thirst with that kind of blood loss and him not being able to get back to her by now. Of course, unless he has an accomplice that has her holed up somewhere."

"Accomplice!? You think there is more than one person responsible?" Margot asked with a shudder.

"We don't have any evidence of that. But I'd appreciate you not sharing that idea with anyone."

"If there is one, maybe that's who has been sending the messages…"

"Now hold on. Let's just take it slow. Again, there is no evidence of any of that. Based on what we have, he simply dumped the body…sorry, that was a little crass. Look, I really do appreciate you coming down here and sharing what you have."

Sensing she was about to be ushered out of the station—because Bolt looked as if he were about to do just that—she blurted out, "I have more!"

"More what? Balloons and cards?"

Margot quickly pulled out her laptop and opened it, "Look, I know what I shared about '33' seems hokey to you. I get it. But I want you and I to take a look at the video that I gave you Friday night."

"Ms. Landry, we here at the station have watched that video a thousand times. Those big green eyes of his are on full display. Creeped me out, really, if I'm being honest. I don't think…"

"No, it's not his eyes. It's Connie."

"What about her?"

"Look, just let me show you."

Bolt let out a deep exhale and sat back down.

"See that? See that right there?" Margot had paused the video at the midway point of Bradly closing the laptop. She put her index finger to the screen at the middle of the right-hand side, "That's blood."

"Oh yes, I was at the scene that night, remember me telling you about it? It was a gory mess."

"Yes, but Lieutenant, how is there blood there if he just pushed her off that stool a few seconds before he shut the laptop?"

Bolt looked as if he wanted to pat Margot on the head and tell her to go home and play hopscotch and marbles, "That's a tiny part of the screen, Ms. Landry. If that was where she started to bleed when she hit the floor, I mean, you know head wounds bleed a lot in a short amount of time, right?"

"Look again, that's her hair and it looks to be in a pool of it."

"Ms. Landry, I appreciate you trying to help. But where you will be the most helpful is during trial. You are going to be one of our star witnesses," Bolt said as if he was a used car salesman on a lemon lot.

"Detective, don't patronize me!"

"Please forgive me. How 'bout this? I'll take a look at the evidence you brought, and I'll also have the geeks take another look at the video. Maybe a fresh set of eyes could answer this question for you...us, I mean."

"Thank you, Lieutenant. Promise me you will."

"I do and I will…I will take another look. However, I need you to promise me one thing, too, Ms. Landry."

Margot's look of hopefulness defused to one of concern, "What is it?"

"If these messages turn out to be nothing, and I suspect they will or they will at least stop now that he's in custody, please keep them to yourself. We have what amounts to a slam-dunk case and we don't want to, well, you know, muddy the waters."

"Yeah, nice, okay. But if I get another message from '33'…"

"You call me right over; you have my cell."

Margot nodded and left feeling like she had just been shown to be an irrational female. And that pissed her off more than she could ever remember having been pissed off before.

30

Guilt Is In The Eye Of The Beholder

It had been only one and a half months since the Connie Minae incident, but to Margot Landry it felt like a lifetime.

Margot had taken a leave of absence, and she was about midway through what she could take and still get paid part of her salary. She had been wise and had signed up for long-term disability insurance when she started her position at Ochsner. Mike and Prestin had worked in tandem to make sure all her paperwork was in proper order for her continued mental health leave.

However, she was true to her private clients, and she believed that any therapist worth their salt would do the same. Regardless of what happened during her final Connie Minae session, Margot was able to do good work with her online clients. It helped that she didn't have any distraught families to cry with during a day job. The clients she was seeing via Telepy helped keep her financially afloat and, in many ways, had kept her mind off the trial that was to begin that day. The weather was turning hot. It was the 12th of May.

Margot sat on a bench in the Orleans Parish Criminal District Court building and looked up some of its history on her laptop. The building was ostentatious in size and classic looking in wood and marble.

The historic structure was completed in 1910 and sits on the corner of Tulane and Broad Street. Seventeen years after its completion it was the site of a murder trial that shocked the citizens of the parish. *The Trunk Murders*, as they came to be known, happened in 1927. The murders occurred, or at least the evidence of the crime was found, at a French Quarter apartment on Ursulines street.

The evidence—discovered by a maid—indicated that two women had been dismembered and deposited into steamer trunks. New Orleanians, at the time, were shocked at the apparent lack of feelings, or at least the lack of remorse, from the accused, Henry Moity. The two women were sisters-in-law, Theresa and Leonide Moity. Henry and Joseph were brothers and married to the two women.

The police hunted for both men after the dismembered bodies were discovered, but Joseph turned himself in quickly and implicated his brother and not himself. Joseph said Henry had murdered both women. Joseph claimed Henry had killed his wife, Leonide, and then his own, Theresa. When the police caught up to Henry he confessed and tried to save himself with the insanity defense. Booze and the ladies being *infidelous* had led to the crime, Henry claimed.

Henry was found guilty of the murder of his wife. As for the murder of his brother's wife, he just pled guilty and, in doing so, converted both sentences of life in Angola to run concurrently. But after years of gaining trust at the prison, he escaped a light work duty assignment. Something about going to the post office or some sort. But he was caught in California. The Louisiana Governor pardoned him for both murders, anyway. Two or so years later, he shot his new girlfriend—she lived. He didn't. He died in Folsom prison where he was serving out a term for her attempted murder.

In 1969, in the same courthouse, Clay Shaw was acquitted of conspiracy to commit murder, or in this case, the assassination of the President of the United States. That president, of course, was JFK. Jim Garrison, the New Orleans D.A. at the time and who was a dogged proponent of all manner of conspiracy theories regarding the JFK assassination, had his office in that building—an office that is still there today. It was in '67 that Garrison claimed he had solved the crime of the century.

Garrison maintained that Clay Shaw had used the name Clay Burtrand and conspired with David Ferrie and Lee Harvey Oswald to kill the president. Ferrie died in '67 and Oswald died in '63, of course. So, Shaw was the last man standing of a supposedly overheard conversation that Oswald, Ferrie, and Shaw had taken part in. That conversation was noted as being overheard by Perry Russo. However, he later undermined his own testimony because it was different under "truth serum" and hypnosis. Margot just rolled her eyes when she read that to herself. Garrison continued to hound Shaw but nothing substantial came of it.

In 2010, proceedings started regarding a murdered New Orleanian, Henry Glover. Glover was shot, presumably for looting, by NOPD's David Warren days after hurricane Katrina. Then he tossed the body in the trunk of an abandoned car and burned it. He did it with some accomplices, or that was the original charge, anyway. They were all found guilty.

Then in 2013, the appellate court granted a new trial citing Warren should not have been tried with his alleged co-conspirators. He was acquitted of all charges. The jury didn't hear a word about any alleged cover-up because it was ruled he had to stand trial on his own now and the evidence from the previous trial was tossed out.

Jerrett Paulus, in 2025, was accused of a double homicide. There was overwhelming evidence, so he pled guilty and got 55 years. But like Henry in 1927, Margot pondered, Brad LeBlanc appeared to be a controlling man. From what Margot had come to know, based on what she saw on her laptop that night, he was also a psychopath. She felt guilty for having those thoughts about Connie now that she knew her to be a victim of domestic violence and murdered. However, unlike Henry, she doubted Bradly would be pleading guilty to anything.

Earlier, when Margot was reading about the "Trunk Murders" she learned Henry tried to escape on a train after his brother accused him of the crimes. He was caught and brought to that 1927 trial date and found guilty. However, after spending years in prison, he escaped successfully this time and spent several years free then got pardoned for all his trouble only to kill again. She figured Brad was capable of that, too. He certainly had the money to get away with plenty.

Therefore, it was cold comfort to her that he was in jail because there were all sorts of moments at that courthouse that happened over the last hundred years that could cause Bradly to be a free man—a free man like many of the rest—to kill again. People do all manner of horrible things and are found not guilty.

Sometimes they are found guilty only to get off later. Or they get found guilty and haven't done anything at all. Orleans Criminal District Court at the corner of Tulane and Broad is a depository of a long, sordid, and storied jurisprudence history. Margot was on her way to becoming a resident of that gory and twisted timeline. And once it all unfolded, Joni would be living there with her, too—permanently.

"ALL RISE!" The bailiff, Jerome DuBoise, bellowed as he began to call the court to order. It was 8:30am sharp. It always was when he crowed out his favorite part of the job, the rising of the gallery. Judge Carmen Brown's Section C was a tight ship and with that came Judge Brown's propensity to demand punctuality, respect, and decorum in her courtroom and in her life.

Margot shut her laptop but remained in the hallway when she heard the bailiff's "all rise". In some ways, she couldn't wait to get into that courtroom, but she wasn't yet allowed. She was warned of the witness sequestration rule long before this trial began and had been reminded by the prosecution that morning. She had not learned much about what evidence had been found nor how they planned to get the guilty verdict that Lead Detective, Lieutenant Bolt, was so sure of. She wanted to see and hear it for herself. Bolt never followed up with any of the evidence she had brought him. However, the notes from '33' or anything pertaining to that number hadn't come up again in the last six weeks. She felt lucky that Brad was held so quickly. It was the part of him possibly being found not guilty or escaping were he to be found guilty, like so many others in that court house's history, that concerned her most. Though, at least the fear of a 401 release was behind her now.

"Court is now in session with the Honorable Carmen Brown presiding. God save this Court and the State of Louisiana."

Judge Brown took the bench, looked around the court to make sure that both parties were represented, and said, "You may all be seated."

The court was packed, so the sound of everyone taking their seats in those historic pews was near deafening—almost military in motion and sounded like a platoon taking instant formation.

"Are both parties ready to proceed?"

The State was represented by Gil Andrews, "Yes, your Honor."

"Defense?"

"Yes, your Honor," Brad's defense table of three answered in unison.

Alexander Argan took the lead, "Your Honor, if it pleases the Court, we would like to request a change of venue."

"Denied, Mr. Argan, I've ruled on that twice already and you won't be wasting anymore of the court's time with that request. Especially not with a jury now seated. Speaking of which, bailiff, you may call them in."

After all jurors were seated, Judge Brown put on her reading glasses, looked over at Gil Andrews and said, "State may proceed with opening arguments."

"Thank you, Your Honor," Andrews stood and buttoned his coat, walked over to the jury box, and began, "Ladies and gentlemen of the jury, please allow me to take a few moments of your time to tell you a story. It's the story of the Defendant and his live-in girlfriend turned victim…"

Argan shot up from the defense table, "Objection, Your Honor!"

"Overruled! This is opening arguments, and State hasn't yet even suggested what she was a victim of nor that it was your client whom was the perpetrator…you know what? Ladies and gentlemen," Brown said as she looked toward the jury box, "please let me have you step out for just a moment."

After the confused jury filed back into the deliberation room the Judge spoke, "Maybe we have started off on the wrong foot Mr. Argan. Please let me make myself clear, if your intention is to stymie this process with a bunch of needless objections I promise you, you will run out of them before I run out of trial and you're two objections down already. One that I ruled on a total of three times now for change of venue. And now another after a single sentence of opening arguments. Here's the worst part, you KNOW that after the first time you asked for a change of venue, and I ruled against your client the other three objections or requests or whatever you want to call them were bogus. You are not going to make this jury," she pointed toward the door of the deliberation room, "believe I am biased against your client by having me overrule stunted objections. If you do that, I'm going to make you explain each and every one you make in front of said jury thereby causing me to site more case law than you will ever know in a lifetime ergo causing you, and not me, to look like a fool. I'm warning you not to act like a beaten fighter hugging on their opponent to smother their punches."

All the defense and prosecution lawyers just looked at one another. Seeing their confusion, Brown noted, "Yeah, my uncle was a flyweight champion in Mexico. And that smothering of legal punches, and I mean that both literally and figuratively, is your right but it will make this take much longer and make you look like you are throwing darts in the dark. We are here to find and solidify the truth, not to win at all costs. Are we clear?" Brown scanned the sullen faces of the defense and the elated faces of the prosecution as they all nodded and said, "Yes, Your Honor".

"Gooooood. Bailiff, please return my jury," Brown instructed with a smile.

"Yes, Your Honor."

Once the jury was again seated, Andrews resumed, "Please forgive us for taking a moment to reset." To make sure that the jury knew that the Court had ruled in his favor he started the exact same way as before, "Ladies and gentlemen of the jury, please allow me to take a few moments of your time to tell you a story. It's the story of the Defendant and his live-in girlfriend turned victim, Connie Minae."

Andrews walked from around the prosecution's table.

"Connie, for whom we are here today to seek justice for, met the Defendant while serving him. She was a barista near where the Defendant worked as a financial manager in the CBD. As you will hear during the course of these proceedings, she was taken in, at first, by his green eyes. I don't mention that simply to give the jury any sense of romance. It's because the Defendant's eye color will be a critical piece of this puzzle. Though, we contend, it will be a puzzle with many pieces that all come together to form a picture of guilt. The guilt of Bradly Ray LeBlanc."

"By the way, did any of you know that across the entire world, less than 10% of people have green eyes? But that's not the half of it—literally. Because in the U.S. it's even less than that—much less. Only 2% of the population in the United States have green eyes. That's only two out of every hundred people you will ever meet. Well, let me introduce one of them to you, ladies and gentlemen—Mr. Bradly Ray LeBlanc," Andrews motioned with his hand toward the Defendant without turning away from the jury.

"Anyway, by the Defendant's own account, it was a whirlwind connection that quickly resulted in the two living together in the Defendant's palatial mansion. Once there, Bradly, the Defendant, convinced Connie to quit her job. The prosecution believes this was the beginning of the Defendant's attempts to control her financial independence. She, however, we believe, found it to be kind and a gesture of security given by a man with the means to do so."

Andrews rested his palms on the jury box before he continued. As he spoke, he looked, one after another, into each of the juror's eyes, "Then he began to systematically remove her from her friends. You will hear from her own therapist, Ms. Margot Landry, who will testify as to Ms. Minae's state of mind and to the state of the relationship. But I digress, as you will also hear from Ms. Minae, herself. You will see and hear the recorded sessions as Ms. Minae goes on to note how the Defendant would make claims that her friends were stealing from him and forbid them from visiting Connie at *his* estate. We are prepared to show that not a single police report was filed regarding any missing items during that time period."

Andrews lifted his palms from the jury box railing and put his hands in his pockets. "And that, ladies and gentlemen, is when the real trouble started. Connie started to push back a little and tried to reassert her independence—tried to gain back some of her personhood. That's when, and this is according to Connie Minae's own statements—recorded statements—that the Defendant, Bradly LeBlanc began to verbally and then physically abuse her," Andrews went to the witness box and laid his arm, elbow to hand, on it before concluding.

"And we have mountains of evidence that you, the jury, will be able to climb high enough to see the whole forest and not just a tree or two that the Defense is likely to *plant* in an attempt to get in the way of our progress towards truth. It's a mountain of evidence that, by the way ladies and gentlemen, was found..." Andrews started to hold up a finger for each point, "...in his kitchen, in his car, and even on video." Andrews paused for effect with his three fingers up and his thumb and pinky clasped against one another in a "scouts honor" gesture. That bit of dramatic effect and priming of the jury was not lost on Judge Brown.

"I'll finish with this: in all my twenty-four years as a lawyer, I would be hard pressed to think of any case that had more evidence against a Defendant. Thank you for being here today and in the days that follow. We believe you will find the Defendant, Bradly Ray LeBlanc, guilty of murder."

Gil Andrews sat and said nothing further.

"Defense, please begin your opening statement," Brown said, now settled and calm.

Alexander Argan stood, straightening the vest of his tight-fitting three-piece suit, and circled around from the defense table in a saunter toward the jury box.

"Good morning, ladies and gentlemen of the jury." Argan stood straight as an arrow, held up his left hand in the same "scout's honor" gesture as Andrews had, and continued, "Mountain of evidence?" he questioned as he looked at his scout's honor pose like it was a finger puppet. Well, lemme tell you what they ain't got on that mountain…" Argan closed his hand into a fist and finished, "…a body." During Argan's pregnant pause, he surveyed the jury and noticed more than one person smiling back at him.

"But that's not all. Let me tell you more about that mountain. All around the prosecution's mountain," Argan made air quotes as he said "mountain", "is 7,253 other New Orleanians that have green eyes. That's right, ladies and gentlemen, 7,253. Now that's a mountain. But that's not all. Notice how Mr. Andrews never mentioned what that evidence is other than eyes and a car? Because it's going to be so convincing, that's why. 'What?' you say? 'Why would the Defense's lead attorney say such a thing?'" Argan held out his palms and looked around as if he were one of the people asking such a question, "Well I'll tell you why, and it's actually clear in the prosecution's opening statement. Oh, there's a mountain of evidence alright—oh yes. But it's a mountain of *circumstantial* evidence. And there's so much of it that it's going to look like guilt—well, it will at first glance. But it's not, it's not guilt at all. It's so much evidence that it's clear that someone is trying to frame my client! Now, if I may, please allow me to tell *you* a story."

Alexander Argan walked closer to the jury and began again, "And mind you, it's not the story I want to tell. The last thing I want to be is that guy blaming the supposed victim. Oh no, not me," Argan said while waving his hands and shaking of his head, eyes fixed on the floor, "No, I'm not going to be that guy at all. And I couldn't be that guy even if I wanted to, because, I say again, there is no victim of homicide that we can find. And

I don't want to focus directly on the evidence in this case right now, regardless. NO! Because all of you will be far too inundated with that tomfoolery and nonsense during these proceedings. Pfft, evidence? Please. We, the Defense, will pick apart each piece of that so called mountain of evidence as this trial goes on. No, the story I want to tell you is the story of Bradly LeBlanc."

Argan now put his hands in his pockets and started to pace as he continued to orate. As he did so, he moved slowly from one side of the box to the other.

"Brad LeBlanc grew up on the West Bank in a trailer park near a huge bar that was popular in the 90's. Though the name of that bar isn't important to Brad's story, what is important is that you know he grew up poor. He grew up in close proximity to debauchery, and he grew up wanting more from his life than his—and I'm sorry to put this so bluntly—alcoholic mother wanted. Every night, Brad's mother, during his teen years, would go to that bar. At some point, she would stumble in with the boyfriend of the night. If all were lucky it would be the boyfriend of the week. If all were unlucky it would last a month. That's when the fights and beatings would start."

Argan continued pacing in front of the jurors, "Let me describe for you a typical week in the LeBlanc household trailer. Young Bradly would wake up, on his own, to catch the bus to West Jefferson High School. The evening before, he would wash the one pair of jeans he had and dry them with his mother's hair dryer. Then, he'd pick a clean shirt he had washed two nights before from the three of those that he owned. Underwear, socks…you get the picture. His mother was not the motherly type, so she was not the one to be washing his clothes nor feeding him. He never knew his father and he's not sure his mother did, either. He can't ask her because she refused to ever talk about it and she died two years ago of cirrhosis of the liver." By this time, the jurors were shifting in their seats a little.

"Let me be clear before I go on," Argan stopped pacing and looked at the box, the people in it, and raised his finger, "Bradly is not asking any of you to feel sorry for him. No, not at all, and neither am I. I'm drawing a mental picture of Bradly's upbringing, or lack thereof, for you to see where this story leads. Stay with me and it will all fall into place."

Argan returned to pacing, "So, you have this kid, Bradly, who's neglected and abused. Some of that abuse at the hand of some of the men his mother brought into the house. He's got no clothes to speak of and lives on a diet of ramen noodles. But ladies and gentlemen of the jury, what does this kid do? Does he get angry? Does he get into a life of petty theft? Does he steal cars and start using heroin? No, ladies and gentlemen, no…he…doesn't! He finds that he is good at math and calculations. He hangs around the right people at school. He studies hard. He gets a high enough score on his SAT to get a full boat ride to Tulane. TULANE, ladies and gentlemen. You bet! My alma mater!" Argan brings his tone down several notches.

"While at Tulane he continues to study hard and graduates with honors. Now Tulane asks if he would like to get his MBA there. Of course he does. He promises himself he will never be poor nor dependent on anyone again. No sir! Not to mention, he is living on campus and working full time. Bikes everywhere he goes—stays out of the bars and stays outta trouble. After his master's, he is picked up by the firm that he interned for and amasses a fortune then buys a big uptown house. Now he's ready to share it with someone. He wants to fall in love and fall in love he did, oh, yes…head-over-heels, he did. Tucking and rolling head-over-heals so much so he looks like a gymnast." One lady of the jury is tickled and lets out a slight 'ha' and covers her mouth with her hand. Argan looks at her, he's trying to gain traction. He says directly to her, "I know, right?", and she shakes her head up and down with a smile.

"So, he wants love but he's not looking. He goes down to have a coffee after leaving work. And mind you, ladies and gentlemen, he is a one drink maximum kind'a guy." The jury crack smiles, "His drink of choice is coffee because he has seen what can happen when one takes too much of the bottle. It's the only thing his mother ever taught him, and that's a life of sobriety. HIS words, not mine," Argan points to Brad and he nods his head.

"Objection your honor!"

"Sustained, the Defendant can't testify without being on the witness stand and sworn in."

"My fault Your Honor, totally my fault."

"The jury is to disregard that exchange."

"Thank you, Your Honor. It won't happen again."

"Please proceed."

"Yes, ma'am. So back to our story—Brad's story. So, there he is minding his own business and there she is—a vision of loveliness—our missing co-star, Ms. Connie Minae. She starts chatting him up and he does the same."

"Careful Mr. Argan…"

"Yes, ma'am. So, the two strike up a relationship and within a short amount of time she moves in and quits her job. Now, my client, the defendant, Mr. LeBlanc, sure didn't want…okay, let's just say he is going to testify to the fact that he didn't want her to quit her job. But, and again, he will testify to this…"

Some of the jurors began to look around at one another. An accused taking the stand was a rare treat in televised trials. The prospect of seeing such a drama unfold live obviously intrigued some of the jury.

"…my client is going to get on that stand and let you know, point blank, that he has a work ethic second to none and if someone is going to be living with him, he doesn't want it to be his mother!"

The gallery started to whisper in hushed tones and Judge Brown spoke up without the gavel, "Gallery! I need quiet, and I need you to save some of that passion for the actual trial, Mr. Argan."

"Yes, Your Honor. Okay so there it is but here's the problem, he is willing to take care of her—lock, stock, and barrel. No problem, right? And he will testify to that as well. There is passion, there are trips, there are good times, great times. Again, he will testify to that. He asks her to marry him even after some of that passion cools. He will testify to thinking that may spark things up again. He is in love, according to his statements that he has shared and, again, Your Honor, and prosecution, he will testify to this as well, he believes they need a jump start and concludes a ring and a promise will do it. But what does she do? She turns him DOWN! And how do we know this? We know this because he has the proposal recorded on his home security cameras. He proposed in his living room, folks! Look, he may not be the most romantic fella in the world. He didn't take her to Paris or Hawaii to propose. He's going to testify that this was an act of desperation and not planning." Argan stopped his pacing and put his hands on the jury box to mirror what his opponent had done, "You are going to see a desperate man, trying to save a relationship. The only one he ever cared for with a woman who had grown cold, and he didn't know why. Our psychiatric professional is going to testify that his mother showed him no love at all. He had never seen an appropriate relationship except on television. Connie was always by his side and then one day she wasn't. He buys a ring and proposes in their living room out of desperation to recapture the love he once got from her and that he never got from his mother. Then what does she do…well you already know what. Weeks go by and they continue to NOT be intimate—just to be delicate here—in any way, shape, or form. They argue constantly and he will testify to that, as well."

Argan took a breath before he continued, "Then a strange thing happens that has my client here today. He goes to a friend's house, and he comes back, and the police are there. Crime tape everywhere, blood everywhere, and in his car, there is a plethora of items that implicate him," Argan pounded on the jury box to punctuate each of the next seven words, "BUT NO BODY TO BE FOUND, ANYWHERE!"

The prosecution chose not to object. They counted it as a point for their team because it spooked two of the ladies in the front row of the jury box.

"Now, I'm going to ask you. What man proposes to a woman…and we have the video, like I said, and weeks later decides he's going to murder her in front of a WITNESS? He could have done it a million other ways, and it would have cost several million less. LADIES AND GENTLEMEN OF THE JURY! I CRY FOUL! I SAY THROW A FLAG ON THE PLAY! THIS IS TOTAL AND UTTER NONESENSE OF THE HIGHEST ORDER!

MY…CLIENT…HAS…BEEN…FRAMED!" Argan pounded again.

Brown looked over for an objection, but the prosecution table didn't flinch. The courtroom was stunned and some even thought that the overweight lawyer was about to have a heart attack as his face had turned chili pepper red.

Judge Brown knew that if Argan was starting out with this much vigor, his tactics would grow tiresome. As a prosecuting attorney for several years before becoming a judge, she knew this was not going to work in his favor and she figured that he had already lost 25% of this trial. The prosecution figured closer to 35.

Argan slowly looked up and had started to sweat, "Please forgive me for my outburst. I'm passionate about this case because, while the prosecution appears to believe they have never seen such a large mountain of evidence, I don't see it as a mountain at all. Regardless, I ask you all to come along with the Defense. Yes, yes indeed, let's climb that big ol' mountain together and see three things: how high it really is, what we can really see from the peak, and what it's really made of. I believe it's made with lies, I believe we will see the truth regardless of the size, and I believe it's no mountain at all. I believe it's a molehill. And I believe that you, Mr. and Mrs. Jury, will see it that way, too. Thank you for your time and attention, ladies and gentlemen."

31

Trial And Error

Judge Brown called to the prosecution's table, "State, call your first witness."

"Yes, Your Honor. The State calls Lieutenant Detective Bolt to the stand," Gil Andrews said with pride.

Bolt was sworn in and the usual cursory discussion about how long he's been a cop, his career path, and his vast experience, followed.

"Thank you for that, Lieutenant Bolt. Now, can you give this jury the rundown of, just in general, what you saw that night as you arrived on the scene?"

"Blood and a lot of it."

"Well, let me just back you up a moment. Right after you pulled up to the scene, let's start from there."

"Sure sure, uhh, yeah so, I go to the address; it's a well-known one."

"Well-known? Had you been there before?"

"Oh no, it's just that it's a very large house in a grand neighborhood so, you know, on a cop's salary and then detective, you wish and hope to win the lottery at some point to get a house like that. But, well, I don't play the lottery."

"Ah, got it. Okay so you pulled up to the scene and some other cops and detectives had already arrived, correct?"

"Yes."

"And you get there and who catches you up to speed?"

"Officer D.D. Robinson."

"And does she tell you what is going on or, ya know, what's the situation?"

"She does. She says that a therapist called 911 and explained that she has been seeing a client that lives at this address...oh, and that she saw a man kill her."

"Objection!" Argan stood.

"Grounds?"

"We have the 911 recording and so does the prosecution and so does the NOPD. We have all heard it several times and she never once said that she knew that she had seen any one kill anybody. If anything, she makes it clear she's not sure what she witnessed."

"Sustained. Detective, we'll let the witness that made the call testify to her own words."

Gil Andrews had been doing this a long time. He knew where to go next, "I believe that may be a great idea, Your Honor. Lieutenant Bolt, I'd like you to step down from the witness box but stay with us in the courtroom as we listen to the 911 recording, if that pleases the Court?"

194

"Defense?"

"We have no issue with that Your Honor. It's going to sound the same regardless of who is in the witness box."

Andrews continued, "We are so glad to hear that from the Defense, Your Honor, because we'd like to call Margot Landry to the stand."

"Defense?"

"Again, Your Honor, it makes no difference to us."

Judge Brown nodded over to, Jerome, her bailiff.

Margot was in the courthouse hallway, minding her own business, when she was called. She instantly tensed up. She didn't expect to be called this early. Jerome waved her over while saying her name, "Ms. Landry?"

"Yes?"

"Please come forth and present yourself to the Court."

"Yes, sir," Margot said with as much of a question in her voice as an answer to the call. Once entering the courtroom, she was instructed to take the witness box and was sworn in.

"You may proceed," Brown said while accompanying it with a wave of her hand.

"Thank you, Your Honor. Ms. Landry, you were Ms. Minae's psychotherapist, correct?"

"That is correct."

"Would you mind telling the jury of your credentials?

"Certainly," Margot faced the jury, "I have a four-year degree in psychology from the University of New Orleans. Once completed, I went on to gain my master's degree in clinical social work from Tulane University. I then completed two years of clinical supervision under a board approved supervisor and have been in private practice for approximately ten years, post licensure."

"Thank you, Ms. Landry. Your Honor, I would like to now have the Court consider Margot Landry an expert witness."

"Any objection from the Defense?"

"None, Your Honor."

"Thank you. Ms. Landry, we are going to have you listen to your 911 recording."

Andrews looked over at his partner, Chelsea Brussard, and asked if she would use the remote that she had at the ready to play the recording.

The two were partners in other ways, as well. It hadn't affected their work. She was smart and supportive. If anything, it made work and Gil's life a thousand times better. It made him better in every way a man could be. He felt he could conquer anything with Chelsea. But he abhorred her first name, and she had no middle name, so he only called her Che-Che. She thought *Che-Che* was cute, and she never asked, and he never told her anything different even if she had.

"The State would like to share with the Jury State's evidence A-1." He gave Chelsea a nod.

The staticky audio began to play for the jury.

"911- what's your emergency?"

"Yes! I'm a therapist and, um…oh Christ, I think I just witnessed a murder. Or at least a…"

"Okay, ma'am, just calm down and tell me if the person is still breathing."

"They aren't here! They are at...oh, wait, wait...umm."

"They aren't there? Did they leave?"

"They were never here, it's...it's a woman! And then this thing, this man, came up behind her..."

"Where ma'am, where are they?"

"I'M LOOKING FOR THE ADDRESS!"

"Ma'am, just take a breath. What's the address?"

"I'M LOOKING, GODDAMNIT!"

The jury could hear the shuffling of papers as Margot had been looking for the address.

"HERE, HERE IT IS, 2112 OAK! HURRY! HE'S PROBABLY STILL THERE."

"2112 Oak-where, ma'am?"

"UMMM, UHHH, UPTOWN!"

"There is a lot of 'uptown' ...wait, I found it. A large residential house?"

"YES! That's it! They were in the kitchen...I saw it when I was doing therapy!"

"You were doing therapy with them in the kitchen?"

"ONLINE!"

"Okay, I understand. I'm sending over emergency services now."

"Thank you!"

"Just stay on the line with me, ma'am, to make sure we have everything correct and emergency services get to the right place."

"Okay, I will."

"...yes, 2112 Oak...Okay, they are in route, and they are close."

"Thank God!"

The same few minutes of static and hearing other 911 operators in the background was also heard by the jury. Andrews didn't want to alter the audio and let it play out.

"...okay, yes, that's probably the one...", OHhhhh..."

"What? WHAT? WHAT'S THE MATTER! I THINK IT WAS HER BOYFRIEND, WHAT DID HE DO? IT'S HIS HOUSE!"

Andrews gave Che-Che a little nod and she closed the file.

"Now, Ms. Landry, I'd like to show you something else. I'd like you to take a look at State's exhibit A-2."

Without any warning to anyone other than Che-Che, he had her start the Telepy video.

The picture was frozen. Margot was in a little box on the bottom right-hand side of the screen. As the video started to play, Connie came to life, again.

"Hello, Connie."

"Hi, Margot. Yes, I know I'm being recorded, and my address is 2112 Oak Street. And how are you?"

"Not too bad. And you?"

"Oh. jus' livin' the dream in this fuckin' prison."

"Give me the rundown of the last two days."

"Same shit, different days. He came home and nearly caught me on the laptop. Luckily, I heard the garage door start to open and it gave me enough time to stow it."

"Connie, I was thinking. I'd like to do a little role-playing with you. That is, if you are willing."

"Role-play? What's that going to do?"

"I want to play him, your boyfriend or whatever you want to call him, and you play yourself. It's to help you be able to speak to him about how things are."

"Like shit will get any better. Are you kidding me?"

"Right now, it's not about getting better. It's about getting out."

"Oh, you *are* kidding me; there's no way…"

"Let's just try it. Now, I'll be…,"

"Brad. His name is Bradly LeBlanc."

"Brad, okay, I'll play him. I want you to talk to me—talk to me like you would him…just freewheel it…just let it go. You can say whatever you want to say and as I'm playing like him you can just correct me when I say anything that he wouldn't."

"He wouldn't say that."

"Say what? We haven't started yet."

"He wouldn't allow any conversation like this to even occur. He would never say, 'You can say whatever you want to say' or 'correct me when…'"

"Okay, you just use me as a body to say to him whatever it is you *want* to say."

"Fuck you!"

"Is that for me or have we started?'

"Can it be both?"

"Whatever you like."

"Okay, we'll start now. Fuck you."

"Keep going."

"Is that him saying that or you?"

"Both."

"He wouldn't say that."

"You just keep talking."

"Now that, he would say. He would say that just before he had enough."

"Go ahead…just keep going with it."

Andrews focused on the jury and found them riveted by the video.

"Fuck you, Bradly. Fuck you and the Porsche you rode in on."

"What, are you upset?"

"He wouldn't say that."

"Well, what would he say…"

The entire jury box looked like nothing but twenty-four eyes and there was another eight where the alternates were seated.

The shape looked right at the screen after pushing Connie to the floor.

"You really want to know what I would say, Margot? I'd say, 'I'm going to kill you'."

The video ended with the darkness of a closed laptop. Now it was just the picture of Margot, in her little box, with shock being her predominate facial feature.

Bradly, sitting ramrod straight in his chair, had no reaction at all.

Margot was irritated; she was nearly vibrating. Bolt had never gotten back to her about any of that stuff she gave him. And now, the prosecution didn't pause the video to show Connie already in that blood. Yes, Margot understood that everyone, except maybe the jury, knew that Bradly was guilty. Maybe even some of the jury had already made up their minds, as well. Hell, maybe even his own lawyer would have convicted him.

However, the deal with Bolt was she promised not to say a word about what she believed she saw and the possible implications. But the agreement he made to gain her promise was that he would investigate '33'. Then Margot simply slumped. The messages had stopped, anyway, and the bastard was on trial. But now her face was on that frozen screen, and she thought she looked stupid. Though, she did take solace in being alive and not in a pool of her own blood.

Andrews continued, "Okay, Ms. Landry," Gill turned back to the jury box, "let me be clear to the jury. I know that seems a little odd that we played the events in the opposite order. However, I know you all understand what you just saw and heard. You're a group of smart folks. Let me point out something as we look at the last moments of that again."

Margot sat straight up and thought, *They are going to point it out! But why? It can't possibly help their case.* She sat with lips pursed and wringing her hands.

"Ms. Brussard, please back it up just a little."

Che-Che did as she was instructed, and she went right past Connie being on the floor. Margot wanted to jump up and scream but thought better of it.

"Pause…right…THERE! Okay, Detective Bolt, please retake the stand as Ms. Landry steps down. Ms. Landry, you have been considered an expert witness and may now remain in the courtroom."

"Objection, Your Honor!"

"Grounds?"

"It may taint her testimony to see the testimony of others."

"Prosecution?"

"We only intend to use her as an expert witness, and the rules of witness sequestration no longer apply as Your Honor has deemed her an expert witness."

"Overruled. Ms. Landry, you may stay seated in the gallery. However, Mr. Andrews, you have limited yourself to only her professional opinion, henceforth."

"Yes, Your Honor."

"Okay, you may proceed."

"Now, Detective Bolt, and ladies and gentlemen of the jury, I want you to notice that two-percenter on the screen. Eyes as green as jealousy and possession."

As had been discussed a few minutes before and in hushed tones, the female part of the Defense team made the next objection. The decision had been made so that they were all equally as irritating to the Judge and that no one person on the defense took all the hits.

"Objection, Your Honor," exclaimed Kathy Kennedy— another Tulane law grad.

"Grounds?"

"Prejudicial."

"While it may be close to the line, it's a colloquialism and it is their case," she thought for a moment, "Sustained. Jury is to disregard the State's characterization."

"Thank you, Your Honor"

"Okay, Lieutenant Bolt. Now, if it would please the Court, continue from where we began. I believe it was officer D.D. Robinson who filled you in on the scene you were about to walk into. Please describe what happened next."

"Well, I made my way into the front door, and the metallic smell of blood was heavy in the air. It's not an unfamiliar smell to me because I have been to so many crime scenes I've lost count."

"Please go on."

Bolt described the scene and was asked a few questions about odds and ends. Andrews went on to ask about Brad.

"So, I understand that at some point, the Defendant arrived after you did."

"Correct."

"About what time would that have been?"

"I couldn't be sure enough to testify either way."

"Would it help if I refreshed your recollection with the time log that was kept by Officer Robinson?"

"That would be helpful."

"Your Honor, I'm reading from State's exhibit G-9."

"Understood," Judge Brown said with a nod.

"It reads here that it was at twenty-fifteen hundred hours. Is that military time for 8:15pm?"

"Exactly."

"Okay, so the Defendant gets there at 8:15pm, that sound correct?"

"I'm sure that's correct. Officer Robinson is a solid record keeper."

"Okay, so 8:15pm and what happens next?"

"He comes up the embankment of the lawn and we chat. Officer Robinson is keeping notes of what he is saying."

"And when was he a suspect?"

"Oh, right away. I mean, he wasn't there, then shows up and seems nervous. He was all tearful and then wasn't when he saw all the blood on the floor."

"Right, let me move this along for the jury if that's okay. So, he seems like something's wrong. What about his video cameras?

The whole Defense table grinned at one another. Che-Che saw it. And she knew why they did. Bolt had just made a major mistake. He had noted that Bradly was a suspect from the start.

"Yeah, he goes to show us the camera of his living room and it's blank. Like it had been shut off."

"Oh, so, as we heard the Defense note earlier, his cameras were working when he went down on one knee to propose but not when this crime took place?"

"Objection, Your Honor!" Vinnie Rizzo had shot up when he spoke. He was the third on the Defense team. However, he was a Yale grad.

"Grounds?"

"That has not been introduced into evidence yet and we reserve the right to withhold it should we see fit. It was only offered in our opening statement and may not be used by us at all. But certainly, it may not be noted as fact by the State before we have even shown it."

"Sustained. Jury is to disregard the State's last statement about the camera and the knee."

Andrews continued, "Suffice it to say, his cameras were turned off or, at least, unobtainable, by the Defendant nor anyone else that we know of, correct?"

"That was his claim, and we saw nothing when he attempted to pull it up on his phone. Then, when we pulled the footage, it turned out that the cameras had been turned off for weeks."

"How do you know it was for weeks?"

"The digital recording was still running but there was no feed. It just recorded blank screens for every camera that was once connected."

"Were you able to ascertain who pulled the camera feed?"

"No. As far as we could conclude it happened at some point, according to our computer specialists, at 3am or so weeks prior. From what we could tell, both Connie's and the Defendant's cars were in the driveway, neither Bradly nor Connie were in frame, and then, just like that," Bolt snapped his fingers, "all the camera feeds were gone."

"Could any other vehicles be seen before the feed went down?"

"A car or two passed not long before, but no."

"What did detectives conclude?"

"We pulled the computer that controlled the cameras, and someone logged in at around 2:55am and then by around, like I noted, 3am, the cameras stopped giving a feed, but the recording kept going."

"Was anyone seen around the computer that controlled it?"

"As it turns out, it can be done remotely. And so, a phone or a laptop can do it. We checked IP addresses. It was the same IP address as had been used many times before in the house. So, again, no one could be seen tampering with the cameras nor the controllers."

"And would you please tell the jury whose device was used to turn off those cameras?"

"The Defendant's, Bradly LeBlanc. The IP address was matched to his iPhone."

32

Rally Points And A Fault

The State felt this was a good time to request a break and Judge Brown granted it, "Court is in recess until 9:45am sharp," Brown swung her gavel and went into chambers.

The court was buzzing. They had learned about green eyes, the amount of blood found, the 911 call, the therapy session, and even that Brad's own phone had been used to turn off cameras while the video controller continued recording blank screens. It was a blistering opening. But they also learned that there was no body and that the person who shut the lid of the laptop had a face that was fully covered. Except, of course, for those striking green eyes.

At 9:45am, Judge Brown opened the door that led from her chambers and briefly stood waiting for Bailiff DuBoise to call the court to order. He did so right on cue because he had been standing there just waiting for her to emerge.

"ALL RISE, this Court is back in session."

Brown took the bench and noted, "You may all be seated. I take it the State wants the Lieutenant back on the stand?"

"Yes ma'am, we do."

"Lieutenant, please remember that you are still under oath."

"I do, Your Honor," Bolt said as he retook the witness box.

"State, please proceed."

"Yes Ma'am, Your Honor," Andrews said as he stood, rebuttoned his suitcoat, and strode toward the witness box.

"Lieutenant, there was a time, after Bradly showed you, via his phone, that his cameras were down, correct?"

"Correct."

"Can you tell us about what happened near the time you searched his car and what you found?"

"Certainly…"

"First, let me ask you this; did you have a warrant?"

"We didn't need one because the Defendant tossed me the key fob and said we wouldn't find anything."

"Was that true? Did you find nothing?"

"Oh, far from it."

"Please tell us what you found."

"When I opened the frunk, and I know that is a strange name, but for cars that have the engine in the back, it's a frunk for 'front trunk'."

"Understood. And what did you find in the front trunk?"

"When I opened the, well, once it was open, there was a blanket and it was covered in blood. We later concluded, through DNA testing, that the blood was a match for Connie

Minae's. Also, laying on the blanket was the knife that matched the set that was in a block in the kitchen of the Defendant's home. There were shoes. A print in the blood in the house matched the shoe print and size and there was Connie's blood all over those shoes. I didn't mention before, but it was definitively Connie's blood in the kitchen. And shoe prints that went out of the back door from the kitchen were also a match. Oh, and there was the ski mask seen in the video. We found a hair in the ski mask that matched the color, the type, and the Defendant's DNA."

"But the defendant shaves his head bald, and his mug shot shows that he was bald at the time he was arrested."

"Yes, but he still had facial hair and thus it was consistent with beard hair."

"Ah, okay, thanks. Let me take you back for a second to something you said. The knife, did it have blood on it?"

"Oh yes, and it was a DNA match to Ms. Minae's, as well."

"You mentioned the kitchen. Did you find anyone else's blood in there?"

"Yes, we did. There was a strange swipe of blood on the wall above the splatter of Minae's."

"Can you please tell us who's blood that was, if you know."

"Yes, the blood was positively identified as the Defendant's."

"So, let me recap this for the jury," Andrews began to count with his index finger as he ticked off the list, "You find the blanket, the knife, the shoes, the ski mask, and the hair, all in the front trunk of the Defendant's Porsche 911, correct?"

"Correct."

"You also find the defendant's blood swiped on the kitchen wall. The same kitchen that has a knife missing from the block that matches the same style knife found in the car. And you find shoes in the car that matched the tracks in the blood trail from the crime scene, correct?"

"Correct."

"Your Honor I'd like to introduce State's evidence numbered B-1. It is a picture of the front truck of the Defendant's car."

"Any objections from the Defense?"

"None, Your Honor."

"So entered."

"Detective, please take a look at this and let the jury know if it's an accurate depiction of the way you found the evidence in the car."

"It is."

"Did you find anything else in the car when it was completely searched?"

"Only a cigar butt. It's how we were able to obtain the Defendant's DNA because he refused to give us a buccal swab."

"Thank you, sir. I believe that will be it for now, Your Honor. I tender the witness to the Defense."

"Cross?"

"Yes, Your Honor," Argan rose and said while he, again, pulled his vest down because his girth had caused it to ride up. Around the defense table he went and up to the fixed-in-place podium that was in the center of the court approximately fifteen feet from the front of the Judge.

"Lieutenant Bolt, thank you for being here today and bringing your considerable expertise with you," Argan opened with a slight sneer. Bolt said nothing because he knew the gesture offered by Argan was not genuine. He also knew what was coming. He knew because the prosecution had clearly attempted to avoid it during direct. But no matter what, it was never going to be ignored. Andrews said as much during pretrial preparations. Argan was going to try and capitalize on the faux pas both tables noticed from the testimony regarding Bolt's actions that night.

"You and I can agree that there was a considerable amount of evidence in that car, correct?"

"Yes."

"And that all that evidence pointed directly at my client, correct?"

"That's why we are here today, yes."

"Let's go over that evidence, it shouldn't take long, though the list is fairly lengthy. Argan stepped out from behind the podium where his notes were and stopped halfway between it and the witness box, "And we have the video, of course."

"Yes."

"During your investigation, was it ever discussed why a man that was going to kill his girlfriend who lived with him would sneak in a window dressed in dark clothes and a ski mask?"

"It was."

"And what was the conclusion?"

"We didn't have evidence of it but thought he may have known she would be on video. That was her regularly scheduled time for therapy."

"So, you are saying my client, if he were the killer, wanted a witness?"

"My team theorized he may have wanted the therapist to see the event and that it must have been someone other than him because he said he had an alibi, though we didn't know what it was at the time."

"We'll get to that during his testimony but right now let's stick with the fact that a man that could take his girlfriend anywhere in the world at any time and with no witness around to see the act, instead chose to kill her on camera, in his own house, with…well let me go through the list. So, let's look at this picture of his trunk," Argan pulled out a laser pointer from his vest pocket, "That's the knife that is assumed to be from the kitchen block, correct?"

"That is the knife, and we were fairly sure that the empty slot in the block—that was otherwise full—would hold that size and length. Through research, we found another set and the knife appears to fit the style, shape, and size."

"Okay, understood, now let's see what else we have here. Oh, the mask. Okay, I guess that makes sense…umm, hum…Oh and here are the shoes. I understand that there are shoes that appear to be missing from his closet, correct?"

"There was a space for several shoes, and two spaces were empty. One in a row of sneakers and one in a row of dress shoes. He had dress shoes on and those are the missing sneakers, we believe."

"Right, right…well, okay. So, all these things are on top of the blanket, no?"

"Correct."

"And this reddish-brown staining? Blood, right?"

"Correct and it was matched with Ms. Minae's blood."

"Right, okay, got it. So, Lieutenant, we have a mask, hair in the mask, blood, a blanket, shoes, and a knife all in this little trunk. I suppose you all have done the measurements and determined that Ms. Minae could fit in the trunk of a Porsche 911, correct?"

"Correct. She was 5' 4" and 110 pounds."

"So, let me make sure I understand this. We have ALLL this evidence in the trunk of this car. Well, the frunk of the car, as we're calling it, and it ALLL links my client so some unknown and certainly unproven crime of some sort, correct?"

"Correct," Bolt said but wouldn't allow himself to smile.

"Then where's the body?"

"We don't know, but we suspect, that your client does."

"Well, now, let me ask you this, then, and it's all hypothetical of course. And with your considerable experience, you may actually have an answer for the jury."

"I'll do my best."

"Oh, I believe you will. Okay, so, one more time and not to belabor the point but let's see…hypothetically, someone has the blanket, I mean, we wouldn't want to get our frunk dirty. Anyway, we have our blood-soaked blanket, we have our ski mask, we have our hair in the ski mask, we have our shoes—

also blood soaked—and we have our knife, also caked with blood. Alllll that, and we leave that all in our frunk. But we take the body out and leave it somewhere else? In all your years, Detective Bolt, investigating crime, have you ever seen such a thing?"

"Yes."

Argan was stunned, and he had made the error of asking a question of a witness on the stand for which he didn't know how they would answer. It was his arrogance because he rarely lost a trial. "Well, okay then. I'm surprised."

"I thought you might be," Andrews said as he cracked a smile.

"Please tell us when and why, if I may ask that of the witness, Your Honor."

Brown responded, "It's at your own peril, Mr. Argan. You possibly got yourself in a little deeper than expected. I wouldn't plan on objecting to his answer to your own question."

"That's fair, Your Honor. Though, I reserve the right to do so."

"And I reserve the right to overrule it…but I'll be fair and impartial, of course," Judge Brown smiled as she said it.

"Okay Detective Bolt, please answer my question."

"It was fifteen years ago and it's quite simple. There was a body. But it wasn't a dead one. The fella had brought his girlfriend and the evidence in his car back to his house. However, it was in an actual trunk of a car. He took her battered but very much alive body and locked it down in his house. When he came back to get the other items of evidence from the trunk, his neighbor was walking his dog and decided to get chatty, you know how those types of neighbors are. Anyway, it turned out it would have ruined his alibi if he had stayed much longer. He simply ran out of time. He left; she got out of the house and called us—that was that—case closed."

"Ahh, I see. I understand it. Well, as the evidence will show…"

"Objection, Your Honor," Che-Che said without even standing up.

"Sustained, your opening arguments are concluded, Mr. Argan."

"I withdraw the statement."

"Thank you. Have you concluded cross?"

"Maybe just one more thing, Your Honor."

"Proceed…with caution."

"Yes, Your Honor, thank you. So, Detective Bolt, you have seen this once in your career…"

Bolt interrupted Argan, "Maybe twice…"

"Another time?"

"Maybe this time."

"Objection, Your Honor," Argan was flustered now.

"Overruled, I warned you, didn't I?"

"Fair…well, I'll ask outright. Do you feel that our client has Ms. Minae holed up somewhere?"

"If he does, it's likely he thought he would get back to her before now. However, she would be dead from blood loss, dehydration, and no food…unless there is an accomplice keeping her alive."

"Any evidence of that?"

"Yes."

Goddamnit, Argan thought. "Okay, I'll bite. What evidence is there of an accomplice?"

"Her truck is gone."

"Meaning?"

"If he loaded Connie up in her own truck, and it doesn't look like it based on our evidence of all the blood and tools in his car, then someone else must have driven the truck and that's maybe where the rest of the evidence you asked about is. Like maybe…"

"So, you have her truck?"

"No sir. We haven't found her truck."

"So, no body but all that stuff left in the front of his car?"

"Yes."

"Okay, that should about do it…" Argan walked back to the podium then raised his finger before turning around. This was where he was going to try and cash in on Bolt's earlier mistake, "OH YES, there was one more thing. Let me see here," Argan rifled through his notes, "Ah, yes, here it is. I noticed something that wasn't brought up during direct but it's in the police report…hummm, yes, here we are…you said in your testimony today that my client was…how did you say it…oh yes, 'a suspect in the first five minutes' or 'right away' or something to that effect, correct?"

"…yes…"

"Then why did you and D.D. Robinson allow him to enter the house, his bedroom, look through his safe and out toward the back where the bloody footprints and drag marks were?"

The Jury who had just settled down from the body discussion was interested again. Bolt slowed his answers for the first time.

"We… well, we believed that it may make him relax enough to make mistakes if we played like we didn't consider him a suspect. And it appears to have worked because it made him confident enough to just toss his key fob to me. And in that moment, I believed he thought I would toss it back and say, 'Naaa you have been cooperative, no need' so, like I said, I think it worked."

"It may have worked at nothing more than tainting your crime scene."

"Objection!"

"I withdraw the statement, Your Honor, I only have one more question and it should be an easy one. Detective, you are aware, as we all are, that there are contacts that can change the color of one's eyes, correct?" Argan asked with a satisfied smile.

"Yes, I'm aware."

"No further questions at this time."

"Redirect?"

"Yes, Your Honor," Andrews continued, "Detective Bolt, I'm sure you have seen in your many years on the job that a perpetrator would come into a house they were familiar with *and* intended to kill someone *and* be so prepared to do so that they would don a ski mask and dark clothes and line their car with a blanket… not only that, and it's been determined though pictures obtained from older home video surveillance, it turns out that it was a blanket from the house. However, all that preparation but not bring a weapon? I mean I guess it's been done before where someone might just get one from the knife block, right?"

"Not unless it was their own house. And those are typically crimes of passion with little or no planning."

"Thank you, Detective, no further questions, Your Honor."

Argan stood, "I have another! Detective, what clothes and shoes were my client wearing when he got back to the house?"

"Black dress pants, a white dress shirt, cufflinks, and dress shoes and socks."

"So where did the black pants and shirt that went along with that ski mask go?"

"We never located those. Maybe they are in the truck we can't find and maybe someone was walking their dog and got chatty. Maybe he ran out of time. The card game he was to be at got canceled. Maybe he was going to dispose of the items he had left in the car, there."

"You have a lot of 'maybes' for such a seasoned detective…anyway, you said there was my client's blood swiped on the wall, correct?"

"Yes."

"There were no injuries found on my client nor recorded, were there, Detective?"

"No."

"Thank you, Your Honor. No further questions."

Andrews stood, again, "Actually, we have another, Your Honor. Those drag marks that were mentioned. Dragged to where, Detective?"

"Out the backdoor that led from the kitchen."

"And where did they end?"

"In the grass and we assume that Connie's body, lifeless or not, was put into the back of her truck and driven away."

"Your Honor, we were going to show this video later, but we feel it important enough to present it now. We would like to enter two videos. Please enter them as State's exhibits G-3 and G-4"

"Any objections from the Defense?"

"None, Your Honor, we are aware of the videos and have reviewed them."

"So entered."

Che-Che went to work with her clicker.

Andrews started his narration, "Please take a look at this first video. It's a video of a traffic camera that catches speeders. We are all familiar with these...pause right there, Ms. Brussard. Well, how about that. There's Ms. Minae's truck there. We have positively identified her license plate." The screen had paused a video that displayed Connie's black Escalade going down a highway. "Is that correct, Detective?"

"Correct."

"Now look at State's exhibit G-4, Chelsea, please. Thanks…now pause. This is approximately thirty minutes later. Correct, Detective?"

"Yes, that was our determination based on the time stamps."

"That's the defendant's Black Porsche 911, correct?"

"Yes, we have determined that is not only his car, but we believe that is him driving while talking on his phone."

"So, maybe all those maybes may amount to something more than a maybe, after all."

"Objection!"

"Sustained, jury is to disregard Mr. Andrews' commentary."

Throughout the rest of the day prior to the lunch break, various experts were called. Tire track impressionists, hair, fiber, etc. All the paid talking heads were there. But they went quickly. There wasn't much to defend against. Nothing said on the stand thus far relating to the evidence played well for either side. The Defense had done a good job of countering the State and raising doubt at every turn. But the blood spatter analysis hadn't happened yet. At least not on the stand.

Julie Morgan was an important witness for the State, and she was good—damned good. Though, only in her 30's she had worked for the State for eight years and was even known as the not-so-secret weapon. But Argan wasn't worried because he had Kathy Kennedy.

"State calls to the stand Julie Morgan." A woman that had the same petite stature as Connie stood to be sworn in. Her hair was dark brown and pulled tightly back into a ponytail. She had sharp cheekbones and a tight pantsuit. Margot had to do a double take as she looked strikingly similar to her former client.

"Please state your name for the record and tell us who you work for and what you do there."

"My name is Julie Morgan, and I work in the forensics department as the chief of blood spatter analysis for the NOPD."

"Thank you, Ms. Morgan. Please tell the jury how long you have worked with the NOPD in that capacity."

"Nearly nine years."

"Worked a lot of cases?"

"Yes, certainly, it's been well over two hundred."

"Needless to say, you have been on the witness stand often, then, correct?"

"Around seventy-five or so times, yes."

"With regards to this case, what makes it so special?"

Morgan spoke matter-of-factly, "Well, not much."

"Please take the laser pointer that's been placed in front of you. We are going to put up a picture on the screen. Now, if you would please tell us, in your professional opinion, what, if anything, is important regarding this part of the crime scene."

A semi-closeup shot of the wall and floor was shown, "Well, as you can see here, there is a large amount of blood and a spatter pattern on the wall."

Margot took notice. *This can't be where they mention anything I have tried to point out,* she thought.

"Using your expert analysis, what is that spatter pattern indicative of?"

"It appears to be cast-off droplets surrounded by a light mist and some slosh marks on the baseboard. I determined this is where a person who was on the floor at the time would have had their throat cut around the jugular, with a sharp object..."

"A knife perhaps?"

"Perhaps a sharp object, like a knife, could have cut the jugular and if the person was frightened and had a quickened heart rate, that may have spurted blood, thus creating a slight misting upon the first slash."

"And the droplets?"

"That was likely created by the perpetrator quickly pulling the knife across the throat like this," Julie laid her head down on the stand. She used the laser pointer to pantomime what it would be like for someone to slit a throat and then Julie finished with a little flick of her wrist. "See, it's that little flick at the end that would create what you see here," she said as she pointed to the picture of droplets that had been cast off in an upward motion and then ran down the wall to create a sideways checkmark. They looked like a chart of a booming market suddenly gone bad. "It's a stroke up and then the droplets went down due to gravity, of course."

"Thank you. Would you touch on what created the sloshing marks?"

"The body had likely sat there for several minutes and when the perpetrator turned her around..."

"I'm sorry, turned her around?" Andrews feigned confusion.

"Yes, I have determined that the body, and we can see this in the still shot pictures like this and in others, the blood just before the door is in a big circle as the person was turned around and dragged by the feet. But based on the therapist's video, we know she was first on the floor, with her head pointed toward the entryway or exit, in this case, after having been pushed off the stool. The person cut her throat here and drug her a little way before he turned the body around to drag her by the feet. Then the drag marks continue…"

"Next slide please, Chelsea," Andrews motioned.

"Yes, there, you can see the circular motion plainly here. Then, it looks as if she was dragged by her feet and on her back the rest of the way up to the grass."

"Understood. Thank you."

Andrews asked a few more innocuous questions that were of little value because he had what he needed and then concluded his direct examination.

Judge Brown spoke up, "This may be a little gruesome, but I believe this is a good place to stop for lunch."

Margot was shifting in her seat. She couldn't wait to see if the Defense would notice what she had regarding there being more blood than what Bolt thought there was in her video. She still would calm herself quickly by knowing that this wasn't her area of expertise. Blood evidence wasn't her forte, trusting her gut was. She also wondered if they had ordered Italian for lunch. *Now that* would *be gruesome*, she thought and wished, only in that moment, that Joni was there to make the kind of face only she was capable of making in response to such a comment, that is, had Margot said it out loud.

Margot had stayed away from everyone during the break and simply went and had coffee at the shop that was a few blocks down from the courthouse. The street was lined with different New Orleans cafés and, though it was an entire block down, she heard that same metallic sound hit a table at one of the other restaurants that had outdoor seating. It gave her a slight jolt of electricity because it sounded nearly identical to the one she had heard two months before when she was at the cafeteria at the hospital. She looked around and saw nothing she could recognize as unusual. Margot, again, shrugged it off just as she had the other times she had heard the sound. Though, not fully because all that blood analysis had her a bit unnerved.

At 1:30 sharp the "all rise" was called by the bailiff and all did just that. Argan tugged at his vest again and out came Judge Brown, called for everyone to be seated, and all complied— except for Kathy Kennedy.

Brown spoke, "Would the witness please return to the box for cross-examination."

Ms. Morgan returned, and as she climbed in the box she was reminded by Judge Brown that she was still under oath.

"The Defense may proceed with cross."

"Thank you, Your Honor," Kennedy said as she went to the center podium and opened a brown leather padfolio.

"Ms. Morgan, please take a look at this photo here."

It was a picture that had been taken further back than the one before. It was of the same wall, but the hallway and part of the counter could be seen.

"I'd like to call your attention to some of the undisturbed pooling of blood, here," Kennedy had a pointer of her own and was using it to direct everyone's attention to the blood and the edges of the pooling, "Please tell me what you see here in Defense exhibit C-3."

"I see blood."

"Correct, thank you. But here, where the pointer is, right on the edge of the pooling. What do you see?"

"It's darker."

"Yes, and what does that indicate, if anything, to you?"

"The blood has started to dry where it is thinnest."

"Yes, thank you. And using your considerable experience, what does that mean to you?"

"Well, it means that by the time that picture was taken, the blood had started to dry a bit."

"And did the NOPD decide how long the blood had to have been there to dry like that?"

"I would have to know the ambient temperature of the room, if there was any type of warming coils laid under the tile, like in some bathrooms, and if they were on, and what time the picture had been taken…I'd have to know at least those facts to determine with even the slightest degree of certainty before I could conclude how long the blood had been there."

"Those are all fair facts for you to need to know. Luckily, I have some notes here that may be helpful. The thermostat was set to 74 degrees Fahrenheit. The floor has no heating element built in it. The temperature outside was in the low 60's and the picture was taken, based on the digital metadata, at 8:27pm."

"I'd really have to perform some intricate calculations. I don't feel comfortable saying anything more than a range with that amount of information."

"Ok, how about a range, then?"

"Objection, Your Honor. This is requiring science that shouldn't be done on the stand."

"I'll allow a range, if the witness feels she might be able to give it since she is considered an expert witness. You may answer the question," Brown concluded.

"With that information and not being able to run calculations nor having been to the scene myself, I'd say the blood had been there twenty to forty minutes when that picture was taken."

"Can you narrow that down?"

"Your Honor, badgering the witness!"

"Sustained. That's enough. She gave you the range."

"Yes, Your Honor. Ms. Morgan, let me show you Defense exhibit C-4."

This picture was one of the same area but taken even further back than the first. It showed more of the blood pooling as well as the circle and drag marks that were on the far right.

"How about now? Does it help now that you can see nearly all the edges of the blood pool?"

"Your Honor, objection, same grounds."

The Judge made her ruling of "sustained" but Margot didn't hear it. Something was wrong. Something was wrong with that picture. Something was wrong with what was being shown. Something was not as she remembered it, but she didn't know what, and as she scanned the photo to figure it out, in a flash, it was gone.

After a few more badgering questions. There was a short redirect by Andrews, "Ms. Morgan, we have the same picture as States exhibit H-2. Please take a look at it again…"

Margot tuned out the testimony and was furiously scanning. She was trying to put her finger on what was wrong; what was out of place. What had been there before but wasn't now. She just couldn't figure it out.

"…and as you can see, the backdoor is wide open the way it had been found when the police arrived on the scene. And, presumably, the *front* door had been opened a little later. And it was a rare, cool New Orleans evening. Please tell us and the jury, would that effect your earlier calculations?"

"Yes, absolutely it would," her ponytail bobbed up and down as she tried to shake her head out of the lawyer's noose.

"And what would that mean if you add all of that together?"

"Objection! It assumes facts not in evidence."

"Overruled, we can see that the backdoor is open and the police report, noted earlier, did conclude that the door had been left open. I'll allow it but keep the scope limited."

Andrews prodded, "You may answer the question, Ms. Morgan."

"Let's just say that… well, that could really limit my ability to nail it down, but it would be a shorter timeframe. Dry air would likely cause blood to clot at a quicker pace than if it were a humid night."

228

"Thank you, no further questions."

The defense was all abuzz once that second picture of the prosecution's had been displayed. Rizzo had noticed something. He had noticed something that even caused Bradly LeBlanc to take part in the excitement that started amongst his team.

Margot noticed what was going on with Rizzo and thought, *MAYBE THIS IS IT! MAYBE THEY SEE WHAT I SEE OUTTA PLACE! BUT WHAT IS IT?*

"Your Honor, we would like to ask that the prosecution do us a favor by leaving their exhibit up for another moment, please," Rizzo said and didn't wait for an answer, "You're a blood expert so let me ask you a question about the drag marks we can see in this photo," he used his own pointer, "Tell me if you notice anything odd about them from this angle."

"I mean, just the circular pattern where the perpetrator turned the body around and pulled her by the feet."

"Yes, correct. But what else do you notice?

"I mean, it looks consistent with someone who had been dragged by the ankles, I suspect but I can't tell more than that."

"With all your years of experience, you don't see it?"

SEE WHAT? WHAT DOESN'T SHE, NOR I, SEE THAT IS THERE? Margot wanted to shout.

"Your Honor…" Andrews began.

Brown held up her palm to signal for him to wait. She was intrigued, "Please, Mr. Rizzo, get to your point quickly."

"Your Honor and ladies and gentlemen of the jury, here is what I see and all of you will see it, too. I ask you this, Ms.

Morgan, as a blood expert, if my client's girlfriend is being dragged through all this blood, spun around, and then through a narrow doorway, mustn't we then ask ourselves where are all the hand marks?"

"I'm sorry?" Morgan questioned.

Rizzo got on the floor. He was a thin man and would do anything to prove a point.

"Mr. Argan, please drag me by the feet."

"YOUR HONOR!" Andrews exclaimed.

"This better lead to one hell of a good point, Mr. Rizzo. I don't like stunts such as these in my courtroom."

"Please bear with me, Your Honor. Like you noted this morning, we are searching for the truth."

"Careful Mr. Rizzo, you have ten more seconds of this before I shut down your display."

"Thank you, Your Honor."

Argan had already been on his way over and had heaved down his girth to grab Rizzo's ankles. He started pulling and Rizzo's arms, that had been on the floor, went out by his sides and then halfway above his head.

"You see the point of my question, Ms. Morgan?"

"I think I do, but I'm not sure what you are getting at?" Morgan said as if she wasn't sure because the one thing she was sure of was that she was the State's witness and not going to help Rizzo one bit.

"I agree," Rizzo continued from the floor but sat up and reset.

"Three more seconds, Mr. Rizzo!" Brown was interested but didn't want anyone to know to what degree.

"Mr. Argan, drag me again."

This time Rizzo held his arms together across his chest.

Everyone was lifted out of their seats to see the point. And it was clear…to most, anyway.

"Your Honor, the Defense is asking a question so simple we almost missed it. The sides of that door opening have absolutely no blood on it whatsoever. There should be contact marks where her body that had purportedly been dragged past it would have made contact and left blood on the door frame, no? And the drag marks leading all the way to the grass has not a single, and forgive me you all for using this term, but not a single Jesus Christ pose."

Rizzo got up, fixed his rumpled suit, and asked again, "Ms. Morgan, are you not surprised to see not a single swipe of blood anywhere on that door? Does your experience not inform you to the degree where it should be a question in your mind why arms that have been dragged through that amount of blood were not splayed out…that is, if the body was lifeless. Because if it was a lifeless body, should its arms not made swipe marks on that doorframe!?!"

Andrews nor Chelsea could think of a single objection that would stick. Though there was one. But it would only force the Defense to further their arguing, and Rizzo would likely win this point, anyway.

"I, I have to say that it does give me pause."

"No. Further. Questions."

Chelsea had one, "Ms. Morgan. We know that Connie Minae was of slight build and only half the width of that doorframe. If her arms pulled straight above her lifeless body and head on her way through, and if the person dragging her knew he only had a few minutes and kept pulling and never stopped, the dragging of her body and all that blood would have left nothing but a straight line all the way through that door, on the cement patio, and through that grass, correct?"

"I would assume so."

"So that means she was either unconscious or dying or dead but most certainly limp, correct?"

"Correct. Based on that scenario."

"No further questions, Your Honor."

Rizzo popped up, "It could have made her something other than dead."

"I don't know what you're implying, Mr. Rizzo," Morgan shot back.

"It could have made her complicit."

"OBJECTION, HE'S TESTIFYING!"

"There was a question mark at the end of that sentence, Your Honor, but please consider that question withdrawn."

Brown was pissed, "Jury is to disregard," she said through gritted teeth, "Court is in recess for 15 minutes! Council, I will see you all in my chambers…NOW!"

And while they waited, Margot had come to a conclusion. That anything to do with blood was not what was wrong with that picture. It was something else, but she still wasn't sure what.

The Defense had their ass handed to them by Judge Brown while in chambers. The Judge's venom spewed so wildly, and there was so much of it, that the prosecution got some of it spattered on them, as well. However, whatever damage was going to be done had been done already. And there would likely be more to follow. Argan and his team knew they were scoring points with the jury, regardless—they were raising doubt. They were making the prosecution do their due diligence. Andrews and Che-Che would discuss during pillow talk, some time after the trial was over, that they had to admit, it was a fantastic stunt. For years later, the two would joke and use the term, "Complicit" as a throwaway word. *This guacamole is complicit, Ew, this fuckin' coffee is complicit, or Wanna get complicit?* It could be used in any situation and mean anything—good, bad, or whatever. After that trial the pair couldn't hear it anywhere, especially not in a courtroom, without having to hold back cracking up. When Rizzo later wrote a book about his work on the trial, he included it, and that took up nearly a whole chapter. In the end, it didn't affect the outcome of the trial at all, but he was still proud of it.

After Judge Brown had completed dishing out her major ass-chewing, returned to the bench with a smile and sense of satisfaction that she had reasserted herself—for the moment.

"The prosecution may call their next witness."

"The prosecution recalls Margot Landry to the stand."

Before this morning, Margot had been on the stand in a few other cases. But she had never witnessed an assault, much less a murder—if that's in fact what it was. She was questioning everything now that she was on her way to the witness box. Margot figured that if she had some reasonable doubt, and she did, then the jury most certainly must have some. They must have had some because they were mostly lay people and making twisty faces at the evidence. Being able to read people was what Margot considered her best talent. However, she was having a hard time nailing down this defendant.

But most of all, it was the nagging feeling that something she always notice when she was doing therapy with Connie was now missing from any photo of that kitchen.

After she had been reminded that she was still under oath, Margot retook her hotseat.

"Thank you, again, for being here with us today, Ms. Landry," Chelsea greeted.

Margot was steeling herself in preparation, so she just nodded. However, she wasn't bracing herself for the prosecution questions. It was the Defense table that worried her. As it would later turn out, it was for good reason.

"Now, Ms. Landry, what I would like to do is go through the four sessions with you and get your thoughts as a licensed clinical social worker.

"Yes."

"Ms. Landry, please allow me to call your attention to the screen and let's watch together what has been described in your notes as the 'goodness-of-fit' session. However, before we do, would you please explain to the jury what that means?"

Margot pulled the mic to her level and cleared her throat before beginning, "So, it's a free session that is given to a prospective client so that they may see if my clinical specialties, style of work, and demeanor would be a good fit for what they are looking for."

"Um, hum, and who makes the determination of 'goodness-of-fit'?"

"Well, almost always it's the client. However, it can be that the therapist is not willing to work with them for any number of reasons."

"Very good. Okay, we can skip the reasons for now, if that works for you."

"Certainly."

"Okay, so, now, let's take a look at that first session and then I'm going to ask you some of your thoughts."

"Okay."

Everyone in the court looked on as the video played. Folks shifted in their seats because they were getting bored. The last act was a hard one to follow.

After the video concluded, Margot had that nagging feeling again that something wasn't right when comparing that session and the crime scene photo that she seen just a half hour before. But she needed to stay focused, so she tried to put it out of her mind.

Chelsea inquired, "Ms. Landry, please tell us what your first impressions were of Ms. Minae."

"I found her to be somewhat charming at first."

"At first?"

"Well, I'm not a proponent of the therapy that she mentioned several times. But I knew then, as I do now, that it's popular and that she had every right to explore it. Mostly though, she appeared to be questioning me, as is also her right, why I wouldn't be using it in my practice."

"Are you speaking of EMDR?"

"Yes."

"As an aside, and before we go through my other questions, just for clarity's sake, would you mind sharing with the jury what EMDR stands for and what it is?"

"Sure," Margot said and turned toward the jury box and continued, "EMDR stands for Eye Movement Desensitization and Reprocessing. And a therapist would use what's called bi-lateral stimulation, creating a fixed point for a client to stare at and then moving that fixed point back and forth, like this," Margot put two crooked fingers up and moved them in a pendulous motion. "This is not quite meant to put a client in a trance-like state but, rather, in a state where the practitioner can get past the trauma response defenses when talking about traumatic events. That's where the reprograming comes in. A new thought or belief about the traumatic event is, and I use this term loosely, offered."

"And you don't believe it works."

"My short answer is it's clearly a gimmick that is simply an add-on to traditional therapy. But practitioners can charge more for an EMDR session, so they believe in it wholeheartedly. However, to be fair, many clients claim it's the only thing that works for them."

"Thank you for that. Okay, so what other professional thoughts were going through your mind during this initial, goodness-of-fit session?"

"I saw a woman who was being thoughtful about what she wanted in a therapist. And, quite honestly, I believed that she wasn't going to choose me, and that EMDR was going to be the reason why. It was clear to her, as you saw in the video, that it wasn't something I was going to offer, and she wanted to explore it anyway."

"Understood. Anything else you wanted to add before we move on?"

Yeah, that creepy fuckin' door turned out to be my worst nightmare, EMDR is still bunk, and I can't figure out what is wrong with that fuckin' kitchen picture!

"Nothing of note. It was a fairly typical first meeting, otherwise."

"Okay, let's go to the next session and we'll see if I have any questions after that."

After the next video was over, the one where that damned door slowly creaked opened, the jury looked more engaged when Margot peeked over at the box.

"In this session it appears that Connie never went the full, what's it called…"

"Clinical hour."

"…right, clinical hour, anyway, here Ms. Minae talked about wanting to separate from a relationship which wasn't a marriage."

"Correct."

"What did you take from that session, in your professional opinion?"

"I saw her as a client who was not happy in her current relationship, wasn't sure how she was going to leave—feeling stuck—and that she appeared afraid of him but not ready to talk about those fears."

"Did you believe her?"

"I didn't have a reason not to. She had sought me out and was tentative about even discussing it."

"Very well. Now let's move on to the next one."

This video was the longest of them all.

"So, what did you think when she shared that he raped her after she turned down his proposal?"

"Well, I was horrified, of course."

"And this was the first time you learned of the marriage proposal, correct?"

"Correct."

"And, as she noted in the session, not only did she turn him down, but she shared with you that she had no intentions of marrying him."

"Correct."

"So, a client shares with you she has been raped. Don't you have to report that, and if not, why not?"

"Actually no, a therapist is not required to report any domestic abuse if the client is unwilling to have us do so. We may report it if they want us to, but we attempt to get them to report it themselves and we work to get them to a safe place.

Child abuse or elder abuse would be different. For those circumstances we are mandated to report within 24-hours. We also would have to report if a client threatened to kill someone. We would have to report it to keep the intended victim safe."

"Right, Tatiana Tarasoff, 1969 and 1976, correct?

"Correct."

"Objection, we are not here for a history lesson regarding therapy nor the law."

"Overruled, but I would leave it there, Ms. Brussard."

"Yes, Your Honor."

"So, later in the session you ask her something that may have been jarring for the jury to have heard—something about her health insurance?"

"Yes, when a client appears to be rejecting all other appropriate options, we, as therapists, may try what is called a paradoxical intervention."

"And that is...?"

"Objection..."

"Overruled, I believe the jury needs to know why Ms. Landry seemed so uncaring and crass at that moment in the session."

The Judge's statement shook Margot, but she understood the sentiment, "So, it's what most others call reverse psychology. It's a way to get the client to see their actions as incongruent with what they desire. This is intended to hear how absurd their situation is, so they contemplate doing the opposite."

"Understood, and I believe the jury could see, in that moment, it appeared to be working."

"I felt progress had been made, yes."

"Anything else you would want to add about that session?"

"I don't believe so. I just felt that she needed to get out of that relationship and that house if he had sexually assaulted her."

"Let's go to the next session."

After everyone in the court had watched the next-to-final session, more questions were asked by Chelsea, "That was intense. What is your professional opinion of that one?"

"I narrowed it down to a few conclusions, but the one that stuck out the most to me was that she was in fear for her life. And when he came home and she hurried to leave the session, she seemed totally out of sorts."

"Did you believe that she was becoming more afraid of him?"

"Yes, I did. That was my thought, for sure."

"Did you believe, based on what she was telling you, that he was capable of murder?"

"Objection!"

"Grounds?"

"She can't say if she believed that a man she has still yet to meet to this day, in any private nor professional capacity, is someone she believes is capable of murder."

"Your, Honor, that is not what I asked. I asked if she believed he was capable of murder based on what her client was telling her."

"Sustained. Although it was clear these were statements made during the 'heat of excitement' which would normally lead to an exception to the hearsay rule, I will not allow the witness to answer because she would be basing her opinion on the opinion of another. Next question, counsel," the Judge commanded.

"I suppose, then, we should go to the last session."

After the ghoulish final act, Chelsea Brussard knew what to do next.

"So, after that night and after seeing this session, if that's what we want to call it, again, did you then and do you now believe that he was capable of murder?"

"OBJECTION!" Kennedy shouted.

"OVERRULED! SHE IS NO LONGER GOING TO BE ANSWERING BASED ON ANYONE'S EXPERIENCE OTHER THAN HER OWN!"

"Your Honor, all due respect! We don't know who that is under that mask."

"And that will be for the jury to decide. Right now, regardless of if they believe it's your client based on an entire morning of evidence, Ms. Landry may still answer the question as to whether or not she believes the man, or woman, for that matter, in that video was capable of murder—it's her opinion. And frankly, she can use her professional judgment, right, wrong, or indifferent to answer as it's her opinion based on someone she has met. She met him in that moment, no matter who that HIM is!"

"But judge, it's prejudicial to my client."

"HOW IS IT PREJUDICIAL IF YOU CONTEND IT'S NOT EVEN HIM AND MAY I REMIND YOU THAT YOUR CO-

COUNSEL SUGGESTED THAT A CRIME DIDN'T EVEN TAKE PLACE AND MS. MINAE WAS EVEN NOTED AS, AND I QUOTE, 'BEING COMPLICIT'! IT CAN'T BE PREJUDICIAL IF IT'S NOT EVEN HIM, AS YOU CONTEND!" Judge Brown lowered her tone and shoulders, "So, what's it gonna be? If it's prejudicial, then are you conceding that it's your client? If it isn't your client, she is only giving an opinion regarding the man in the video."

"I withdrawal my objection."

"Ms. Brussard, please proceed."

"Ms. Landry, in that moment, did you believe that that man was capable of murder?"

"Yes."

"No further questions, Your Honor," Chelsea smiled and walked back to the prosecution's table with a sense of satisfaction.

"Defense?"

"Yes, thank you, Your Honor," Kathy Kennedy would be continuing her lead for this witness, "So, you testified just now that you believed that this *person* in the video was capable of murder."

"Yes."

"And you based that on what? Your keen sense of observation?"

"I don't know how keen one's sense would need to be after seeing that, but he looks threatening enough to me."

"Threatening or murderous?"

242

"Threatening for sure, *murderous* is to be determined."

"Let's move on since we don't even know who the man behind that mask is and without a body we don't even know if a person is dead."

Che-Che raised up, "Objection, Your Honor! We believe we established this morning that anyone Ms. Minae's size who lost that amount of blood would have died in the pool of it. The wounds that the blood spatter indicated was likely created by the slitting of her throat," Chelsea's objection was more about reminding the jury what they had heard that morning than it was to be awarded a point from the Judge.

"Well, now that you have both testified to facts already noted to the jury this morning, I will sustain the objection so we can all move on," Brown ruled. She knew what both attorneys were doing.

"Yes, Your Honor."

Kathy continued, "Ms. Landry, in your earlier testimony, you noted that…," Kathy had moved back to her notes, "…and I'm paraphrasing, that you had a few thoughts regarding Ms. Minae's behavior, correct?"

"Yes…"

"Using that keen sense of observation, what else did you think?"

"I don't know that I understand your question."

"Well, what was your final diagnosis?"

"I didn't settle on one."

"Oh, that's fine, just tell us what your working theories were."

Margot knew she had to be honest because she had written it in her notes. And they had all been subpoenaed and were in the possession of nearly half the people in that courtroom, "Okay, well, I had not settled on any one diagnosis. One thought was that she was an abused woman who was becoming more panicky as the sessions went along. I also theorized that because of her trauma that she had fallen into learned helplessness and that had caused her to become a help rejecting complainer…"

"Please explain those last two points to the jury. And before you do, I would like it noted that the trauma you are referring to was what she told you happened at the hands of my client, for which there is no evidence, correct?"

"Correct."

"Please continue with your answer."

"Well, learned helplessness is a term used to describe when someone has tried so many different ways to escape, or at least thought of them, that they believe nothing they do will make a difference, so they quit trying…"

"And the second term?"

"A person may then reject all options presented."

"Is that the only time a, well, a help rejecting complainer may complain and reject the feedback and options offered by a therapist?"

"A client sometimes, and I didn't settle on this being Ms. Minae's issue or not, but to answer your question, sometimes the client is getting a secondary gain from staying in whatever situation they are complaining about. Or, it may be better said, they are gaining the attention they want by someone showing care and concern for their complaints. They don't want out of whatever the issue or issues are. If they got out, then they would lose their identity of being a victim, and it may be the only identity they have."

"Ms. Landry, you have noted symptoms but not noted any diagnosis about her personality yet. Would you mind letting us know what your thoughts were on that?"

Chelsea chimed in, "Your Honor, what does a diagnosis or, frankly, any of this testimony regarding Ms. Minae's state of mind have to do with the fact that she has been murdered and the Defendant is accused of said murder."

"Your Honor, I'd like to respectfully remind the State that we don't have a body, and we don't know who was behind that mask. We don't know if Ms. Minae was involved in any way with what happened that night. Let me be crystal clear, and not because we haven't been already; we contend that isn't our client on that video, nor behind that mask, nor that harmed Ms. Minae in any way, shape or form. And if there were a ruse, our client wasn't responsible for that, either."

"Your Honor! The defense has gone to victim blaming here! It's disrespectful!"

"We don't even know IF she was a victim of anything other than her own behavior and planning," Kennedy began to say before Che-Che was even finished with furthering her objection.

"ENOUGH! Ladies and gentlemen of the jury, please disregard all that you have heard during that exchange," Brown bellowed and then looked at Chelsea, "Your PSEUDO-objection, as none was ever made, I'm still giving thought to. Secondly, I'd like it noted that it was put on the record this morning that there is enough blood—also known as connective tissue—as well as both hard and circumstantial evidence connecting the defendant to the crime that the State was able to secure an indictment for murder against the defendant. That is what we are here to evaluate. However, the Defense is correct, we have not positively identified who is in that video nor that a murder has even taken place. That is for YOU, the jury, to decide. I am totally impartial to the outcome. And to that end, it is for the Defense to question the evidence. Ms. Minae is on video and has been assessed to some degree by this witness. Therefore, as to your objection that was never quite raised— State—it's overruled. The witness may answer the question."

"Would you mind repeating the question?" Margot asked timidly.

Brown was not chancing more nonsense from the Defense nor the prosecution on this one. So, she decided to pull an ace from her sleeve. That ace was her court reporter.

Judy Perkins died many years ago a Huntsville, Alabama juris prudence legend as a court reporter. Her niece had followed in her footsteps. She didn't have half the reputation that her Aunt did. But she was good enough. Though, no one would ever be as good as her Aunt.

Brown asked her, "Mrs. Daltry, would you please read back the last question?"

Daltry did as she was asked, "STATE: Ms. Landry, you have noted symptoms but not noted any diagnosis about her personality yet. Would you mind letting us know what your thoughts were on that?"

Brown prompted Margot, "Please answer."

"So, I had concluded by the third session, the fourth time I had seen her, that she was in a manic phase of bipolar disorder."

"Please explain to the jury."

"I was theorizing that by her pressured speech and flight of ideas that she was in the phase of bipolar disorder that caused her to look out of control."

"Would bipolar disorder, specifically in a manic phase, cause someone to act irrationally?"

"It could."

"Is there any other diagnosis you were theorizing?"

"Yes," Margot said reluctantly.

"Please reveal to the jury what that diagnosis was," Kennedy used the word "reveal" for effect.

"Borderline Personality Disorder."

"Could that cause someone to act irrationally?"

"Yes."

"Even more so than someone with bipolar disorder?"

Margot sighed at having to admit, "Yes, even more so in some cases."

"Could either bipolar disorder, manic phase, of course, or borderline personality disorder cause someone to self-harm?"

"Yes."

"Could it cause them to cut themselves on purpose?"

"YOUR HONOR!" Chelsea objected.

"Overruled. The witness may answer."

"Yes."

"No further questions at this time, Your Honor."

Chelsea "Che-Che" Brussard couldn't get to the witness box fast enough, "A little rapid-fire round, Ms. Landry...what is one of the major reasons that someone would struggle with borderline personality disorder?"

"Real or imagined abandonment."

"Give me the main one. The one that you wrote in your notes!"

"Trauma. Childhood trauma."

"And for women, what often is the cause of that trauma should they struggle with this disorder?"

"Childhood sexual abuse."

"And did the client say that the Defendant raped her?"

"She did."

"Could that trigger an episode?"

"OBJECTION! Assumes facts not in evidence. We have no clue if Ms. Minae had been sexually abused as a child or not."

"Sustained. Please rephrase the question."

"If someone had been sexually abused as a child, suffered from trauma, and it led to the disorder known as borderline personality, could a rape trigger an episode of the symptoms of that disorder?"

"OBJECTION!"

"Overruled, you may answer."

"Yes."

"And, hypothetically, is it possible that someone who is living with someone struggling with borderline features or bipolar disorder could feel stressed—just absolutely have enough of the roller-coaster ride—that they might harm the patient?"

"Your Honor, objection!"

"Overruled, the witness may answer the hypothetical."

"Not only hypothetically, but I'm actually aware of situations such as that, yes."

"Do you believe it is possible then, since the Defense has gone to blaming the victim, that Bradly LeBlanc could have had enough? Could he have had enough of the type of behavior—behavior you witnessed—to have SLIT HER THROAT?"

"OBJECTION, THIS IS OUTRAGEOUS!" Kathy Kennedy had stood up so fast that it banged the Defense table so hard that it nearly knocked over the water pitcher.

"SUSTAINED!"

"I withdraw the question and have none further."

Brown glared at Che-Che on her way back to her boss and lover who looked up at her with a glare that was filled with caution.

Judge Brown gnashed her teeth, "Recross?"

Yes, and thank you, Your Honor.

"Do you know, for a fact, if that is our client in that video?"

"No."

"Do you know for certain of any diagnosis that Ms. Minae has or had?"

"No."

"Do you know if she is alive or not?"

"No."

"Are you willing to stake your license to practice psychotherapy on…"

"Careful, Ms. Kennedy, I've had about all I can take."

"No further questions, Your Honor."

"State?"

Both, Gill and Che-Che, shook their heads 'no'.

"The witness may step down."

Margot was about as relieved as she possibly could be, though it would be short lived. She left the witness box like a Slinky.

"I think this is a good time for us to break for dinner and the day. May I remind you all, ladies and gentlemen of the jury, that you are to stay away from any media, print or otherwise, while this trial is in progress. That certainly includes talking to any of the media outlets—print or otherwise. Ms. Margot Landry, you are still under oath, and you could be called again tomorrow, as sometimes happens even after there are no more questions by either party the day prior. I am instructing you to also stay away from the consumption of any media and certainly do not speak to anyone regarding these proceedings until this trial has concluded."

Margot had not sat down yet and was still facing the judge. She simply muttered, "Yes, Your Honor."

After a short drive to Joni's house where the ladies had earlier agreed to meet, Margot poured herself out of the car and into a wineglass.

Joni had prepared a Greek pasta salad for herself and her ragged and worn friend. Margot kicked her heals off under the dinner table as the ladies started to eat.

"That bad, huh, sweetie?"

"Worse..." she lamented while Adler tried to interweave himself between her ankles. It brought her almost as much comfort as the first bite of food after her third sip of wine, "It was horrific enough to have to sit through all that evidence...but to have to testify, too? Jesus, this is good."

"Glad you like it. Adler helped...so, is he guilty?"

Margot finished chewing, took another sip, and looked up.

"No...maybe...I don't know."

"I'm no lawyer but while working at my old company, we had to sit through a few of these things. Boring really...all numbers and whatnot but I do know this..."

"What's that?" Margot questioned as she took another bite.

"That means the defense is creating doubt. And if you are in doubt, then that jury surely is. You lived through it...they are only getting the revisionist history of it."

Margot nodded with a half head tilt and a half shoulder shrug as she took another bite, "I did give that some thought, too, Jonesy."

She hadn't realized how hungry she was, and the wine was starting to hit her all-but-empty stomach.

"Lawyers and our judicial system are a funny thing, Margie. Here's my take, not that it matters much to what you are going through…well, not that it matters much at all. Simply an old broad's opinion."

"Joniii…"

"No, really, it's okay. I know I'm old, I know I'm not an expert in anything legal, but I also know I'm old enough to have a well-formed opinion. It may be wrong, but it's well-formed. And husband number one was an attorney."

Margot giggled for the first time all day.

"There was a time—long before I was born—when the judicial system had very little justice in it at all. They would just find someone they believed was guilty and string 'em up. I know you know all this, but I want you to just eat right now. So, I'll continue to yammer."

Margot took a swig and held up her glass hallway from the table to the ceiling then slowly swayed side to side, "Preach Sister Joni, preach!"

"At some point, of course, there were laws put into place. Now, I'm speaking of American law—law based on our Constitution. There's way too much history to go into regarding that, but it's not needed to make my point," Joni took her glass, swirled it around, then took her own swig.

"At some point—and I don't exactly know when and I don't know that I give a shit—but at some point, it was decided that the accused should have representation because law is so...fucking...complicated. So, you had all these people who were accused and the law just churning them through the system. Now, of course, now they needed representation so that system didn't just chew 'em up. They needed a person who knew the law. They needed a lawyer."

"I need more wine," Margot said with a chirp while shaking off the day.

"So, the lawyers showed up...not a new concept and, again, not the point. They were there to represent a client—guilty or not. And then the shit hit the ceiling fan. Lawyers must be paid. And you don't pay a lawyer that doesn't get you off, so to speak," she finished with a wink. "Now it's a competition. It's not about truth for the defense. The truth doesn't set the guilty free. But money and obfuscation will."

"Oooh, 'obfuscation'"

"I may be a broad, but I'm not an uneducated one, honey."

"Truth!" Margot felt the alcohol washing over her in a cleansing baptism from the hell that was her life right now.

"So now we have a system where defense attorneys are not paid to keep that system honest and shepherd some poor slob through a process they don't understand. They are paid, and it's where the real money is, honey, to get the guilty off scot-free."

After dinner the ladies sat and chatted a bit more then did the dishes. Joni put on a pot of coffee and the two stood in the kitchen while Margot finished sharing her experiences of the day. The two ladies and Adler retired to the living room. Joni turned on the television and said, "It's almost time for the 10pm news."

Margot made her own objection, "Oh crap, the judge told me not to watch anything about the trial."

"Would it change anything you are going to say in court if you did?"

"No, I suppose not."

"And besides, you're not watching it, I am."

"Right…I'll just avert my eyes and not listen."

"Atta girl."

Of course, the trial was the lead story. A middle-aged anchorman with a nice head of hair made the call, "In our lead story tonight, wealthy New Orleans businessman…"

"He's not a businessman," Margot objected.

"I thought you weren't gonna watch."

"I'm not but my hearing is too good, I guess," both ladies just smiled at one another.

"…Bradly LeBlanc is on trial for the murder of his girlfriend, Connie Minae, but there's only one problem—her body has never been recovered."

The camera cut to the co-anchor, a woman in her early 30's with a blond bob who wore a red dress. She was standing in front of a large LCD screen. There was a picture of the accused and next to it a charming picture of Connie who was actually smiling in the photo while sitting on the grass with a large white Samoyed next to her.

"That's right, Roger. The City Of New Orleans D.A., Daniel Whitmire, spoke to us last month when news of the decision to take this case to trial first broke."

The screen went to file footage from the interview that occurred nearly a month prior. The interviewer was the same woman who had just introduced the video, "So, D.A. Whitmire, we understand the decision to take the LeBlanc case to trial was an easy one."

"Yes, well, charging someone with murder is never an easy decision but the evidence uncovered is so overwhelming that, honestly, even without a body we believe he will still be found guilty."

The interviewer continued, "But how rare is it to get a conviction without a body?"

"Honestly, it's rare to even have charges filed without the body of a victim. However, in cases where there is a large amount of blood a prosecution team can get a conviction as long as all the other evidence lines up. And in this case, well, I have rarely seen it this close to what is known in our field as a 'slam-dunk'."

"I don't mean to belabor the point, but you say a 'slam-dunk' even without a..."

"Here's something that most people don't realize; in law and in medical science, blood is considered connective tissue. And connective tissue is considered a body part. And there was so much blood left at the scene, we were able to conclude that the person who lost that connective tissue is no longer alive. The blood, in effect, *is* the body."

After the clip was shown, the second chair anchor in the red dress took back over from her own interview, "Standing by live outside the New Orleans courthouse on Tulane and Broad is our own Liz Bowman. Liz…"

"Yes, thank you Tammy, today there was blistering testimony from prosecution witnesses and tempestuous back-and-forth from both sides of the court that set off Judge Carmen Brown on more than one occasion. Cameras were not allowed in the courtroom where we heard from several expert witnesses regarding blood spatter analysis, tire track impressions, and even Connie Minae's own psychotherapist who, at times, seemed confused about what she thought regarding the victim's behavior that led up to the night of her disappearance in the wake of her own blood."

Margot was pissed, "Oh, that's just fucking great! There goes my private practice."

"Sources close to the investigation who agreed to speak off camera told Eyewitness Four news that quote, We have a heck of a case and the fact that the Defense was willing to rush into a speedy trial is telling of the guilt of their client, end quote. However, sources close to the defense when asked why they wanted to have their day in court so quickly simply said quote Because Bradly is innocent and we will show that our client has a large amount of evidence against him because he is being framed, possibly by some very important people, end quote. The trial is expected to resume at 8:30am sharp tomorrow where we will bring you more. Tammy, back to you."

"Thank you, Liz. Roger, we have received word that it's not looking like a slam-dunk at all for the prosecution, however, the defense appears to be on shaky ground, as well."

"Thank you, Tammy. This is definitely one to watch as it appears to have all the makings of a documentary special from all we have heard leading up to this trial."

Joni left the television on but turned down the sound. Margot still looked stunned.

"I'm sorry, hon. I'm sure it will be fine. Maybe there will be plenty of folks willing to pay you just to hear about your story and just simply call it 'going to therapy'."

"Even if that were true, that wouldn't last long."

"Well, the good thing is, neither does the public's memory. So, when that runs out then you have the real clients showing up again, no?"

"No, because they would think that if anything they are going through lands in court, they will think I'll just blab confusing information about them—they will think I'm a hack."

"You could always write your book about this experience."

"Well, it would be a short one, because there is almost no time that I spent with Connie."

"I'm sure it'll work out. Hell, you write that short book, and it gives you time to write the one you really want to finish."

"I don't know that I want to do anything but take a hot bath and go to bed. I have to be there again tomorrow. And it won't be for the press to sing another round of my praises," Margot looked at Adler who was between the two ladies and started to pet him. He flipped over on his back and exposed his belly for her to give it a good scratch and a rub.

33

Skullduggery

At 8:30am sharp the court was called to order and Brown took the bench. Che-Che stood up, and most were only mildly surprised when she said that the prosecution rested.

"Defense, please present your case."

"With pleasure, Your Honor," Kathy Kennedy stood and continued, "The Defense calls Ms. Lexi Jade."

The whole gallery, who wasn't already facing the back of the courtroom, turned around as the Bailiff pushed open one of the double doors and called out into the hall, "CALLING LEXI JADE!"

There was no response.

"Calling LEXI JADE!"

Still no response nor appearance of Lexi. Jerome turned to his judge and shrugged but stayed by the door with it cracked.

Brown raised the eyebrow that was always half raised because it was stuck in that position from her using it so much as an expression, "Defense? Any clue where your first witness is?"

Bradly LeBlanc looked on nervously while Kathy put her hands on the table, looked down, and said nothing. She only added to her nervous look by shaking her head "no".

Che-Che whispered to Andrews through the side of her mouth, "She's probably in the same place where Connie's body is."

Echoing through the hallway, the sound of heels could be heard over the anticipatory silence that had settled over the courtroom. The bailiff, Jerome, looked out of the same door he had left cracked as the sound of those heels got closer; louder. Jerome looked at Judge Brown and gave two quick nods with his eyelids closed.

Brown lowered her brow, "It appears you may be in luck, Ms. Kennedy."

Lexi Jade rounded the corner, and Jerome pushed the door open wide. There stood a statuesque woman who was well endowed, dressed classily, and with an hourglass shape that caught the attention of men and women alike. Her raven hair was half to her waist with a cascade of loose curls. She wore a tailored dress that went just below her knees, and she carried an Hermés bag. She looked as if she had double the money of everyone else in the courtroom combined. A classy gold cross hung around her neck, stopping just at the cradle of her exposed cleavage making it look slightly sacrilegious.

"Ms. Jade?" Brown asked.

She answered in a smoky voice that had just the right amount of southern flair to it, "Yes."

Brown stuttered, "Please…uh…please come forth to be sworn in."

Jerome, who had stayed behind for an extra second, let the door go and trotted past Lexi Jade and grabbed the Bible that, as a married and Christian man, he needed so desperately right now.

Lexi sashayed up to that Bible. Some in the court, based on the fact that she was dripping with sex, may have thought would burst into flames once she put her hand on it.

Through the haze of perfume and visuals, Jerome did his best, "Do you, Lexi Jade, swear to tell the truth, the whole truth, and nothing but the truth?"

"No."

There was a slight but audible gasp throughout the courtroom.

"My name is not Lexi Jade. That is my business name. My God-given name," Lexi looked down at the Bible with ice blue eyes as if it were a naughty item and then back up at the visibly shaken Jerome, then finished, "is Alexa Midland."

"Oh, um, yes ma'am. Do you, Alexa Midland, swear to tell the truth, the whole truth and nothing but the truth?"

"So… help me God," she answered and then winked at the awestricken bailiff who's mouth upturned into a stupid, shit-eating grin.

"You make take the stand, Ms. Midland." Jerome managed to stammer.

Che-Che side eyed Andrews who just stared at his notes. He was thankful they had decided she would be taking point on this one after Alexa was discovered and shared by the Defense during pretrial preparations.

"Good morning, Ms. Midland," Kennedy opened, "You've already stated your name for the record. Can you please tell us what you do for a living?"

Everything that Alexa said was slow, smoky, and deliberate, "I'm a pharmaceutical sales representative."

"Anything else?" Kennedy asked even though she would have rather it not have to come out. But no matter, the prosecution already knew the answer.

"Soap."

"Might you explain that a bit more for the jury?"

"It'll be my pleasure to do so. It started as…well, let's just call it a hobby. I started making high-end soap with unique textures and scents."

"Do you have many clients who purchase your soap?"

There were no objections from the prosecution's table because they knew where this needed to go to get to where they needed to be.

"No, not many, and that's by design, and not many can afford my product, anyway. Like I noted, it started as a hobby, and it still is, in many respects."

"Is, or shall we say was, Mr. LeBlanc one of your clients?"

"He was," Lexi said as she looked over at Bradly who refused to meet her gaze and wry smile.

"Did he happen to purchase product from you often?"

"Let's just say he became a regular patron."

"I see. How regular?"

"My soap business occurs at night and some weekends because my day job continues to get in the way. Regardless, Mr. LeBlanc sampled my soap every Friday evening at 7pm."

"About how long would these sampling sessions last?"

"One, maybe two hours, at most."

"So, on the night in question, was Mr. LeBlanc sampling your soap?"

"He was."

"And was that a one- or two-hour sampling session?"

"It was barely one. He made his purchase quickly."

Some in the court laughed audibly and Margot just shook her head. Though, she didn't care who or what was said on that stand as long as it wasn't her.

"And do you have a store for your soap?"

"I do but it's not your typical storefront. It's an upstart business, so I run it from an apartment that I rented. I would never want anyone to know where my actual house is, of course."

"Where is it located…the 'storefront', that is?"

"Uptown."

"And that's where Bradly was soap sampling that evening?"

"Yes."

"So, he left around 8pm?"

"Sometime near that. I'm not a clock watcher when I'm with a client so I can't totally be sure. But I had another patron interested in my product and he was to be there at nine. I like to

262

get set up for the next customer, you understand, so it was probably no later than 8:15pm."

"And how long has my client, Mr. LeBlanc, been a…a well, a client of yours?"

"About a month and a half or so before his beloved went missing."

"And on that evening, between seven and 8:15pm, he never left your sight?"

"Only for about a minute when he excused himself and went into the restroom."

"Thank you for that, Ms. Midland, that will be all for now."

"Cross by the State?" Brown asked.

"Oh my, yes, Your Honor," Chelsea couldn't wait for this one and she plowed right in.

"Soap, huh?"

"Yes, I've brought a sample. May I show it to you?"

"By all means, please do!"

The pews in the court made an audible creek in unison as everyone leaned forward to get a look. From her $25,000 handbag, Alexa Midland pulled out a small, hinged box and opened it as if she were about to make a marriage proposal to the whole gallery. It contained a block of white and pink marbled, hand cut, soap. The presentation alone was worth the clear and ever-present sultry bullshit she was actually selling.

"That's quite something, Ms. Midland. How much does a bar like that go for?"

"Objection your honor. This is immaterial."

"Overruled, she brought in a sample. I believe we would all like to know how much this soap costs. However, Ms. Brussard, after we get the price tag, we need to move on."

"Yes, Your Honor. You may answer the question, Ms. Midland."

"Well, some pay just to look, but It's one thousand per bar."

"At that price you must not sell many of those."

"Oh honey, I sell as much as I care to."

"And because time and the whereabouts of Mr. LeBlanc is important to this case let me ask, why would it take an hour, or two, to sell a bar of soap?"

"I sell by the hour. One bar an hour."

"Ahh, I see. So, this was a one bar night for Mr. LeBlanc, correct?"

"Correct."

"Ms. Midland, I'm going to be frank with you—it's obvious you are not selling soap—you are selling sex."

The courtroom erupted in everything from laughter to knee slapping and Brown struck her gavel but said nothing.

Alexa Midland was unflappable, "No, ma'am. That would make me a prostitute and that's illegal, immoral, and it would call into question my character."

"Ma'am, if you are not selling sex, then why would someone buy soap at that price and why would it take so long to sell it?"

"Ms. Brussard, since you have been frank, please allow me to do the same; it sells itself, it doesn't take that long to convince the buyer that it's worth it, and with the rest of the time, if I'm interested, my clients and I may get to know each other a little better."

"Oh, well, how well did you know Mr. LeBlanc?"

"Do you mean that biblically or personally?"

"Personally."

"Not very well. Though, on a few occasions he did complain about his homelife."

"Ah, I see. And what were his complaints about?"

"Objection!"

"Overruled, it goes to state of mind, if this is going where I think it might. I promise to mind the storefront should the lights go out, Ms. Kennedy."

Argan nor Bradly were pleased, and Rizzo was just simply entertained. They were all getting paid, anyway.

"Please answer the question; what were his complaints about?"

"Not being cared for at home."

"In what way?"

"Romantically—sexually. According to him, there wasn't much he was happy with, and he said her behavior had become more erratic. He said he was afraid she was back on narcotics."

"OBJECTION!"

"Overruled."

"Judge this is hearsay."

"Not quite, Ms. Brussard. This is testimony about what Mr. LeBlanc was telling the witness regarding what he was experiencing at home. Not what someone told him and then he was repeating."

"Thank you, Your Honor," Chelsea said satisfactorily. "So, she had a history of taking narcotics?"

"Objection, that would be hearsay."

"Possibly. I'll sustain the objection; however, it is in evidence that she was in recovery from addiction as she said so in a recorded session with Ms. Landry."

"Thank you, Your Honor. May I rephrase?"

"You may attempt to do so."

"Did he say he was concerned she was using again?"

"He did."

"And he noted that he was concerned—and this goes to his perception—that's what was causing her behavior to become more erratic?"

"He did."

"Thank you, Ms. Midland. I believe that will be all for the moment."

"My pleasure, Ms. Brussard."

"Redirect?" Brown asked of the Defense table.

"Yes, Your Honor. Ms. Midland, did my client ever say he wanted to kill Ms. Minae?"

"Not to me, he didn't."

"Did he ever say to you that he told anyone else that he wanted to kidnap or kill Ms. Minae?"

"Not to me and not that I'm aware of."

"Did he ever say to you he wanted to harm or had ever harmed Ms. Minae?"

"No. I would never abide keeping company and especially not selling soap to a person who even had the appearance of that type of character."

"Thank you, Ms. Midland. That will be all."

"Anything else from the prosecution?" Judge Brown asked.

"Just one question, Your Honor. Ms. Midland, did Bradly LeBlanc ever say to you personally or imply what he wanted from his relationship with Ms. Minae?"

"Yes."

"And what was that? What did he tell you directly?"

"He told me that he wanted to marry her."

"Did he ever tell you that he proposed to her?"

"Yes."

"Did he tell you what her answer was?"

"Objection! Hearsay!"

"I'll rephrase; did he say anything about getting married?"

"He said he was thinking about what it would be like to have a big New Orleans style wedding but that he wasn't planning one now."

"Okay, well I know you can't tell us how she answered when he proposed. But if he wasn't planning a wedding, did he ever tell you what he was planning?"

Bradly started to bang on Argan's arm hard as a signal for him to object but Argan didn't know what he would use for the grounds to do so. He stood up quickly, anyway and shouted.

"OBJECTION, YOUR HONOR!"

"Grounds?"

Still not knowing why he was objecting nor what he was objecting to but knowing that Bradly must have told his soapy sex worker something he didn't want to get out, did his best.

"Leading the witness and the scope of the question is far too broad."

Margot was hanging on the edge of her seat with her mouth open because *this* was body language she understood easily. It was panic Bradly was showing.

"Sustained. Narrow your scope, Ms. Brussard."

"Yes, Your Honor," Chelsea said and leaned into Andrews to confer. She nodded her head in understanding as the two had decided to swing at a curveball.

"Ms. Midland..."

Argan had remained standing and Bradly had his hand at the ready to bang on Argan's side in anticipation of what response would be elicited by Brussard's next question, any question. Every second counted to beat Lexi Jade to the punch; a punch she was about to throw without meaning to. But she was a woman of honor—regardless of her soapy business—she would always tell the truth. Though, she had to talk herself into *her* "truth" to keep them in line with *her* beliefs, from time to time.

"…would you please tell the jury, and whatever the answer is will be fine, what, if anything, did Bradly LeBlanc share he wanted from the relationship with Connie Minae after he proposed."

Bradly started banging on Argan's side again.

"Objection," Argan said sheepishly.

"Grounds?"

"Again, scope is too broad."

"Sustained. Brussard, you got one more shot at this."

Everyone at the Defense table was at the ready and armed to the teeth for whatever may come, though there was no time to ask Bradly what it would be.

Chelsea Brussard took a breath and let it out slowly then asked a specific question she didn't know the answer to. It was one that could be career making or a total flop. But based on Bradly LeBlanc's behavior and the evidence that was overwhelmingly against him, at this point, she went for broke, "Ms. Midland…did Bradly LeBlanc ever tell you he wanted Connie out of his life?"

"He said he wanted her gone for good."

Argan shouted, "OBJECTION! OBJECTION! OBJECTION!"

But it was too late. He had faltered. He was too slow. He had made the mistake of trying to think of the answer to, what would have been, the judge's next question regarding grounds. And, as it turns out, it wouldn't have mattered.

"Overruled!" was the Judge's call on the play. She shouted it like an umpire over the roar of the crowd and her own gavel. The gallery was so loud that it made the courtroom sound like the home team just made a buzzer beating goal…and it was a championship game.

The Defense never knew this utterance was a risk because Bradly never told his team he had said it. As for the prosecution, it was watching Bradly panic and a bit of dumb luck.

"Thank you, Ms. Midland. I have no further questions, Your Honor."

Kathy Kennedy was still standing, as was the whole Defense team.

"Any further questions, Defense?" Brown asked after the courtroom came to a hush.

"Yes, Your Honor. Ms. Midland, you have testified, under oath, that our client, Bradly LeBlanc was with you from seven until 8:15pm on the night in question, is that correct?"

"Yes."

"Is that still your testimony?"

"Yes."

"No further questions," Kennedy finished as she sat down, knowing her efforts had amounted to little because if Brad didn't tell them he said that he wanted Connie "gone for good", and he hadn't, then what else hadn't he told them?

Not only would the Defense team never find out what Bradly knew, nor didn't know, nor say, but by the end of the trial—and

Brad's life—none of it would matter. But most would all soon come to know a *version* of the truth.

And though only one person would ever know all of it; all of *that* truth. Margot, Joni, and Connie would all be neck and neck in second place.

34

A Peek at the Peak

The Court suggested a 15-minute recess, but the defense asked for thirty, which was granted. No one knew any better, but for that entire 30 minutes, Bradly was grilled by his own team behind a closed and locked door. During that time, it was decided that Bradly Ray LeBlanc would not be taking the witness stand, they would not be presenting any more evidence, and they had none, anyway. All they had was soap and an hour and a half of alibi—an alibi that kept him only a few minutes from the crime scene.

Bradly maintained his innocence with his team—as he would for the rest of his days to anyone that would listen. The walls were closing in and everyone behind that locked door knew it. Bradly admitted to nothing other than saying that he wanted her gone for good. He reassured his team he didn't mean for her exit to be via death. That meant little to them now, though. However, they were going to throw a Hail Mary. And even if someone caught it in the endzone as the game clock ran to zero, it was most likely only going to end in a tie game. But at least that tie game meant a hung jury.

The Court's recess was over. Everyone had already piled back into the courtroom and Jerome called the court to order. After all were reseated, the Defense dropped their bombshell that was nothing more than a dud.

"Your Honor, the Defense rests," Argan took the lead and the hit. Though, for this defense team, none of their careers would be any worse for the ware. No team would have wanted to defend a client with this much evidence leaning against them.

When Argan argued earlier that he believed his client had been framed, he didn't believe that—not when he said it, and even less now. His job, like the rest of the team's, was to make sure the evidence had been solidly collected; that all the bags and tags were perfect—that the science wasn't in question. It was also to raise doubt in the minds of the jurors. He believed his team could do that most in their closing arguments. That boulder was going to fall on Kathy, but he had faith in her.

Kathy and Argan had worked together only once before but she was known all around the firm to be quick on her feet. All they needed was a hung jury and then they would back out of this case, move on, and never care again who went on to defend Bradly the second time around. Promises had been made in the Defense's opening arguments that could never be fulfilled now—nor ever. Their efforts had performed like a cocky surgeon that tells the whole family that the patient will pull through, then begins surgery only to find the cancer has spread in ways and in areas they had never dreamed of. Now they needed to suture up the patient and give them over to a social worker who would be tasked to find good hospice care.

Judge Brown spoke up, she wanted the circus that this case had brought with it, and would continue to bring, off her docket, "Prosecution, you may begin your closing arguments."

Chelsea stood with the knowledge that both sides knew they needed a female in closing; they needed to sway the jury one way or the other. It's considered tactless by some to play the game this way. It's considered by some who are not in the profession—like a Joan Pierse—to be crass. But in the profession, itself, it's considered a necessity to do so. One woman to play to the others in the jury as the voice of the victim. The other side needed one to play as a woman who trusts the accused and thus, so should they.

Though the prosecution had been ready for closing arguments since day one because the evidence they had was so overwhelming, Chelsea Brussard wanted the "oh, gee whiz" effect and went all in, "Your Honor, this is rather sudden as we thought we'd have more time to prepare our closing. We believed we would hear from the Defendant, and other witnesses because the Defense said so very confidently in their opening. However, we're willing to go forward with our closing now, if we must."

"Excellent, Ms. Brussard. Please proceed," Brown said with that perpetual eyebrow raise as she knew what Che-Che was really saying. She was telling the jury that they didn't get their promised sideshow; she was saying that Bradly was exercising his Fifth Amendment right because he was as guilty as a henhouse fox.

Chelsea "Che-Che" Brussard picked up her legal pad, walked over to the podium, laid down her notes that she didn't need, then walked over to the jury box to begin hammering nails in Bradly's self-made coffin.

"Ladies and gentlemen of the jury, I'm as shocked as many of you might be. We were promised a tremendous show of force from the Defense yesterday. And, during some of their

274

cross of our expert witnesses, I believe we got some of that. However, we also believe that you will find that our mountain of evidence—the one the Defense poked a bit of fun at during their opening—only grew taller as this truncated trial went on. We also believe that this, and the damning statement shared with us by Ms. Midland not even an hour ago, has put you, the jury, in the position to see the truth. The truth that the Defendant, Mr. Bradly LeBlanc was a man that—in the State's opinion—was clearly distraught that his girlfriend, Connie Minae, had turned down his marriage proposal. We know this from the video shared with us by her therapist, Ms. Margot Landry. We also know from those videos that Connie believed that he was controlling her financially, emotionally, and then, physically."

Brussard paused and looked around the box before continuing, "The State believes you will deliberate thoughtfully and come to the same conclusion, the Defendant, who is clearly used to having the finest of things in his life and being in control of all of them, had found himself not in control of the thing he may have wanted most—Connie's love and affection. What he wanted from most from Connie was so out of his reach that he had to buy soap weekly."

Brussard started to pace, "And by the way, that is not meant to impugn the character of Ms. Midland as it was never established that anything other than soap was looked at nor touched during those Friday night meetings. What it does say, however, is that Bradly LeBlanc was willing to pay one thousand an hour for the company of a listening ear—and listen she did."

Brussard stopped and looked at the jury again, "Let me also say that this part of our closing arguments is ALSO not to suggest that Ms. Minae should have been doing anything

275

different. She didn't want to marry the Defendant. Ladies and gentlemen, for some people, to marry someone is to wholly possess them. Not H-O-L-Y, but to possess them entirely. It's the final act for those who need to possess a person completely," Che-Che paused as if she were thinking. But it wasn't about having a second thought, it was to deliver it with a slight bit of flair, "On second thought, there is one deeper but less meaningful way to possess someone. It would be to own their soul forever. Ms. Minae's own words from beyond wherever she is right now—and that resting place is a location only the Defendant knows—is that she was not to be possessed. We have presented the evidence to show this. Though, it appears he wholly possessed her, after all. Possessing someone in life is one thing, but to possess them their entire afterlife, is much deeper."

Chelsea started pacing again and counting on her fingers, "Blood, the connective tissue of the body and—in that amount—is the body itself. It's no different than if we had only found her heart. Could she have had a heart transplant, in this scenario, and be living on a beach somewhere with a stack of Mr. LeBlanc's money? Sure, she could, I suppose. But does that make sense? Had we found both of her legs and nothing else, we could surmise that she is still alive. Had we found both arms, we could surmise that, as well. But that amount of blood loss means we do have a body. No question. She was 5'4" and 110 pounds. That amount of blood loss would mean there was hardly any left. Our experts estimated by the blood evidence found, that she had lost over four pints of blood. That would cause her to pass out, go into organ failure, and die without immediate medical attention. The only *attention* we have evidence she received was that of a blade," she held up a second finger.

276

"So, not only do we have a body of connective tissue, but we also have the blade—the knife from the kitchen. Ladies and gentlemen, who shows up to murder someone and not bring their own knife? Unless it is their own knife from their own kitchen, of course—the Defendant's kitchen. Forensics experts who examined that knife testified it was Connie's blood. It was concluded definitively through DNA testing to be hers. And where was that knife found? It was found in the car of the Defendant, Bradly Ray LeBlanc."

Chelsea moved closer to the jury box and held up a third finger, "We have the mask. And where was it found? Yet again, in the trunk of the Defendant's car. And in that mask?" Another finger went up and she moved closer still to the jury, "A DNA matched hair of the Defendant's," then another finger, "We have the shoes that match the defendant's size and an empty spot in his closet next to other sneakers. What else do those shoes match? Sole prints that are in the bloody drag marks. Those shoes were in the car, as well. So was the blanket—a blanket that has been identified as identical to one seen in pictures taken from older video footage of the house. We were able to obtain that because Bradly had not yet turned off his own cameras to conceal what he was going to do to Connie on the night in question."

Che-Che held up a ninth finger. "And then there is the video itself. The video shared with us by Connie's own psychotherapist, Ms. Landry, of a masked figure. The same mask found in the car possessed by the Defendant."

Chelsea was so close to the jury box that she put her hands down on the railing and finished, "That masked figure running down the hall to grab Ms. Minae, throw her to the ground, and with 2% worth of green eyes said, "'I'm going to kill you'".

And that's exactly what he did, ladies and gentlemen. The Defendant killed Connie Minae."

The Defense team had to hold down and console Bradly. Margot could tell he wanted to rise and say something but, she had no idea what. He was clearly more emotional than he had been through the whole first day and now this morning. *Well, except when his lady of the soap sold him out,* Margot thought.

"All the evidence is there, folks. All of it. The eyes, the mask, the blood, the knife, the shoes, the shoeprints, the hair, the blood on the blanket in his car. The car that came down the road not long after, the State believes, he drove Connie in her SUV up the road to a place still yet to be determined. Yes, all in the car of a man of many possessions. The only thing he couldn't possess was Connie Minae. And now, he's done that, too."

Bradly LeBlanc went to shoot up out of his chair. Rizzo on one side and Argan on the other kept him in his seat. When they did, he growled in a low and animalistic tone. Rizzo clapped his hand over Bradly's mouth. Margot got goosebumps when she heard the commotion.

"Thank you, ladies and gentlemen of the jury," Che-Che concluded by not looking over her shoulder but a simple nudge of her neck while saying, "And that noise you hear, the one behind me. That noise is of a man possessed."

Judge Brown spoke up quickly, "Defense, please present your closing arguments."

That task was left to the only person not holding Bradly still—Kathy Kennedy.

"Thank you, Your Honor. Ladies and gentlemen, I'm not going to ask you what would possibly *possess* a man of my client stature to care enough about a marriage proposal that he would kill over it. That is, if it did indeed happen at all. Because we only have the testimony of Ms. Midland to suggest that the proposal occurred. Mr. LeBlanc could have any number of women. As a matter of fact, since he's been jailed pending the conclusion of this case when you set this framed man free, Mr. LeBlanc has received numerous proposals of his own from women all around the country. And some men, too, just to be inclusive and to tell the whole truth, of course. No, if possession was what was on the mind of Mr. LeBlanc, that would have been no problem. But possession was not his goal."

Now Kathy started to pace, "Okay, so we have all that evidence pointing to my client. Fine. We concede every bit of it, no question. 'Strange' you note to yourselves? Strange that we not refute the evidence one piece at a time? Not strange to the Defense, not strange at all. Because we continue to contend that our client was framed. We have said so since our opening arguments and although we may never know *who* framed our client, let me tell you why we believe he was."

After she stopped pacing, Kennedy looked at each and every juror as she spoke, "Are you all going to believe that any murderer who's as intelligent as our client drives Connie's own SUV, with all the evidence in it AND her body, if she is in fact dead, an SUV we still don't know the whereabouts of, and just leaves it somewhere? It's not a needle in a haystack, folks. Or he takes her body out of that SUV and leaves it somewhere else? Not only that, but this person takes most of the incriminating evidence out of the one vehicle that we can't find and stuffs it in the trunk of their own car only to drive it right back to the murder scene and toss the lead detective the key fob allowing him to poke around warrantless? Does that sound like a multi-millionaire who made his money by using his brains?

And why would my client do it right on camera with green eyes staring right back at us? Pfft. This is preposterous, folks. Green eyes, indeed."

Kathy started pacing again, "Contacts to make my client a suspect, we say. Video at just the right time to be seen and recorded, we say. Frunk full of evidence to complete the frame job, we say. Knife from the kitchen block, they say, when a killer could have brought any weapon they wanted to. Whomever this killer or abductor or frame artist this was must have had to use it to set the scene later because we never see that knife in the therapy video. Now, we say it wasn't used but, rather, 'have someone drop you off at the house, climb in the window, and do your best to Ms. Connie', we say. Leave a mound of evidence, we say. His blood on the wall…a swipe? But no cuts nor abrasions. Bizarre, we say. Enough is enough, we say! Ladies and gentlemen of the jury, what do you say? Would any of you perpetrate a crime such as this and leave this kind of evidence laying around and, what's worse, leave it in your own possession? Would any of you be foolhardy enough to put evidence in your car and drive it back TO THE SCENE OF THE CRIME…AND WHAT CRIME? WE! DON'T! KNOW! And neither does the prosecution. Connective tissue, indeed. Nonsense! No body, no crime, we say!"

Kathy Kennedy pushed her fingers together at the tips and put them up to her chest, "Thank you all. We know you will come back with a not guilty verdict because Bradly LeBlanc is not a stupid man. He didn't get rich by being stupid. And none of you will do the wrong thing and vote guilty because none of you were picked for this jury because we, NOR THE PROSECUTION, believed you were stupid. Common sense tells you something is wrong here. But it's your intelligence that tells you this was a frame from the start."

Kennedy sat and folded her hands while looking straight ahead. If the pay wasn't so good, she thought, she would almost feel guilty at having, again, raised the specter of a frame job when everything she knew about this case told her otherwise. Bradly's behavior was also telling her something was very wrong here.

Judge Brown looked over at the prosecution table and asked, "Since you, the State have the burden of proof, you may have one more closing argument."

"Yes, Your Honor," Che-Che said coolly and swaggered over to the jury, "As your intelligence tells all of you, getting love letters in jail is nothing new. BTK, Jeffery Dahmer, Manson, Gary Ridgeway, Ed Kemper, heck, even Ed Gains, no doubt. They all got love letters, dirty pictures, and Hallmark cards while they were in jail and even convicted with all of the bones of their victims exposed. Please! No, what most of us want is what we can't have. We want what has value. And the harder something is to achieve the more we want it, the more valuable it appears to be. Yes, we all want what we can't have but most of us are not willing to kill for it. But Bradly LeBlanc? He wanted Connie Minae and, in all ways, possible. No job, no friends, no freedom. But he couldn't have her hand, so he took her life! And our evidence? Yes, they must concede it because it's overwhelming. They say, 'no body, no crime'. The rule of law is corpus delicti. No literal body is required for a murder to be proven. But framed? It might help to have someone they want to point to who has done that to their client. Have they named anyone? No!"

Che-Che stood and looked at the jury box as she continued, "There are a few stories that *our* evidence tells. One story could be that the crime was clumsy and not clearly thought out. The only evidence the D.A.'s office is surprised we didn't find was a list of things he needed to remember to do. You know, like that murder many years ago in Metairie where a man ambushed and killed his wife after her therapy appointment—left a to-do list in his trailer he was having to stay in after he was put out of the marital home," several jurors nodded, indicating that they were familiar with the case that Che-Che was referencing.

"Okay, so, the Defense has the right to raise the specter of framing, and we have the right to refute it. We could have raised an objection during their closing arguments as it assumed facts not in evidence—it's a 'what if' scenario they raised. Since they brought it up, I'll answer it with another mystery; what did Bradly do? Did he frame a guilty man? What if that guilty man is himself? Let's think about it—if I wanted to get away with a murder and thought that the evidence that was left in my haste was so sloppy—shoe prints and whatnot—why not just keep as much evidence as possible and leave it in my car, pay the best lawyers around, and posit the frame job conclusion to raise enough doubt in your minds?"

Chelsea paused and looked smugly at the jury, "I mean, the known romantic partner connected to most any decedent is often raised to the top of the suspect list immediately. If I were Bradly LeBlanc and, being a smart man, knew that I would be the primary suspect and then knowing I left a sloppy crime scene in my haste and in my house, why not frame myself? I mean, if I believed I had a good alibi witness in Ms. Midland, maybe who I paid a sum like, oh, I dunno, let me just pull one from the air, nearly a quarter million dollars to testify where I was during a murder that I knew was caught on video, why not? Why not take the frame all the way? Or maybe part of the plot to frame himself was in play the whole time and that would explain the therapy video—maybe it was just a little insurance. Then, I just take it all the way to the conclusion and dump all that evidence in my car. Do any of you, ladies and gentlemen, know how many murders are solved because of a poor clean up job? I'll tell you; it's a lot. Why not forget about any clean-up at all? Maybe Bradly felt there was enough evidence pointing his way he might as well point *all of it* his way and claim someone framed him with planted evidence."

Chelsea was nearing her close, "The Defense is correct. None of you were given the responsibility to be on this jury because any of us thought you were stupid. But we also don't believe it would take a rocket scientist—nor a financial manager—to see through this foolishness. Mr. LeBlanc is guilty of murder. And he is sitting atop our mountain of evidence that proves it. He's sitting there and simply waiting for you to shout up to him, 'GUILTY'!"

And with that, Judge Brown sent back the jury for deliberations, and everyone began to wait. Margot rushed to Joni, eager to stay away from the media.

35

Not Seeing Leads To Believing

Margot got to Joni's house around 1:30pm and filled her in on the day of trial watching. Joni was surprised but not shocked because she had learned the day before about all the evidence that was stacked up against Bradly.

"To be honest with you, honey, I'm glad it seems to be over this quick. I've had about all I can stand of hearing his name and anything to do with the whole sordid mess. Hung jury or not, at least it would be outta the news for a while, sheesh. Anyway, how are you holding up, toots?"

"Meh, I'm good, I guess. I still can't shake…"

"Oh, honey, I love you dearly but not that again. The picture?"

"Yeah, I just can't get the image out of my head but it's not clear enough for me to make out what's wrong with the picture they showed in court. Jonesy, look, all I ever saw was whatever was on the computer screen. And it was always in the same place. That fuckin' creepy-ass door, the hallway, Connie's smug face…"

"Ooo, speaking ill of the dead, are we?"

284

"Well, is she Joni? Is she dead? I mean I know of no one, including you who seems to think there was blood already on the floor when she hit the deck. But what if? What if she set the whole thing up?"

"Yeah, enough blood so that she would be dead just laid out on the floor for some creeper to help her cover up her own disappearance. Sure thing. Sounds logical."

"Look, I get it, it sounds stupid. But unless I get to see that picture one last time that the Defense put up on the screen during trial, I won't let this go."

"Why don't you just ask them for the damned thing?" Joni said with the wave of her hand like it would be the most easy and logical thing to do.

"Pfft, yeah right! They already think I'm a kook and they…well, humm, maybe once a verdict comes down. Maybe I can sweet talk one of 'em… I mean Bolt thinks I'm a clown, but Andrews doesn't know me. Or maybe I can go to Chelsea."

"A little woman to woman, heart to heart? That might work."

"Maybe I should tell them that I concluded they are screwing based on their body language in court and that I'll keep it to myself."

"You know, years ago there was a book that came out called, *How To Win Friends And Influence People*…you should read it sometime."

"Nice…look, I wouldn't do that, I'm just saying…Oh, I really don't know what I'm saying. I just know I need to see that picture."

"Maybe you should just open your laptop and watch the videos again. Maybe the answer is in there. Or maybe, just maybe, the prosecution already gave you the answer and now we just need to wait for the jury."

"I might as well look at them for a bit. I feel like I've seen them so many times that I can't see the forest for the trees. Oh, that reminds me, I need to write an email to Mike and Prestin to say thanks to them for the time off they afforded me. Fuck, but soon I'll need to go back to work and definitely back to therapy."

"Well, one outta two ain't bad."

"Yeah. I'm so happy you don't have to go back. But I'm going to be so lonely without you there."

"Well, I've been giving that some thought. You are more than welcome to live with me if you like."

"Oh Jonesy, I couldn't impose like that..."

"No imposition. And if it were, I wouldn't have offered."

"I dunno. Let me think about it. And what about the little creamsicle?"

"Oh, honey, you have been in your own world so much you haven't noticed he's my cat now. He'll be going nowhere. So, think of it this way, you'd be moving in with him and not me."

"I'm not going to tell you I love the idea. But I do."

"Well, we can settle on it later. Me and Adler may change our minds, anyway. And not to tempt you but I'm making 10 once filets tonight...so, no pressure."

"You're the fuckin' best."

"All the husbands said the same thing."

Margot was scrubbing through all the videos, one by one. Joni had the television on mute, reading a several month-old copy of Vanity Fair, sipping tea, and petting Adler. Margot just couldn't find what she was looking for and was even now questioning if the dark splotch on the floor was anything more than a video artifact and not blood. Going with her gut was becoming harder after the prosecution had tied up the case so tight that it was clear to the Defense just how tight, they just gave in after the soapbox admission of what Bradly had said about wanting Connie gone out of his life. *Did he say permanently?* Margot wondered.

Margot had been so lost in her own thoughts and her own videos she didn't notice the breaking news coming on, but Joni did because she had been waiting for it, "Don't look now, honey, but I believe we have a verdict!" Joni said with excitement. Adler got spooked and ran off. Joni leapt to her feet even though she didn't need to move to hit the mute button to get the sound back on. She had never let that remote leave her side the whole afternoon.

"...so we go live to the New Orleans Courthouse with our own Travis Warren. Travis..."

"Thanks Ron. Well the jury was out less than an hour and a half and have returned a guilty verdict—murder in the second degree. Close sources believed it was a crime of passion, although, they also believed that planning was involved. The jury still decided to forgo murder one and went with the lesser charge. It still carries a mandatory sentence of life in prison without possibility of parole. The accused, Bradly LeBlanc reported shouted at the Judge as he was being led away to serve that mandatory sentence. As the cuffs were being put on the well-dressed LeBlanc, he reported shouted, I didn't kill that no good, expiative! She set me up!" Judge Brown, the sitting judge in this case, ordered LeBlanc out of her courtroom immediately and tacked on another six months to an already lifelong sentence for his outburst and for her good measure. Both sides declined interviews citing the inevitable appellate process that the Defense promised they would bring soon, as they were, quote, going to the office now to being writing, unquote. Back to you, Ron."

"Thank you, Travis. We will bring you more developments as they unfold. Again, Bradly LeBlanc, found guilty of murder two and received a mandatory life sentence without the possibility of parole."

Joni allowed her eyes to leave the screen and looked over at her best friend, "Margot, shut your mouth, you're letting the flies in."

Margot sat at the table with the look of shock as the speed and heft of the sentence washed over her. She looked back down at her computer and saw the masked monster that just went into a holding cell awaiting transfer to Angola prison.

Margot slammed the laptop lid down and exclaimed, "Fuck it, I'm going to get that damned picture, and I don't care who I gotta shtup to get it."

"There's that rebel I love about you!"

Margot rushed down to the D.A.'s office and asked to speak with Gil Andrews. The front desk called up to his office, and they put the call through. Margot heard all the exuberant celebration in the background.

"Yes, Ms. Landry, I take it you heard. Good job on your testimony. And let me be the first to say that this case wouldn't have gone as well if you hadn't recorded those sessions. We can never repay you."

"Well, Mr. Andrews, maybe you can."

Within a few minutes, Margot was in the office of Gil Andrews. It was stacked with banker's boxes and papers everywhere.

"Now tell me again what it is that you want, Ms. Landry."

"There was a picture. It was evidence that the State, you and Ms. Brussard—lovely lady—and smart, too…anyway, it was State's evidence, but it seems that the Defense put it up on the screen, too. I just wanted to see it again. There was just something about it."

"What, like a memento or something you're wanting? Hell, I'd sign it for you, but I can't give that kind of thing out."

"Oh?"

"Yeah, I mean, we know they're going to appeal and that takes years to get through. If he's granted a new trial on some technicality, well, they are going to want that. Hell, we may even need it."

"Well, maybe if I could just take a look at it here."

"Pfft, sure, if I could find it," Just then, Brussard poked her head in the doorway and gave Gill, then Margot, a look. She started to speak before taking her eyes off of Margot, "Gil, you coming to join the celebration…and hello, what was it? Oh, yes, Ms. Landry. So nice to see you again so soon."

"Likewise."

Gil appeared to grow nervous, "Um, yes, I sure am. Just finishing up a little business with Landry, here."

"Huh…well, don't be too long."

"Nope, ha, not at all."

Che-Che shut the door but not all the way.

Margot looked back at Gil, "Well, I wouldn't want to keep you from Ms. Brussard too long," Margot finished by pointing to the copy machine, "That thing work?"

In under thirty minutes, Margot had her picture but refused to look at it in the car. She wanted her and Joni to do it as a team. God, she just loved her some Joni. She made life more exciting.

36

Now You See Me, Now You Don't

Joni met Margot at the door, "Did ya get the goods, toots?"

Margot held it up with a shit-eating grin. It was so close to Joni's face she couldn't see anything but colors, so she leaned back and focused, "Ew, I don't even know if I will let you bring that bloody thing into the house."

"Like hell you won't!" and Margot went through the door and passed Joni with a bounce.

The ladies had wine, cheese, the laptop, and the picture all spread out, "Okay, let's see what we got. It's a photocopy, of course, but it should be enough to satisfy my curiosity."

"God, I hope so. Let's put this shit to bed."

"Trust me, no one wants to do that more than I d..HEY!" Margot said with a snap of her fingers and scared Joni half to death.

"Je-SUS!"

"Sorry, I had an idea. I'm going to take screen shots and send them to you via email, and you print them out on your desktop!"

"Okay okay, just don't scare the bejesus out of me like that again."

"Sorry! I'm just so fuckin' excited! I need to put this in a file in my head so I can move on. I need closure to this shit."

Minutes later, all five pictures were laid out. Joni and Margot took each one and laid it next to the crime scene photo. Both ladies' excited eyes scanned the evidence over and over. This went on for an hour. Joni kept looking with her readers on and Margot with Joni's old metal and glass magnifier.

Nothing.

Neither one of them saw anything different.

"Honey, I'm so sorry. Honestly, I can't keep looking at all that gory shit. However, I'm getting hungry. How rare you want your steak after looking at that river of red?"

"FUCK!"

"Okay, well done it is."

"No, I'm sorry. I was just so fuckin' sure it was there."

"What was there?"

"Something, anything, everything!"

"Honey, maybe putting this to bed means that you admit to yourself that there is just that—nothing there."

"Maybe so. Make mine medium-plus."

"Honey, I'm a good cook but that is a tall order."

"Surprise me."

Joni busied herself in the kitchen with butter and rosemary, salt and pepper. Margot busied herself by simply staring off into the distance. Adler was mewing in the kitchen smelling all the goodness that his Aunt Joni was tending to.

Margot, lost in thought, felt defeated. But at least she had done her due diligence. It didn't help, though. That nagging feeling in the pit of her stomach was still there. Maybe it was just hunger. She hadn't eaten all day. At least the baked potatoes were smelling good.

"Dinner will be ready in about 15 minutes." Joni called from the kitchen. "Just seared the steaks, they go in the oven, and then five minutes of rest. Then, sheer perfection, Margs!"

Margot was sorting the pictures in order and stacking them as she cleared the table. Joni was pulling out the serving dishes, plates, and flatware.

As Margot stared, one by one, in timeline order, something caught her attention. She shuffled the pictures and looked again. Then faster still. She grabbed the magnifying glass and there it was.

"JONI!" Margot yelled and heard a dish hit the floor. Margot ran to the doorway that led to the kitchen. She saw Joni standing near a mosaic of broken plate pieces, "Kiddo, I thought I told you not to scare me like that again."

"Joni, trust me, you need to see this."

"Let me get these pieces up first."

"Joni, I need you to see this now!"

"Okay, okay."

Margot disappeared from the doorway. She was already standing over the pictures in a stack, "Go through this stack one by one. It ends with the crime scene photo. Then tell me what you see."

Joni retrieved her readers from her dress pocket while keeping an unimpressed look on her face as she did so, "Alright, let's see it," Joni started to flip through the pictures.

"No, ma'am, not like that. Take each one, look for one or two seconds, then lay them face down each at a time 'til you get to the last."

"Sir, yes sir!" Joni gave a salute.

Margot was bouncing up and down with a huge grin.

Joni did as instructed and got next to the last picture with Margot getting more and more excited with each picture Joni put down. She got to the last one and looked. She only saw that big bloody mess, "I'm sorry hon, I just don't see it."

"Not yet you don't, but you will."

"Just show me."

"It's no fun that way, Joni!"

"It's no fun this way, either."

"Do it again."

Joni did it again and got to the last picture, "Shit!"

"YOU SEE IT!"

"NO, THE STEAKS!"

Joni rushed to the kitchen and the noise of metal and the stove clanking about. Joni put the steaks she had saved just in time on a board to rest and came back to the dining room.

Margot had the magnifying glass on the final session picture, "Give me your reading glasses, please."

"Your eyes getting bad, too? They say it happens at 40, ya know," Joni quipped with the truth as she handed them over. Margot snatched them from her hand out of excitement and laid them down on the picture of the crime scene. She had placed the magnifying glass on other picture, but in the same location. Both were on an item that was placed atop the part of the counter that was dropped down. It was where there was a bowl full of loose change.

"Now tell me what you see."

Joni looked down and saw what Margot had seen subliminally before but now in full view. Joni looked up and Margot had that stupid grin again.

Both ladies said in unison, "Keys."

Then Joni burst her bubble, "Yeah, they left in Connie's truck. So…"

"Joni, there is no key fob on the keyring. Her truck was a late model Escalade. They haven't made one of those without a fob in decades."

"Then they are his keys, he took them with him."

"Porsche 911, again late model. Twenty or more years' worth of fobs."

"So, they were there and then moved elsewhere. I'm sorry honey, I just don't get it."

"Joni, those keys are there every session, look. Here, here, here, here, and then they are still there when he pushes her off the stool. But when they take the crime photo, they're gone. No fob! So those keys are for neither one of their vehicles. Not to mention, his car wasn't even there at the time. So, who's keys are they and why are they gone?"

"I think I know why?"

"Why!" Margot was excited. She had Joni riding shotgun in the front seat of this mystery machine now.

"You told me that fine Detective Bolt shared with you that the safe had missing money. Maybe it was the key to the safe."

Margot slumped and said, "Well, I mean, I guess so. Don't they have combinations?"

"Yes, but some models have a key in case you forget the combo or it doesn't work. Some are push-button and if the batteries die, they have a key to those types, too."

Margot just looked at the floor. Joni hugged her and then went and got the steaks plated.

After dinner and light conversation where Joni had convinced Margot that she had solved the mystery and that it wasn't very satisfying to either one of them, Joni said, "You sit here, and I'll pick up everything and put on some coffee."

Margot looked up sheepishly, "Thanks, that would be nice. I appreciate that. I just feel so beaten down."

"It's okay, here, feel free to look at the keys in every picture. Who knows, maybe you will see something more interesting in that bowl. Maybe something else on the mail counter."

"That's what they call those!"

"Yeah, see there, there is a place where a phone used to hang. It's where the phonebook would be and people would sit there and do bills and whatnot. Maybe there's some bills missing."

Margot, looked up with a feigned sad face, "Not funny."

Joni shrugged, went into the kitchen where she busied herself with dishes while Margot looked at each picture of the bowl of change with the set of keys in every picture but the last. She called to Joni who was still in the kitchen after about ten minutes of her loading the dishwasher as the smell of coffee filled the air.

"Maybe *this* means something."

Joni rolled her eyes to herself and stopped just short of reconsidering the offer for Margot to live with her.

"There's something etched into the head one of the keys, but it's hard to make out because they are always in a different position. Then it hit Margot, "Joni, why would someone go into a safe every day?"

Joni thought and then said, "Maybe it's because they always store a nice watch or ring or something in there whenever they get home. Maybe someone tossing change in the bowl disrupts the position of the keys."

"Maybe, I guess. Well, and I did only see her once a week except for that one time where I saw her that one week twice. I guess if the safe was faulty, like you said earlier, they would just use the key every day or week or who knows how many times."

"Yeah, it's probably just a simple explanation."

Margot persisted, "Still, there is some sort of something scratched in this one brass key. But I can't make out what it is. The picture is so grainy and in two of the pictures you can't even see that key at all."

"You want a chocolate éclair with your coffee?"

"Yes. Yes, I do."

"Then step away from the pictures."

"Yes, ma'am."

Joni smiled to herself, went back to the kitchen, and started to plate dessert.

37

All Roles Played

Six Weeks Earlier

Gary Wayne Duratas peered through the vertical blinds that hung in his living room window while waiting for his girlfriend of the last few months to show up. Earlier, during the planning stage, she decided for the both of them that she would park in the free-standing garage in the back of the house. Gary had taken half a day off from work to make sure everything on his end was set. It was 5pm on Friday afternoon.

At 5:05pm his girlfriend backed her black Escalade towards the garage. Not moving from the window, Gary used the remote to his garage door opener to give her access. As the garage opened, she continued to back in. Once the entire length of her vehicle was inside, Gary used the clicker again and shut the door. Everything, thus far, was going as planned.

Gary waited, as he had been instructed earlier, at least five more minutes until finally going out to his garage. Neither he nor his lover wanted anyone to notice she had come there. It was her first time, though, it wouldn't be her last. And Gary planned for the two of them to be together forever. He was head over heels.

He checked his watch. It was time; 5:10pm.

Gary lived out in the sticks, as it is often called when one lives in a rural area. And still, there is always that nosey neighbor who stands by the fence, waiting for conversation. Roger Henson was his name. He was Gary's neighbor. But he wasn't even so much as mowing his acreage this afternoon. Gary had a few acres of his own and lived in a house willed to him. He was an only child. Both his parents had died in an accident. Their boat had apparently sunk in the Gulf of Mexico, and it was never found. But they washed up days later. Mr. Duratas after about a week and Mrs. Duratas several days after that. A duck hunter found the Mr. and a fisherman found the Mrs.

That had been several years ago and between then and now, Gary just couldn't bring himself to get rid of the house and acreage. He only made around seventy grand a year, but no matter—everything was already paid for long before the elderly couple drowned when their cabin cruiser sank. Gary took the gift they left him as payment for how abusive and neglectful they could be because they were perfectionists and never wanted to be parents, anyway.

Gary gripped the handle of the Igloo cooler he had been instructed to load up and went out to the detached garage where his girlfriend had parked. He went around to the door on the right-hand side and unlocked it. It was stark inside after the daylight was shut out when he closed the door. The Escalade back hatch opened and created enough light for him to see that there was a blanket in the back for him to lay under. Without a word from either of them he did so, as planned, and clicked the door opener that had never left his palm. Dying sunlight slowly filled the entire space—a sunrise from a sunset.

His girlfriend drove out and, while he hid under the blanket, he could feel the front tires first, then back ones leave the slightly elevated concrete slab floor and return to gravel. As it did, with the press of his thumb, he closed the door of the large structure again when she began to drive the two back to her place.

"I take it I don't have to ask, but you brought my shit, right?"

His voice muffled from under the blanket, Gary responded, "You know I did. It's the most important part."

"No," she said, "you are the most important part. Well, you and maybe Margot."

"I think maybe *you* might be the most important part of this plan. Almost all of it is your idea. That fucker's gonna get just what he deserves, ain't he?"

"Surely will! And then we will be free to start our new life. A little name change, a little plastic surgery will go a long way for me, and you can just be you."

"And we get married?"

"Oh yeah, you are definitely the man I've been looking for," She was lying the way she always did. She really had no intentions of marrying anyone—ever.

"I know *you* don't like to say it but I'm going to—I love you, Connie."

"I know. Who else would be willing to do this for me?"

Once back at Connie's and Brad's house, it had gotten darker. Daylight savings time was still a week away. But her session with Margot was nearing, and there was much to do—costumes and set dressing must be perfect.

Brad's Porsche, as usual, wasn't there—it never was at that time on a Friday. Irrespective of what Connie had told Margot, the truth was he had never come straight home on Friday evenings. He would leave work in the CBD and go directly to his escort's house and then play cards with the boys afterwords. Connie had known this for several months. The whole dance was Swiss clockworks. She had done her homework and gotten an 'A'. He had been tracked for, what amounted to, a few thousand miles in that Porsche because she had put a device under that car long ago, she knew everywhere he went and when he was going to be in that driveway.

Connie had gotten the idea that she had landed a big fish in Brad. And though she never wanted to get married, she was going to take his cash slowly over time. She was even willing to play along as the dutiful girlfriend. But when she found out he was seeing someone else, escort or not, she was never going to allow any competition. She stopped having any kind of sexual contact with Brad once she knew where he was going and what he was doing before the cards and chips hit the table at whoever's house was hosting the game that night.

She would quickly come to think of that escort as a diseased whore. And Connie took as much pride in her vaginal health as she did everything else that she set her mind to. She may have come from what some might think of as trash, but she swore she'd never be poor again. Though she made some untaxable cash working at the swanky coffeeshop, it also set her up nicely to meet plenty of easy marks. She felt like she had been played a fool with Brad, though.

Connie had never allowed herself to care about Bradly any more than the dozen or so others she had taken for a ride. She couldn't allow it. She was incapable. She was a psychopath but had not yet come to that conclusion. What she had concluded was that she had found another easy mark in Gary. *Yes, he will do nicely* she thought when he started chatting her up in the true crime section of a bookstore.

Connie opened the back hatch of her black SUV and didn't even look around to see if anyone was watching. She was overly confident and that's what happens when one is a psychopath or sociopath, for that matter. They also tend to be able to talk their way out of almost anything. That caused her to be arrogant in execution but swift in conversation.

She lifted the blanket and Gary looked like a lost puppy; he was still gripping the cooler handle. She gave a tick of her neck to signify for him to get out of the back. Gary did so but slowly; looking left and then right while sliding his legs around and placing them on the blacktop driveway. He looked directly up at one of the security cameras that was bolted to the back gable and then looked back at Connie.

"Oh, please. You think I didn't remember to turn that shit off? You know me better than that. It's been disconnected for weeks."

"You can never be too careful," Gary said timidly then swallowed hard. Both walked to the back patio door and went into the kitchen; the one Margot had come to loathe looking at.

Once inside, Gary did as he had become accustomed to doing for the last half-dozen or so Friday trips to that house. He tossed his keys in the bowl. He would normally drive himself and park a block down, come up the left side of the house, knock, and Connie would let him in. The first thing he would do would be to toss those keys in that bowl on the mail counter.

He had developed the habit because during their first escapade in Brad's bed, Connie wanted to make a show of it and lock Gary in by ripping his clothes off. During the slap, tickle, and tussle, his keys ended up underneath her pile of freshly removed clothes that she kicked under the bed, and it had taken nearly five minutes to find them once they were finished with their tryst. He vowed to never let that happen again because it had been a close call when Brad came up the driveway just as Gary found the keys. If they were always in the same place, even if he had to run out the back in the nude, Brad wouldn't catch up to him as he drove away in his green Chevy Chevelle. It was *willed* to him, too.

Connie retrieved her computer and power cord from a Louis Vuitton laptop bag. Brad had never cared that she had it, used it, nor who she contacted with it. He was the one who had bought it for her, including the bag it was in.

She settled the laptop on the counter and then sat on her usual acting stool while she plugged in the computer to make sure she wouldn't run out of battery during the most crucial part of the session. Her laptop was another very important part of the ruse that she had planned for weeks.

She wiggled in the chair, straightened the computer, and looked up at Gary.

He just stood there and stared at her.

She made a face with a twisted mouth and eyes wide open like, 'AND?'

"Oh, okay, yeah. You ready?"

304

"Umm, yeah!"

"Okay, okay…I got cha'."

Gary picked up the cooler and sat it on the counter. He pressed the button on the side and slid the top back. In it were four full pint-sized blood bags. Connie had been having him draw her blood every Friday since she started looking for just the right therapist.

She had found Margot by searching around and her site spoke to Connie. It spoke to her the same as it would if she were looking for any easy mark. She could read the timidness in Margot's online profile. Though, she had no idea that Margot, like many therapists, was observant. A psychopath wouldn't believe a therapist could keep up with them. She was right even though she had simply picked the wrong one, as it would turn out, in some respects.

Gary stood there at the ready to take orders and Connie conducted him like a symphony of dunces.

"Glove up and take the largest knife from the block over there. It has his prints on it," she motioned with the soft stroke of her hand in the air.

Gary pulled two black gloves from a box he had brought from work and put them on with a snap, then waited for her next instruction. Blood bag in one hand and knife in the other, Gary then asked, "Are you sure we should put the blood down first before I, well, push you off the stool? Shouldn't we do it after?"

"She is going to call the cops as soon as you close the lid on this laptop. We don't know how much time we are going to have, Gary."

"Oh right, yes, okay…good."

"Now, cut the top open and start pouring here," Connie pointed to a spot on the floor under the stool, "Get close to the floor and pour it slowly."

"Got it."

Gary walked around to the side she was on and cut the top of the bag just enough to make a small hole. He bent down and poured the crimson lifeforce out slowly. It ran in the cracks of grout and under the chair; all over the tile.

He looked up at her and she down at him like he was a servant; because he was in this very moment, *her* servant.

"Now the next one. I suggest you bring the rest with you because it's going to get more and more difficult to move around."

"True."

Gary walked back around and brought the cooler with him to put the empties in. He repeated the task three more times and put the knife in the cooler.

"I have a pair of his tennis shoes in a bag in my purse. You know what to do."

Gary pulled a pair of shoes that were in a travel bag from her 'neverfull' style purse and pulled one of Brad's shoes out. He removed one of his own and put on Brad's. Gary stepped half of the front part of the shoe in blood and walked backwards out toward the kitchen door and out to the yard then stopped, took off the shoe and walked back into the kitchen.

"Now place it back in the bag but don't close it yet, and put it in the cooler," she said with another conducting wave of her hand. "Take out the knife and coat it well with the blood then place it in the bag with the shoes."

Again, Gary did as instructed, "You don't happen to know how many years we could get for this, do you?"

Connie thought, *None for me, but I don't know about you.* Then she said aloud, "The only thing I know is that it's too late now and the near quarter of a million in cash in that safe you are going to get to next should take care of any feelings of guilt, remorse, or fear you may be starting to feel."

"Ah, yes. The safe."

"Change your gloves first. The combination is 51-50-15. Take my bag with you and fill it."

Gary, again, did as instructed by changing his gloves before going into the bedroom closet and using the combination to a new life for the pair. When he opened the safe it was all there plus some men's rings. During the planning stages with Connie, she had instructed him to not take those rings nor the pistols. Connie said it would look like there was no reason to take them for a man who planned on coming back and who also wasn't thinking right. It was another part of the framing of an innocent man—so innocent, that a murder wouldn't even be committed that night.

Gary came back with the bag and had only taken the money from the safe, as instructed.

Connie sat upon the stool with the metallic smell of her own blood all around it. For her, it was intoxicating. Her elbows were on the counter creating the right height for her fingers to interlace and have her chin rest on them while she waited for her tool, Gary, to finish the first of three parts of her bidding. She had been daydreaming about how this would all play out. It wasn't the first time she had done so; daydream about an outcome, that is.

Connie prided herself on always being ahead of the game and giving a man whatever he wanted to get her needs met, then dumping him when he was all used up. Brad was supposed to be her swansong. Then he had started acting in a way that caused her to become suspicious, though, for her, it didn't take much. She had placed that tracker on his car and then traced the address of "the whore" and found her online profile. She wasn't even upset with the woman because Connie saw her as somewhat of a kindred spirit. She saw "the whore" as a woman just making her money in a similar way, though, just one that she didn't respect as much as the way she made her own. Now, this woman had taken her sexual control away and had put her in jeopardy of catching an STD. Connie had no clue if he was allowed to go bareback during the "sessions". Connie had given thought to making him wear a condom but decided against it because Connie figured that would risk giving away the fact that she had solved the mystery of what he was doing before he would play cards. Connie thought she might tell him that she was afraid of pregnancy, but she had shared with him that she was on the pill and that was early in their relationship. She finally settled on just being pissed and refused to have sex with him at all. Regardless, Connie had become a misandrist years ago. She hadn't really cared about men for at least two decades thanks to her mother and the quality of men that she had brought around.

Connie didn't just grow up poor. She grew up with a mom that allowed too many men in the house. She learned early on that her value and worth was in her femininity. She had been brought into an adult world long before she was an adult. It disgusted her until she found that she could reframe it to her advantage. She didn't know it kept her sick. And she didn't know that she was born a psychopath. The combination of the two, along with her intelligence, had worked for her and she took pride in that. Brad had encroached on her pride of being manipulative and caused her to feel weak and played. He would pay for that with some of his money and his freedom. She considered after she had found out about his Friday flings that she may marry him and divorce six months later just to take half. Louisiana is a 50/50 state, and she would get a sizable amount.

But then there was that vaginal health. No matter. She would take the next one, Gary. He had inherited much after his parents died. Though, they didn't will it to him. They didn't care enough about him to do so. He was just their sole heir and so, by default, he got it all. Half of free would work for her. Connie smiled with pride as she enjoyed the thought of two for one. And what could he do? He was just as guilty as she was and if they got caught, she had decided, she would play the victim and get less time than he. If she did it quick enough after this stunt and married him, they would still be married and he would still be in jail, she figured. She would just use up what he had laying around in his bank account and disappear before he got out. Either way, any part of marrying anyone was never about love for Connie.

There was still more to do before she could get there, though.

"I got the cash," Gary said with pride and plopped the purse on the kitchen island just out of the laptop's camera view.

"Now, on the inside of that bag you will see a gold zipper. Look inside and you will find a bandage there. Shit-wit unintentionally gave me a gift. He cut himself on the back of his head while shaving a while back and I *intentionally* put a small bandage on it and let it bleed through. He's on blood thinners so it wasn't going to be enough to stop the bleeding. I took it off and put a bigger one on the cut. Needless to say, that Ziplock bag you just pulled out has the bandage soaked with a tiny bit of my contact saline applied and wrapped in a paper towel. Take it and smudge some of it on the wall right above where my blood has stopped running," Connie mewed while waving her hand in the general direction.

"When you're done, you will find the green color contacts to replace your own. They will be a little stronger than yours. I know you are 5.5 in each eye—these are 6's. I had to get them as a free pair when I went in a few months ago."

"It'll be fine, sweetheart."

"Don't call me that. You know I hate that."

"I'm sorry, Connie."

"He calls me that after he beats on me and tries to make up."

"I know, it won't happen again."

Connie was lying about every part of that. She just hated anyone to call her any pet names and right now, she was getting into character for Margot, mustering up her angry and hurt routine. It seeped out.

Brad had never laid so much as an angry look on Connie. Even though they hadn't been much of a couple for months. Her choice, not his.

"Okay, that should do it," Connie said as she looked with stern satisfaction at the blood swipe on the wall, "Now put in the contacts and take my keys out of that bag. There is a duffle up front in the Escalade. You know the rest."

Gary nodded and tried to lean over and give Connie a kiss on the cheek and she moved away at the same speed he leaned in. Neither said a word and her partner in crime left out of the side kitchen door.

Connie still had plenty of time before she needed to join Margot on her call, so she looked up a video on how to count your macros and then searched for a crystal studded Labubu.

Before Gary had left the half constructed faux crime scene and Connie on her high horse, he took her keys from her L.V. bag. It also had the spare Porsche fob connected at the ring. He decided not to ask why she had it if her boyfriend had been as controlling and abusive as she was leading Margot to think. He surmised that she just swiped the fob at some point but wondered why she wasn't more careful than to connect them to the Escalade fob and keys. *Maybe she connected both sets just today to make this next step easier for me,* he thought.

Gary went to the passenger side door of the SUV and opened it. He put the cooler down on the floorboard and slid the top back. He then unzipped the duffle bag Connie had left for him on the front seat. In the duffle, there were a pair of black sweatpants, a pair of identical tennis shoes to those now in the cooler with blood on them, two ski masks with only eye holes, a pair of jumper cables, and a black ball cap. Under all the supplies was a blanket. During the planning, it was agreed that it would be the dumping place for all the items to put in the Porsche.

He spread the blanket on the ground and smeared all the blood left over from each pack he had emptied in the kitchen. Then, Gary put in the pair of shoes—the pair where one had been stamped in Connie's blood. Then he added the knife and a ski mask—identical to the one that Gary would use later. This one, however, had Brad's hair collected from his beard comb inside. Gary scooped up the corners of the blanket, closed it up, and put it in the floorboard of the passenger side seat next to the ice chest. He removed his gloves, put them in his pocket, and went to the driver's side. Once he was seated, he put the black ball cap on and cranked the SUV. Gary whistled a tune as he pulled out toward his destination. He had been there more than once and knew the way without a GPS.

Gary Duratas went the speed limit the whole ten minutes. He needed to be expedient, but he also needed to not get caught. He had a whole hour-plus leeway because he knew that Connie had planned to stay on the session the entire time with Margot, if need be. However, the one hitch in the plan could be Margot canceling. Late would be fine and early would work, too. But if anything went wrong before the "on-camera assault", they would have to start all over again. He had a few bags of her blood stored for that contingency plan.

As he drove along, there wasn't a cop in sight the entire way. Gary slowed as he neared the parking lot entrance to the high-grade apartments and spotted the Porsche backed into a spot. When Gary and Connie started tracking Bradly, this was always the type of spot he would pick, and Gary was glad he continued to do so. It was lined with bushes that provided cover for the Porsche's license plate. Gary knew this was going to be a challenge, though. He drove up a little further and backed into a spot several cars away from the target. He needed to look for a few minutes to make sure no one else was sitting on their little porches. Grills and children's toys lined the way, but no people.

Lexi Jade didn't work from home, just like she would testify to, in court, six weeks later. She had rented an upstairs apartment just for her business address and activities. Gary could see a low wattage bulb shining its light through the curtains of what he assumed was the bedroom. Her front room blinds shown no light.

Gary took the jumper cables and wrapped them loosely around his hand—creating fairly wide loops—tugged the bill of the black, nondescript ball, cap, and pulled the SUV out of the parking spot he had backed into. He drove the loop around the parking lot and back to the little black sports car. While making that loop, he scanned the back side of the apartment building. There were identical parking spots and identical apartments. There was one person outside on her porch. She was smoking a cigarette and reading a hardback copy of something. She didn't look up.

Strange, Gary thought, *apartment folk are usually some of the nosiest fucks around*. Though they were upscale apartments, it had no gate and there were no security cameras to speak of. They were apartments where people kept to themselves. A few were used as short-term corporate apartments; a few were used for selling soap.

Gary kept driving until his driver's side door was just by the front of the "frunk" of the Porsche. Exiting the SUV and looking around—quickly scanning the sidewalk and parking lot—he felt confident enough in his safety to shut his door quietly and turn toward the front of Brad's Porsche. If anyone were to ask what he was doing, he would simply note that his friend had called him over to give him a jump.

But no one was in sight while he put on the new pair of gloves he had in his other pocket. Gary felt for the button of the Porsche 911's front trunk release and clicked it. He heard the unmistakable *thunk* of the latch release. Keeping the jumper cables looped around his right hand, he turned, and with his left, lifted the panel. He tucked his hand under the front of the hood and lifted it. Now came the hardest part.

With Connie's Escalade running, lights on high beams, and an armload of a bloody picknick from the front seat, Gary placed the blanket inside the car, and all the incriminating evidence lay bare when the blanket opened and shown a freshly bloomed flower of gore.

After Gary closed the hood of the Porsche, he removed his gloves and laid himself on the ground. Feeling around, he found the tracker easily, removed it, and hopped back in Connie's SUV and slowly drove away.

After another ten-minute drive, he backed the SUV on to Connie and Brad's blacktopped driveway and cut the engine. It was 7:05pm Friday night and all was well.

Gary pressed the button to open the lift gate, hoisted the duffle bag, and hopped out quickly, then went around to the back of the Escalade to get changed into his costume. Everything was big enough to fit over his clothes. He changed into the identical white tennis shoes as the planted ones. They were snug but they fit well enough.

After opening the window and starting to climb through to the back bedroom that had the poorly latching door, he could

314

hear the session in progress. *We are home free all now*! he thought.

"Connie, I was thinking. I'd like to do a little role-playing with you. That is, if you are willing."

"Role-play? What's that going to do?"

"I want to play him, your boyfriend or whatever you want to call him, and you play yourself. It's to help you be able to speak to him about how things are."

"Like shit will get any better. Are you kidding me?"

"Right now, it's not about getting better. It's about getting out."

OH, she'll be getting out, alright, Gary thought.

"Oh, you *are* kidding me; there's no way…"

"Let's just try it. Now, I'll be…,"

"Brad. His name is Bradly LeBlanc."

"Brad, okay, I'll play him. I want you to talk to me—talk to me like you would him…just freewheel it…just let it go. You can say whatever you want to say and as I'm playing like him you can just correct me when I say anything that he wouldn't."

"He wouldn't say that."

"Say what? We haven't started yet."

"He wouldn't allow any conversation like this to even occur. He would never say, 'You can say whatever you want to say' or 'correct me when…'"

"Okay, you just use me as a body to say to him whatever it is you *want* to say."

"Fuck you!"

"Is that for me or have we started?'

"Can it be both?"

"Whatever you like."

"Okay, we'll start now. Fuck you."

"Keep going."

"Is that him saying that or you?"

"Both."

"He wouldn't say that."

"You just keep talking."

That's right, just keep talking, Gary thought further as he creeped toward the door that entered the hallway. A breath of air pushed through the window, and the door started to open before he was ready to make his grand entrance. Or it could be his exit, depending on how one might perceive it.

"Now that he would say."

"Go ahead."

"Fuck you, Bradly. Fuck you and the Porsche you rode in on."

"Why are you upset?"

"He wouldn't say that."

"Well, what would he say…"

Gary took the chance before the door opened too wide on its own, pulled it hard, and ran down the hall. His eyes on the back of Connie's head the whole way. He pushed her down with his right hand.

"You really want to know what I would say, Margot? I'd say, 'I'm going to kill you'."

As soon as Gary slapped the laptop shut, Connie was pissed, "Goddamnit Gary, did you have to push me down so fuckin' hard?"

"I'm sorry, I'm sorry, you wanted it to look real, right?"

Connie was covered in her own blood, and it had already grown a little less viscus. Even still, it had splattered everywhere. She had no idea if it looked how it should or not.

"Fuck it, grab the laptop and the plug and put it in the truck, then come back and drag me outta this shit!"

Gary did as he was told. However, there was no need to have dipped any shoe in blood because it was everywhere. Gary left prints all over the kitchen as he retrieved the laptop and power cord. He put it in the truck and came back. "I'm going to have to drag you so that it smears the new prints I just left outside on the concrete."

"I don't give a fuck if you have to drag an elephant through the French Quarter! Get me outta here, NOW!"

Gary pulled Connie by the shoulders and spun her around.

"What the fuck are YOU DOING?!?"

"It will be easier to drag you by the feet."

"JUST GO!"

Gary dragged her over the new prints and the prints he was now making. Once at the black top he took everything off as she climbed in the back and under the blanket that Gary was once under—only she didn't look like a scared puppy—she looked like a wet hen. She reached up and pushed the liftgate button while Gary was still tossing his costume and shoes in the back.

Gary got in the front, cranked the Escalade, and then remembered…

"FUCK FUCK FUCK FUCK FUCK!"

Connie's muffled voice came from the back, "WHAT NOW?"

"I FORGOT TO GET MY KEYS FROM THE BOWL!"

"DAMN IT, GARY!!!"

Gary was already hopscotching his way over the patio, opened the kitchen door, tripped the light fantastic around the kitchen counter and leaned his body so far over the blood and to the edge of the mail counter that he had to land using his hands with all his weight on them. He grabbed the keys from the bowl and did a gymnastic style push up and away from the counter.

By the time he got back in the car he could hear the sirens. He pulled out of the driveway and went in the opposite direction from where they were coming.

He drove toward his house, that was in the same direction as Lexi Jade's apartment. A traffic camera would catch him speeding. That was all part of the plan. But Brad coming back in the opposite direction only 45 minutes later was not. The crime camera on the other side of the street going toward Brad's house got a nice picture of the black Porsche 911 following all traffic rules and him chatting on the phone. His card game had been canceled.

38

Seeing Is Believing

Present Day

It was Monday morning, and Margot had returned to work. Her two peers were extremely happy. They decorated her space by leaving flowers, cards, and balloons. Margot peed herself just a little when she opened the door to her office. Flowers and balloons were no longer something that Margot cared for. The skull, the balloons, the number 33, and flowers were all attached to her trauma now. She wanted to throw it all away but knew she couldn't until she took all the items home that evening. She knew the ladies and Prestin would come by and she had steadied herself to make a big deal over their welcoming party. But, when she got home, in the trash it would all go. Then she thought she wouldn't even bring it to her house. She knew of a nice dumpster behind a Piggly Wiggly grocery store where she could dump them. And yet, she wasn't even sure if she was going to sleep at the house or not. Joni said she could do as she pleased and stay with her—the offer was still on the table.

Margot didn't have much to do. Prestin had taken over her caseload the day she left and now all those cases were settled since she had been gone so long, and he had taken on any new ones that came up. He would see those through, as well. So, Margot had nothing on her plate nor any calls to return, and only new cases would come to her from here on out. She figured that they would all take some vacation days she would have to cover for. She also figured they were fairly burnt, and she was, too. But there could be no excuses, she had been gone for two months.

Margot left her office after all the, 'Oh my God's', and 'Welcome back's'. She just couldn't be in that room with all the items that reminded her of Bradly and his fucking around with her. She thought about visiting him and asking, 'What does H.H. mean? What does the "33" stand for? What's with the skull?' but knew she would be in trouble for meeting with him if there were to ever be an appeal granted. And she figured he would lie to her, anyway.

What was worse, she wasn't sure it was him. Yes, the messages stopped when he went to jail, but they were definitely messages directed at her. They were specifically cryptic. The best her and Joni could come up with was that they were designed to spook her since she was the one who witnessed the murder. But then Joni and her got stuck on the cryptics of it all. The skull, the H.H., and the 33. What did it all mean? Both decided they just wouldn't ever know. And Lieutenant Bolt wanted nothing to do with it. And if it was Brad, and it most likely was, the D.A.'s office wouldn't want anything to do with it, either. What's more, she didn't even know who the lawyers were for Brad now, anyway. The whole team had either been fired or quit by the end of business on Friday.

Margot just walked around slowly in the common areas and winding her way to the shop where she would have loved to have seen Joni, but the manager was helping a customer and it would have been Joni's day off, anyway, if she had still been working. She ended up at the cafeteria around 11:30am. She put her purse and computer bag down on a booth that was against the wall where she could see everyone hustling to get lunch—white coats and scrubs everywhere.

She went over and got her usual patty melt, a bag of chips, and a drink. After paying and getting back to her table she opened her laptop and the pictures she and Joni had been looking at the night before were tucked between the laptop screen and the keyboard. She had forgot that she left them there. She was doing everything she could to figure out what the etching was on that key. She just couldn't leave it alone. Maybe it was just a number of the mailbox it belonged to or whatever, but she wasn't sure—though, it didn't look like a number. And in only three of the pictures was the key even turned the right way to make out part of what she...

THUNK!

The sound was at the table next to Margot and caused her to look up. A man she thought she had seen before was looking down at her with a smile, "Anyone sitting here?" he asked. He had sat a stack of files down on the table.

"Umm, no, no. Not at all. You feel free."

"Thanks," the gentlemen said as he pulled out his wallet.

"No worries."

The man turned and walked toward the line of people that were now backed up due to it being closer to noon. As Margot watched him walk away, she took note that he wore a short, white coat. A professional but likely not a doctor. His dark hair looked familiar. She just couldn't remember where she had seen him before. It even felt like more than once. She just couldn't be sure.

She looked over at his stack of papers and began to think about the fact that it was a HIPAA violation if those were client files…Margot's blood ran as cold as ice and the first shot of it went straight through her spine. On top of the files were a set of keys, *THE* keys. Margot looked at one of her pictures that Joni had printed for her and then back at the keys again. The brass key was laying on its edge.

Crudely scratched into the head of the key was the same image of that fucked up scull from the balloon and card. On the forehead of the skull were the initials H.H. scratched in just as crudely.

Margot was frozen. She could see him out of the corner of her eye as he turned around and looked at her. When she saw his neck swivel, she looked right back at her computer screen and didn't look up, though could still see him. He had a grin almost as ghastly as the scull on the key.

The line was becoming shorter. So, he turned again. Margot, her laptop, and her bags were gone.

Gary Duratas was disappointed and thought to himself, *Awww, she must have lost her appetite. I wanted a lunch buddy, today. Joni is probably doing the cooking now, anyway. Margot is probably well fed. Connie would be proud of me, I bet. Stepping out of my comfort zone and making new friends. Well, renewing old acquaintances. I'll have to tell her all about it tonight over dinner. I don't want to have to stop for anything, though. Maybe I'll call her and see if we have something worth a shit in the freezer. Na, probably not. I should just stop and grab something fresh to bring home.*

Margot got two floors above the cafeteria and peered over the railing while she waited for the man who's name she didn't know to come out. When he did, she tracked him. First, he went to the giftshop window and then she moved slowly as he looked in.

She quickly realized he was the man in the door that had dropped his keys when the balloon burst and asked if she and Joni were okay. Margot was shaking with fear, rage, and suspicion. *This has to be the fucker in the mask in that video! They're his fucking keys*, she thought.

As she continued to follow him from above, he looked up, but not far enough up nor far enough behind himself to see her. While she tracked him walking over to the bank of elevators, she had another epiphany. He was the one who got in the elevator that day and then said, "No worries." *That fucker was not only mocking me, but he had also been listening in on the sessions. MOTHERFUCKER, THEY SET ME UP TO BE THE WITNESS!*

After calling Prestin and letting him know that she needed to go home a little early, it being a first day back and all, Margot positioned herself at around 3pm near the exit to the parking garage. Not long after 4pm she could hear a rumbling coming down the ramp. It was a hunch, but it paid off. She saw him in a classic green car. Something from the 60's or 70's, she figured. She thought he would peel off like many men driving a machine like that would, but he didn't. He casually put his arm out of the driver side window that was open and drove away, staying under the speed limit.

She slammed her car into reverse, backed out double-time, threw her series 3 BMW in drive, and screeched out of the parking lot. She called Joni on the way and said she was, *coming in hot!*

39

She *Ain't* Shy

On Tuesday, at 11:30am, Margot sat at the same table she had the day before, was eating the same thing, and reading The Times Picayune.

THUNK!

"Anyone sitting here?" Gary asked with a smile and a comforting laugh. It would have comforted most people, but not Margot. She was pissed. She knew she saw more blood on that damned floor; more blood than Connie could have bled in that short amount of time. And she definitely knew those keys connected him to Connie. Margot felt she had not only been mocked but also hounded, followed, frightened on purpose, and worst of all, played a fool—she had played her role well. She had been set up as a bullshit witness; a handpicked sucker for those two to get away with putting an innocent man in jail for life. Margot, the night before, had finally settled on a diagnosis. Connie was a borderline with antisocial traits. She was leaning toward narcissist when it came to the man with no name, a stack of files, and a fucked-up skull key. Then again, it was more likely he was as much of a sap as Bradly and was being used as a delivery boy for Cunt-y's messages. *GO WITH YOUR GUT, GIRL!* Margot thought.

"No one but you. Please take a seat."

"Sorry I ran, ya off yesterday."

"No no, it wasn't you at all. I got paged," Margot said with that familiar feigned look of disappointment shown by poking out her lip and slumping her shoulders.

"Oh, they still have those?" Margot looked confused after Gary said it, so he clarified, "Pagers, I mean."

"On my phone...just old terminologies for new technologies."

"I'm a bit old school myself. I like old cars. Ya know, they just don't build them like they used to."

"They sure don't."

"Sort of like women now days. They just aren't like they used to be."

It took every ounce of Margot's patience to not grab Gary's keys and scratch his face with them, "Looks like the line is getting long," Margot nudged her head up as an indicator for him to look.

"Well heavens to marigolds! I better go get in it or I won't get to eat a thing!" He pulled his keys from his pocket and tossed them on the table, got in line, and whistled a tune.

When he turned around Margot was gone again.

"She's so shy," Gary started to sing aloud, turned back around, and slid along with the line. As he did so, he finished the rest of his melody with a smile of satisfaction.

Margot took the elevator up to the third floor where the skywalk was for the parking garage and ran out once the doors opened, then trotted over to a parked 1990's Volvo station wagon. Joni was in the driver's seat and waving for Margot to get in, "Come on, Come on!", she whisper-yelled with a lit smoke in her mouth.

Margot hopped in, held up the keys with a shake and said, "Drive up the ramp until we see a big ass green car!" Joni would have peeled out if the car had been capable of it. It had needed a tune-up for twenty years.

Up and around they went until they got to the sixth floor, "Where the hell is this thing?" Joni said as she cut the wheel again. Her tires yelped every curve she took.

Margot pointed, "THERE! THERE IT IS!" and Joni jammed on the brakes. Margot hopped out before the car had even come to a full stop. Within seconds she had opened the Chevelle and hopped inside. It was immaculate and all original. The only item that didn't look like it came stock on the car was the GPS stuck to the window with a bracket and suction cup. It had stood out to her when she stalked him the day before. Then the ladies hatched their scheme.

Joni wasn't at all interested in doing what they were doing. But Margot had convinced her that Connie was alive, was part of this ruse, and she was going to prove it. She may not care much for the likes of Brad, but he was an innocent man. Of that, she was sure. She was sure that the owner of the keys she now held in her hand was the man behind that ski mask. She had told Joni the night before that Connie must have put his dumbass up to it. Joni had asked why not just go to the police but didn't finish the question once Margot started to make a face. Joni knew the police, and even herself, had not taken Margs seriously. Then Margot went on to tell Joni that she felt guilty and needed to set things right.

She put the key in the ignition and turned it on. The GPS came on with a chirp. She pressed the 'home' button. It was a longshot but was worth a try. The address and a blue flag marking the spot came up on the screen. She used her phone to take a screen shot, turned off the ignition, and jumped back in Joni's car.

"GO! GO! GO!" she yelled, and Joni put her head out of her open window to make sure a car was not coming; cigarette smoke billowing out of her face. As she went down the sixth-floor ramp, Gary came out to see his car still there, knew Margot had taken his keys, and watched the sun faded yellow Volvo wagon go down the ramp in a hurry. He knew who's wagon that was. He had seen it several times. He had worked there for three years as an orthopedic physician's assistant. The women had a head start and his only set of keys to that car, the other set was at his house—and so was Connie. *She's not going to be very pleased with me when the ladies get there*, he thought, *and neither will they*. He took out his cell phone and started walking back into the building.

40

Joni In The Driver Seat

Margot took the deck of smokes and Joni's lighter that was in an old-style leather pouch with a kiss clasp latch from the console, pulled out a cigarette, lit it, then started to put the address in her phone from the screen shot she had found from the GPS in Gary's automobile. While looking at the phone and typing with the smoke tucked between her fingers and exhaling the first draw she asked, "So, we smokin' in the car now, too?"

"Honey, I have been smoking everywhere I have a hole since you hatched this plan last night."

"Take a right up here!" Margot said as she poked the cigarette back in her face and pointed.

"You gotta give the ol' girl some advanced warning. She used to turn on a dime, now it's taking a buck-fifty," Joni quipped as she cut the wheel hard. She was joking again because it helped calm her nerves. Old habits die hard.

"When we get there, we gotta be quick. Maybe we see her SUV, maybe we see her in the window, maybe she won't be there at all. Who the fuck knows? But if we find her, we get a half mile away and call the cops. No one can know you were there because I'm liable to lose my license."

"Why in the world would that happen?"

"I can't bring someone to a client's house, Jonesy, TURN HERE!"

"DAMN IT, MARGS!"

"Well, former client, anyway," she took another drag as she retrieved her phone that had fallen in the floorboard of the car on that last lefthander.

"Okay, good! We stick to the plan."

"Yup! Two lights up take a right, and we will be on the street. Shit, I'm shaking!"

"Shaking? I think I shit myself two turns back!"

The ladies slowed down a block away and then crept up to the curb of the house. It was a fairly nice one but needed a few coats of paint. At the end of the driveway there was a three-car metal garage.

"Okay, let's make this quick. All Gary needs to do is get an Uber or co-worker to shuttle him here and who knows what happens next."

"Nothing good, I bet."

Both ladies tossed their cigarettes on the ground, each crushed them with their shoe, and started up to the house with a scurried trot.

As they circled the house, they looked in all the windows and saw nothing that would indicate that a woman had been anywhere near that house in years. Bookshelves lined with hardbacks and paperbacks, a leather couch, a large television. There was a downstairs bedroom but one couldn't see in the window. Blackout curtains appeared to be on the other side of the glass. After both rounded the house, they got back to the front door. Margot just opened her arms in a "what now" stance. Joni walked up and snatched the dangling keys in Margot's right hand and walked up to the door.

"What the hell do you think you are doing, Joan Pierse?"

"I want this shit over with and over with once and for all," she said as she rifled through the keys and tried each one. She didn't care much for seeing the skull with the H's scratched in it.

"Joni, we can't do this."

"Honey, 'can't do this' left town a long time ago," and the door opened.

"Okay, we stay together."

"We don't have time to stay together. I'm going upstairs."

"Jesus!"

"He left town a long time ago, too, honey…get moving."

The two opened every door to every room and closet. Nothing stood out and nobody was there. Their search took all of about two minutes. The two reconvened downstairs, dejected.

Joni said, "Well, that was a bust and that about closes the book on this one. He knows you snatched his keys, so you better have one hell of a good story if you want to go to work tomorrow."

Margot was just staring out of the back window while Joni was speaking. Joni looked to see what Margot was so focused on. When she saw it, Joni said slowly, "Oh yeah, that thing."

"Yeah, *that* thing."

Margot went to the front door and looked out. Seeing no vehicles that weren't there before, she felt a slight sense of relief that they may have a few minutes left. She opened the door and the ladies went out then to the left, around the house, and up to the large garage. Once there, they found no locks on the garage doors; only handles. They tried each of the three. The doors gave no quarter but, rather, only creaky moans. They had tried the first one on the left, then the middle, and then the last one on the right. Joni saw a service door on the far side of the building. She marched up to it and Margot scurried behind her, looking side to side like a first-time cat burglar. Joni started trying the keys on the service door lock while Margot peered into the windowpanes. It was pointless, though, as they were blacked out.

The deadbolt gave way with the correct key and a *click*. The two looked at one another, then Joni pushed it open. And there it was, Connie's black Escalade, hood first, all the way in and to the left side of the huge garage. The two women looked at one another, again. And Margot said, "I fuckin' told ya so."

"Okay, so what now, Nancy Drew?"

Without a word, Margot ran over to the vehicle and started looking in the dark tinted windows of the passenger side. Joni stood by the door of the garage and looked at tools that were all hanging perfectly on a peg board. To her left, there were the

333

usual instruments for yard and woodworking. Further over was a huge table at the height of a woodworker's bench. Joni's curiosity got the best of her, and she decided to step in a little further.

Margot had worked her way around to the back of the SUV. She cupped her hands around her face and pressed them against the window, then narrated, "It's a mess back here! There's a blanket and a bag or some shit…"

Margot heard another click so she froze and stopped talking. She slowly lowered herself down beneath the Escalade's liftgate window. She could see a light reflecting on the garage floor then felt the temperature drop slightly. At that same moment, she heard a commotion and a loud *CLUNK*. Suddenly, she saw Joni hit the floor and Joni's head started to leach blood. It was just like what she had seen in the corner of that video two months before, though just a trickle this time. A shovel lay next to her best friend in the whole world. It wobbled to a stop with a scratchy metallic sound.

Connie Minae was looming over Joni with a look of righteous indignation.

It wasn't until after Margot slowly emerged from the back of the truck and stood straight up that she could see what Joni had seen before passing out.

There was a freezer that had been latched with a big brass padlock.

The one Joni had just opened with the skull key before she had fainted and knocked into the shovel hanging on the wall.

On each rack in that freezer, in clear plastic bags and all neatly aligned, were the severed heads of countless women—

all with their eyelids affixed so they stayed as wide open as possible.

And there, centered on the top shelf, with the number 33 etched just below her hairline, was the head of Connie Minae.

Epilogue

One Year Later

Somewhere—anywhere—in Louisiana, there is a television on. And on that television a public interest segment during the morning show is set to interview a person who is promoting their new book.

As the screen fades into focus we see two women sitting in chairs that are slightly facing one another. The women are smiling and speaking with each other as the bumper music fades out.

"We have a very special guest this morning who is here to share her new book that is already a bestseller. She's New Orleans' own, Margot Landry. Welcome Ms. Landry, we are so happy to have you here."

"Thank you, I'm very glad to be here."

Joni was at home, in her bed, sipping tea, while she and Adler watched their best friend, Margot, being interviewed. Joni had given a stipend to her so that she could take the six months off from work to write the book. Although Margot would continue to use a laptop, it would only be used to write books. She would never provide therapy again.

"Ms. Landry, many of us know your story but this book, and I have read it, is quite chilling. It's the account of the man that turned out to be one of the most prolific serial killers in New Orleans history, if not *the* most prolific, no?"

"Yes, Gary Wayne Duratas was able to stay under the radar for years and, to be honest, this volume is only my first in a three-book set. I have started writing the stories of many of the other women whom he killed in the middle years prior to his final victim, Connie Minae."

"Right, as many may remember, her boyfriend, Bradly LeBlanc was the one that was first charged and convicted of her murder. A murder for which they had, up to that point, not even found a body, correct?"

"That's correct. Gary Wayne Duratas and Bradly's girlfriend at the time, Connie Minae, had conspired together to frame LeBlanc. She felt, according to Duratas—and we must take anything that he says with a grain of salt—that LeBlanc, himself, had sullied their relationship."

"Fascinating!"

"Yes, however, after the discovery of Connie, LeBlanc was set free, of course."

"How many other murders are connected to Duratas?"

"Oh, there were 32 other women, and most had loved ones who Duratas was able to successfully frame for their murders—Connie being number 33. However, there may be more. I have been informed by the FBI that they are currently taking another look into the sinking of the boat of Gary's parents. They believe there may have been foul play there, too."

"Many in the audience today may be asking how, then, did you come to title your book H.H. 34?"

"H.H. was the moniker he gave himself, although he never contacted the press for publicity, so it was only learned after he was taken into custody, confessed, and boasted about his story. It stands for Head Hunter."

"Please tell our audience this morning how you were able to get unfettered access to such a prolific serial killer, one that even the most high-profile professionals couldn't get access to? I mean, it's widely known that he refused to tell his full story to anyone but you."

"I asked him the same question after he requested to speak to me. You see, you have to understand the mind of a psychopath. All psychopaths believe they are smarter than everyone else. Cops, lawyers, judges, anyone really. And once they are caught, they have to believe one of two things to keep their ego intact. They need to believe that they gave themselves over to the police and they were never truly caught. Or they need to believe that the person who 'caught them' was as smart as they are, again, to keep their fragile ego intact. Therefore, he said I 'earned it'. He said since I was the only one 'clever enough' to 'nail him down', I was the only one who could understand his mind well enough to tell his story the way he wanted it to be told."

"And the number 34, what was—or is—it's significance?"

"I asked him about that particular number in one of our early interviews and Duratas shared that it was yet another way that I had earned the exclusive interviews with him for this book."

"Oh, how so?"

"As it turns out... I was to be number 34."

A Note From The Author

Thanks so much for your ~~purchase of~~ well, however this novel came into your possession, and I hope you enjoyed it.

I promise, more twisty tales are coming your way. Depending on when you have finished this story, some may already be out and about in the wild.

Please visit **Gasliterary.com** or search for me, **J.T. McNair**, to see what other stories I want you to have.

Well, go on. You should.

www.ingramcontent.com/pod-product-compliance
Lightning Source LLC
Chambersburg PA
CBHW011451170626
46814CB00012B/3012